THE
MARRIAGE

BOOKS BY K.L. SLATER

THE MARRIAGE

K.L. SLATER

bookouture

Published by Bookouture in 2021

An imprint of Storyfire Ltd.
Carmelite House
50 Victoria Embankment
London EC4Y 0DZ

www.bookouture.com

ISBN: 978-1-80019-495-3
eBook ISBN: 978-1-80019-494-6

In memory of Julie Wagg.
Much loved mother, wife, mama and friend.

PROLOGUE

Bridget

April 2019

I stood in front of the full-length mirror in my new ivory silk dress. Simple and classy, it skimmed my curves but crucially remained demure in all the right places.

I'd had a salon spray tan. My moisturised skin looked smooth and youthful, but when I pinched the top of my hand, the skin did not spring back immediately. I'd curled my hair and pinned it up, adding a tiny sprig of fresh gypsophila here and there to soften my look, and applied a pretty pink lipstick, the latest spring shade according to the sales assistant at the department store make-up counter.

Peering closer to the mirror, I studied my reflection. Tiny lines fanned out from the corners of my eyes and lips. My cheeks gave way to a soft sagging that spoiled the razor-sharp jawline I'd enjoyed in my thirties.

In two years' time I would be fifty years old, but age was just a number. Today, I felt young, vibrant and free. I'd planned this fresh start for what felt like a very long time.

Today, I would start a new life with a man twenty years younger than me.

In one hour's time, I would marry the man I loved.

The same man who ten years earlier had killed my only son.

1

2009

To the local residents, retired primary school teacher Mavis Threadgold was a familiar sight walking the streets of Mansfield, a large market town that lay in the Maun Valley, twelve miles north of the city of Nottingham.

Dressed in her honey-coloured mac, tartan scarf and sensible laced walking shoes, she pounded the pavements like clockwork, three times a day, always accompanied by her trusty two-year-old black-and-tan dachshund, Harry. Whatever the weather, the intrepid pair could usually be spotted on one of their favoured routes in and around the town. Not so different to many other dog walkers in the area, apart from the fact that one of Harry's regular daily outings took place at 2 a.m.

It was this walk they were on right now. Mavis stood patiently as Harry sniffed around the base of a lamp post. She often reminisced about her teaching days as she walked. Indeed, this was her favourite time to do so, the streets being so quiet.

Their eye-wateringly early walk had started the year Mavis retired, when she had lost her class of thirty eager, fresh-faced pupils. She'd had a pacemaker fitted for her worsening atrial fibrillation, and with it had gained the most wretched case of insomnia. Every night, after sleeping soundly for three or four hours, her eyes would spring open for no apparent reason. But it wasn't just the heart condition that kept her awake.

Retiring early had scuppered Mavis's plans to live mortgage-free when her annual salary ceased. She'd bought her house late in life and her mortgage was due to be paid off on her sixtieth birthday. Sure, she had a pension, but having never married, and with only one salary to live on, she'd skimped on her contributions over the years and her income wasn't nearly as robust as it might have been. In the end, she was forced to extend the mortgage for another five years to reduce her payments.

Walking was the solution to her insomnia. It was one activity she hadn't had to cut down on to stay within her budget, and even better, following a brisk twenty-five-minute stroll – invariably between the hours of two and three in the morning – she'd take a cuppa back to bed before settling down again for another few hours' shut-eye.

Mavis marvelled how every morning the streets were the same: calm, deserted and completely uneventful. Until now. About to cock his leg against yet another lamp post, Harry froze as an explosion of booming music came out of nowhere about fifty feet away from them, in the middle of the almost silent street.

The rear fire doors of Movers, the only nightclub left in town, were suddenly flung open and two flailing bodies ejected onto the pavement before a muscular doorman slammed the exit closed again.

Mavis bent down to scoop up a startled Harry into her arms and stepped back into the shadows, out of sight of what she assumed would be local thugs intent on causing trouble. But when her eyes adjusted, she realised she actually knew the two boys who were currently dusting off their clothes.

It was none other than Thomas Billinghurst and Jesse Wilson.

She'd taught Tom and Jesse twice, first in her Year 4 class and later, when they were both aged eleven in their final year before they went on to Mansfield Academy.

The boys had been as close as brothers, inseparable from nursery, and yet very different personalities. Mavis didn't mind admitting they had been two of her favourites, largely because of what she affectionately called their double act. Tom would step in as a calming influence when one of Jesse's hyper moments struck, and Jesse happily coaxed Tom to join in activities when his nature was to shrink back. They naturally complemented each other without thinking about it, and both were all the stronger for it.

She did a quick calculation in her head. They'd both be eighteen years old now. That made her feel ancient, although she was only sixty-five.

As they'd grown older, Jesse remained the wild one and the frequent subject of gossip in the town. Often in trouble, and when he wasn't, it would never be very long until trouble found him. Poor Bridget certainly had her hands full with that one, Mavis reflected, especially given that she was a single mother.

Tom, on the other hand, had grown into a bright, sporty type. He came from a good family. Back in his schooldays, Jill and Robert Billinghurst were always first in line at the school's annual parents' evening. Over the years, Tom had developed into the sort of boy who excelled at whatever he turned his attention to. That was currently boxing, if Mavis remembered correctly. There had been a small report of a recent win in the local newspaper a few weeks earlier.

She was about to step forward to say hello to the boys when the two of them, clearly the worse for wear, suddenly squared up to each other. Mavis was accustomed to dealing with this kind of thing in the school playground. It was surprising how much grown men had in common with warring five-year-olds. But here in this quiet, dim street with just the faintest glow of orange sodium light, there was no trace of the two mischievous but likeable boys she'd once known so well, and an icy prickle crept around the back of her neck.

She opened her mouth, anxious to intervene before things got really nasty, but she hesitated as voices were raised, the harsh tones amplified. Then the pushing and shoving started. The look in their eyes, and such terrible accusations flying around. Things Mavis wished she wasn't around to hear.

But she couldn't just stand by. This had to stop right now.

As she moved out of the shadows, the altercation escalated. Their movements quickened, raw fury burning in their eyes and vicious words still spilling from between bared teeth.

Mavis gasped at a flash of something sharp and metallic. Holding a shivering Harry close, she tucked herself behind a large green recycling bin at the back of the greengrocer's, watching with dread from amid the stench of rotten vegetables. What she saw and heard next caused the breath to catch in her throat. Her grip tightened around Harry's soft, warm girth as she backed away into the safety of the shadows behind, her soft-soled shoes scattering loose gravel underfoot.

The boys turned for a split second, as if they'd seen or heard her, but the interruption was forgotten as one lurched towards the other.

Mavis scurried through a concealed alleyway that served as a shortcut to the back of a short row of shops, before emerging on the next street, where she put the dachshund down again and caught her breath. She fished in her pocket for her pay-as-you-go mobile phone and rang for an ambulance, covering the mouthpiece with her hand to muffle her voice.

'There's some kind of incident at the rear entrance of Movers nightclub in Mansfield,' she said breathlessly. 'It looks pretty nasty. There are two men fighting and I think someone might be about to get hurt.'

She ended the call amid a flurry of questions from the emergency operator.

When she reached the top of the hill, she stopped, tipped her head and listened, her heart quickening as the urgent drone of emergency sirens fractured the silence of the usually peaceful early hours. She turned and looked back down the hill over the town and saw several vehicles with blue flashing lights turn into the high street below.

Her heart squeezed, and for a moment she considered turning around and going back to see if everything was all right. She wondered if she'd imagined the flash of metal – her eyesight wasn't what it used to be. Her hearing was temperamental too, and their words had seemed slurred; perhaps she'd misheard the terrible things they'd said, the awful accusations. Just the thought of dealing with the police, enduring the curiosity of the locals and, as a worst-case scenario, ending up as a witness in court … well, she couldn't cope with that. Not after her heart operation. The doctor had told her she must avoid stress at all costs.

Harry pulled on his lead, eager to get home out of the chilly November air.

'Perhaps there's been a traffic accident, Harry,' she wondered aloud, as if acting a part. It was good practice, because that was what she intended telling the police if they came knocking at her door. That she didn't see what had happened because she'd almost been back home when she'd heard the sirens.

Sometimes the truth was hard to bear but even harder to speak, and although as a God-fearing woman she struggled with this approach, Mavis had always recognised the value of keeping silent and letting other people resolve their own troubles.

She knew both boys, she knew their families. Getting in the middle of those two sides – both of which contained rather volatile personalities, if she remembered correctly –wouldn't end well.

Mavis had spent thirty years helping the young charges in her care to recognise the difference between right and wrong. She was a big believer in doing the right thing when one was able, but sometimes the truth was so shocking it was kinder and wiser to say nothing at all.

Hopefully it would prove to be only a scuffle, an alcohol-induced disagreement between two friends.

In Mavis's experience, these nasty little incidents usually blew over in no time at all.

2

The Mansfield Guardian
15 October 2009

Man dies after one-punch assault in town centre

An eighteen-year-old man has died after being taken to hospital in the early hours of this morning in a critical condition following an assault outside a nightclub that led to a bleed on the brain.

The incident happened just after 2 a.m. outside Movers nightclub and late bar on White Hart Street in Mansfield. The two men were ejected by security staff after a disagreement escalated between them inside the venue. The fatal assault then took place outside the rear entrance.

The *Guardian* understands that Jesse Wilson was hit by a man known to him. Police have arrested another eighteen-year-old local man, a middleweight professional boxer who recently qualified for the East Midlands Boxing Championships due to be held in February next year.

Police are appealing for witnesses.

3

Tom

April 2019

The prison staff had done a good job, Tom thought. They had made a sterling effort.

The officers had prettied up the small, drab inmates' chapel with a swathe of white satin draped artfully around the door. Small vases of freesias and pink roses adorned the windowsills and scattered red hearts brightened the small table where he and his new bride would soon sign the register.

Tom had surprised the prison governor when he'd applied for the marriage licence. 'There hasn't been a wedding here for over ten years,' he'd told him. 'But if that's what you want, it is your right and we'll do our best for you.'

He'd proposed to Bridget six months earlier. Put in a special request for a private visit. As he was almost at release date, he was granted use of the small visiting room for one hour. It was a space usually reserved for sensitive visits from family – to notify a prisoner of a death or news of a birth, that kind of thing.

Painted in an awful glossy green, artificial plants dotted the corners. A low coffee table with peeling veneer sat in the middle of a few scratched chairs. But there was a window overlooking the fields at the rear of the prison. While he waited for Bridget, he'd stood staring out at the grass, the sky, a scattering of gulls that swept through the expanse of grey cotton clouds as if to remind him of the size of the world out there. A world he'd soon be part of again.

'Why a private room?' had been Bridget's first words when the officer escorted her in. Her beautiful face looked taut and concerned. 'Tom? Is everything OK?'

'Everything is perfect.' He'd smiled, and they'd taken their seats.

'I'll be just outside the door,' the officer, Barry, said meaningfully. It was against the rules for him to leave Tom and his visitor unattended, but he had been around for Tom's entire sentence and he knew the reason for the visit. He left the door slightly ajar.

Bridget looked back over her shoulder, concerned. 'You're scaring me now, Tom,' she whispered. 'What's wrong?'

'Nothing's wrong, Brid. I've asked you here because ...' He stood up and moved to her side, falling to one knee. 'I want to ask you: will you marry me?'

A small sound escaped her mouth and her hand flew up to cover the bottom half of her face as her eyes glistened. 'Oh Tom ... yes! The answer is yes, of course I'll marry you!'

They both stood and he embraced her, for the first time in the two years she'd been visiting. He buried his face in her clean, shining hair, inhaled the shampoo smell of almonds and vanilla. She pressed against him and his entire body responded, seeming to fill with raging desire as he held her closer, feeling her warm, firm thighs against his.

The door creaked open slightly and Barry craned his head around, raising his eyebrows to show it was time to sit down. Tom took a step back and let out a breath. God, he wanted her so badly. It had been so, so long.

'I secretly hoped you might ask,' Bridget said, dabbing at her eyes. 'But I thought it would be after your release. I never expected this!'

'I ... I had to ask you now. I'm sorry there's no engagement ring yet but I'll put that right as soon as I can,' Tom said, his body still tense and hot. 'I think the last six months of my sentence is going to feel like six years, but now that I know we'll have each other when I'm out, it makes it all bearable.'

They'd sat back down and talked about practicalities.

'I can organise everything my end. We just have to decide when,' Bridget said. 'When and where and ... how we're going to tell our families.'

The stubborn throb of desire drained from Tom in seconds.

'Yeah, I know,' he said. 'I've been thinking about that.'

They agreed it would have to be done soon after his release. 'There's going to be a backlash,' Bridget warned. 'Best not to give them too long to think about how they can cause enough trouble to change our minds about the wedding.'

When Bridget left, Barry escorted Tom back to his cell. 'I'm guessing congratulations are in order, judging by the lady's reaction.' The officer winked.

Tom grinned and nodded. 'We've just got to decide how to tell our families now. I've got six months to work out how to stop my mother starting World War III when she hears the news.'

On the landing outside Tom's cell, Barry hesitated. 'You know, don't quote me, but you could get married in here. Mind you, your good lady might not be impressed. I mean, there are definitely more romantic venues, but it'd solve your problem about family kicking off, 'cos there wouldn't be a thing they could do about it, would there?'

He opened the cell door and went off along the landing whistling the 'Wedding March'.

And now here they were, just minutes away from their nuptials.

The prison staff had more than risen to the wedding challenge.

One of the senior officers had brought in his son's navy three-piece suit and a white shirt for Tom to wear, and Barry had loaned his own brand-new brown leather brogues for the day. Tom's neck felt uncomfortably damp under the starched collar of the shirt.

Jesse's face flashed into his mind's eye, the way it often did when he was nervous. Since the moment nearly ten years ago when the two investigating detectives came back into the claustrophobic interview room to tell him Jesse had died, his friend's image had been forever seared into his mind's eye.

The expression on Jesse's face was always the same too, the one he'd worn the split second before Tom had issued that fateful punch. The exact point in time when he might just as easily have chosen to turn around and walk away. *If only.*

But now he had a second chance at life.

The door opened and the chaplain entered. He was a small, rotund man with thinning hair and dark-rimmed glasses. Around his neck he wore a buttermilk satin cassock. He held regular weekly services at the prison, but Tom had attended none of them.

Today, the chaplain clutched a sheaf of paperwork in one hand and balanced a purple velvet cushion on the other with the ring on it. Tom had worked more hours than he could count in the prison kitchen and also on additional cleaning duties to raise funds and the governor had allowed the chaplain to purchase a modest ring on Tom's behalf.

It occurred to Tom that this, the morning of his wedding, was another of those life-defining moments when it was in his power to slam on the brakes or freewheel all the way into a tempting new life. A better life this time, filled with love and redemption.

The door opened again and there were hushed voices. Reedy classical music began, filling the corners of the room with its thin sound. Bridget walked in and Tom's breath caught in his throat. She looked an absolute vision. Stunning. She wore a mid-length plain white satin sheath that clung to her toned, shapely body. Tiny sparkles played around the delicate straps and she clutched three calla lilies, their vibrant green stems elegantly bound with silver ribbon. On her feet were dazzlingly high silver sandals that showed off her glossy French-manicured toenails and neat, lightly tanned feet.

He knew what the lags and certain officers here were saying behind his back. He had purposely kept himself to himself inside, but there were a couple of guys he trusted and had bonded with. They'd told him things they'd heard when Tom wasn't around. That he must be crazy to marry someone so old and it would never last. That she must be of unstable mind, as the mother of the man he'd killed … no decent woman would ever do that.

But what did their petty, spiteful opinions matter in the scheme of things? Soon he'd be a free man and he'd never have to see these lowlifes again.

People didn't understand that the bond he and Bridget shared was special. Unbreakable. People outside were going to have similar concerns, and as Bridget had said many times when they'd discussed the issues they'd face, that was *their* problem.

In Tom's opinion, Bridget looked a good ten years younger than her age. She'd barely changed from the days when he used to spend a lot of time at Jesse's house. She was still a gorgeous-looking woman.

She walked slowly into the chapel, her eyes meeting his and the hint of a smile playing on her lips. Her ash-blonde hair had been curled and gently pinned up at the back so that soft ringlets hung down here and there. Carefully placed white flowers framed her delicate features.

Sometimes when he looked at her he saw Jesse's eyes, his profile. But not today. Today she was Bridget Wilson, his soon-to-be wife. Mother of the young man he had killed with a single punch almost ten years ago.

Bridget had found it in her heart to forgive him, and through that decision she had saved him. She was his past, his present and his future all rolled into one, and he made a silent vow to himself that no matter how difficult things might be outside, he would let nothing and no one get between them.

He couldn't wait to start their new life together. He just had one final hurdle to overcome.

He had to break the news about their marriage to his mother, Jill. And it would not go down well.

4

Jill

October 2019

I stared at the neat array of paperwork and the foil of paracetamol set out on the polished mahogany coffee table in front of me and felt a warm glow spread into my chest. I'd been waiting ten long years for this moment and now it was finally here. Tom was coming home.

I tapped each piece of paper and mentally checked through the list once more.

Details of a two-bedroom flat just a ten-minute walk away from this house. One call and the letting agency would prepare a tenancy agreement for signature. Tick.

A new bank account with an opening balance of one thousand pounds. Tick.

Details of a temporary job offer, courtesy of my contact at the central library archives. Tick.

Last, but not least, an appointment with a highly recommended counsellor in two weeks' time. Tick.

I sat back and closed my eyes. I'd been thorough and I really needed to relax now to give the tendons in my neck a chance to loosen. I had to simmer down a bit, otherwise the headache I'd had for the last twenty-four hours would never go away. Waking up at five o'clock this morning hadn't helped matters, and that was after popping one of the new sleeping tablets the doctor had recently prescribed.

'All sorted?' Robert walked into the room carrying two cups of tea. He placed one on the low table and sat down in his chesterfield leather armchair with the other.

'It's all done,' I said, swallowing two paracetamol with my tea. 'We're finally ready for him. Have you organised the car?'

Robert performed one of his mock salutes. 'Exactly as instructed, ma'am. Full tank of petrol, his favourite playlist, and enough water and snacks to last us three times the journey.'

But my husband's cynical reassurances did nothing to stop the fluttering in my chest. I just wanted – *needed* – everything to be perfect for my boy's homecoming.

I returned to my list.

'I've bought him two pairs of jeans, a sweater, three T-shirts and a tracksuit, but I wondered whether I ought to get him a pair of smart black trousers and a nice shirt? You know, just in case we go out for a meal or if he meets up with an old friend for a drink. I'm sure he'll have lots to catch up on.'

Robert traced the rim of his cup with a fingertip. 'Tom will have his own ideas about what he wants to wear, and I doubt he'll feel up to socialising for a little while. Hopefully he'll spend some time reflecting on what a mess he's made of his life so far.'

'He's had plenty of time to reflect on that in there,' I said tersely. 'He needs our support now, and to put it all behind him.'

Robert sniffed. 'Started again already, have you? Defending him, making flimsy excuses for him. I've not missed all this one bit.'

'That's not what I'm doing. I'm Just … I'm fretting that I've forgotten something important.'

'Like you always do. Trying so desperately to control every detail before the panic sets in.'

'Nonsense,' I said, but of course, he was right.

I couldn't just let life happen. I'd seen the results of that attitude as a child, when my father had to declare himself bankrupt and we lost everything. At eight years of age I remember him sitting there looking like he'd turned into an old man overnight, endlessly repeating, 'I took my eye off the ball, I'm an idiot. I thought the business would take care of itself.' Except it didn't take care of itself at all. The partner Dad had trusted for twenty years betrayed him.

'You're thinking about your father again,' Robert said drily. 'I can tell. You've got that haunted look in your eyes.'

I watched as he put down his cup and ran a hand through his now mostly silver hair. The day Tom went to prison, ten years ago, it had been raven black. One thing that reminded me just how much time we'd lost.

'I'm just making sure I've addressed everything for Tom coming home,' I said quietly. 'That's all.'

Robert said, 'We've already talked endlessly about this. You should do the bare minimum. You've always had this notion he's a helpless little boy, when in fact what happened all those years ago proved he can be a nasty piece of work.'

I ignored the barb. As far as I was concerned, what happened to Jesse was a very unfortunate accident. Jesse had actually been the nasty one, he'd had a knife; Tom was simply trying to defend himself. Regardless, the jury had delivered a guilty verdict on the charge of manslaughter, though it wasn't a unanimous decision. Upon sentencing, the presiding judge had said, 'Thomas Billinghurst, you were a trained boxer and you used that training to position yourself to achieve maximum harm and to deliver a fatal punch.'

If Tom hadn't boxed, there might well have been a different result. We'd appealed, of course, but lost.

I regarded my husband through narrowed eyes. Tom had never been his father's priority. Robert had turned out to be that baffling type of man: the jealous father. He'd doubted and criticised our boy for most of his life, so it was no surprise to hear the old bitterness resurface now. He'd been quiet lately, nothing I could put my finger on, I just got the feeling he was a bit 'off'. I decided I preferred him quieter than full of opinions like he was this morning.

'I think I've remembered everything,' I murmured to myself, ignoring Robert.

'Well, I wouldn't worry if you haven't. Some ex-cons have no choice but to stay in a hostel when they get out of prison, with zero support from anyone else. Tom's not a teenager any more, he's a grown man who's finally got to face reality. Some might say that's long overdue.'

Ex-con. Would he never let it go? Massaging my temple, I picked up the paperwork and leafed through it yet again, but I didn't take any of it in.

It was no use trying to talk to Robert when he was in this mood. We'd always been very different when it came to discussing our feelings. After a successful career as an architect that was cut short fifteen years ago, he'd retrained as a student counsellor at a local college on the outskirts of town. Considering his lack of empathy with his own family, there were raised eyebrows when he announced his decision, but he'd proven to be a popular, competent therapist able to build a rapport with the students.

As a qualified librarian, I preferred perfect order, leaving nothing to chance, particularly something as crucial as Tom's homecoming. Goodness knows we'd waited long enough for it. I missed my job; it had been one of the casualties of Tom going away. Many times I'd thought about returning to work, but my confidence had gone and I just couldn't see myself performing that role any more.

I'd let a lot of things go this past ten years. One of them had been driving. I was perfectly fine nipping out to the local shops, but I felt too nervous to negotiate the bigger, faster roads, and the motorway was completely out of the question. I'd had no choice but to ask Robert to drive us to HMP Nottingham today to pick up our son, though that had given him the chance to express his poor opinion of Tom. Again and again.

I gathered up the paperwork and gently tapped it on all sides to get a perfect stack before slotting it inside a foolscap folder.

Standing up to leave the room, a new thought crossed my mind. Tonight, Tom would be right here, in this very house. Back home where he belonged after enduring a nightmare. Finally he'd be able to put it all firmly behind him and catch up on life's milestones that had been on hold for the past ten years. A career, reacquainting himself with friends and, eventually, meeting a nice local girl and starting his own family, with me standing at his side to love and support them all.

After years of putting my own life and dreams on hold, this wasn't just Tom's fresh start. It was mine, too.

5

Bridget

I folded the small, checked blanket beneath me and sat on the dewy grass next to my son's grave, then reached out and pressed my fingertips to the smooth biscuit-coloured headstone that a local stonemason engraved a week after his funeral – ten years ago now.

Somewhere down there, way below the dull grey slate chippings, lay the bones of my beautiful boy Jesse.

There had been so many impossible decisions to make, when I'd been half mad with grief. Wood or fibreglass for the coffin? What colour silk for the lining? Many times I'd simply let some faceless person at the funeral parlour make the final call on my behalf. But I'd steadfastly refused to have him cremated as they'd suggested. I'd wanted to keep him whole and substantial. I didn't want my strong, handsome boy, who had been so vibrant, so full of life, reduced to anything.

I couldn't bear the thought that his strong young body would be diminished.

I slid my free hand into my coat pocket and pulled out a small, ornate silver frame: my favourite photograph of Jesse I'd taken about a year before he died, which I always brought here. We lived in the grubby two-bed semi on the rough side of town then that we'd called home since he'd been two or three. I couldn't afford to buy a house back then, but I'd worked two jobs and rented the best place possible.

When I'd had the film processed, he'd looked like a rock star, with his handsome face and mischievous grin. He'd liked the photo and had kept it on his bedside table.

When he died, kind locals set up a GoFundMe page and raised what to me as a struggling single mother seemed like an enormous amount of money. Enough for a deposit on a house in a better area. But I still didn't want to move from the home I'd shared with Jesse. The mere thought of doing that had felt disloyal, as if I'd somehow be leaving his memory behind too.

Coral McKinty, Jesse's girlfriend of about a year, was six months pregnant when he died. Coral was a local girl, pale and skinny. She'd been in the year below Jesse at school and had been around to the house a handful of times with a bunch of other kids for one of Jesse's pizza and movie nights, or just to chill and listen to music in the scraggy square of grass we called a garden.

Coral looked attractive when she made an effort, but was so meek and unremarkable that Jesse's choice had baffled me. He'd had his pick of local beauties, but had chosen to date a fairly ordinary girl he'd known for years.

'Coral's OK, Ma,' he'd told me one time. 'She lets me do what I like and doesn't give me any trouble. She'll do for now, anyway.'

'Hey, cut that out!' I'd said, shocked at his attitude. I'd raised him to have respect for women. Goodness knows, he'd seen me struggle enough as he was growing up. 'You've made your choice and you're committed to Coral and your baby now.'

Coral was an only child and estranged from her own widower father, so when baby Ellis came into the world three months after his daddy's death, Ellis and Coral would stay with me regularly overnight, sometimes several times a week. The time felt right to move on to a modest but slightly bigger house in a better area.

They lived with me for a few months until I got Coral sorted out with a new-build terraced townhouse, just a five-minute walk away from my place. My grandson was the part of Jesse that lived on, and the bond I built with him encouraged me to grow strong again, helped me to start the healing process. Through Ellis, I still felt Jesse's presence in my life, and I needed that like the air I breathed.

When Jesse was alive, my love for him had been like a dazzlingly bright butterfly. Now, it was a quieter, darker love, a dull-winged moth.

A chilly breeze skimmed over the flat ground and crept under my layers of clothing. I shivered now and clutched Jesse's photograph to me, seeking comfort. I knew that today, after Tom's release from prison, there would be stormy seas to cross.

Just before Jesse's funeral, lonely and utterly bereft, I'd reached out to Jill Billinghurst. I'd dialled her landline number and then cut off the call before it connected. I did that what seemed like a thousand times before finally plucking up the courage to allow it to ring.

'Hello?' Her voice had sounded as empty as my own.

'Jill? It's … it's Bridget,' I'd said hesitantly.

'What do you want?' she snapped.

'Look, we need to talk.' I was sure she must have thought the same thing herself. As two grieving mothers, we had to gather strength from each other. We'd been friends for too long not to find a way through the tragedy together. 'Talk about everything that's happened.'

She'd been my closest friend for fifteen years and yet now I'd finally drummed up the courage to make contact, I couldn't seem to string a sentence together that articulated how I felt.

'There's nothing I want to say to you,' she'd replied coldly.

We'd each known the other's son as well as our own. We'd raised our boys together. I knew Tom's likes, his dislikes. I knew about the strawberry-shaped birthmark on his left shoulder. I knew he'd had two wisdom teeth removed and that, up to the age of about fifteen, he sometimes used to sleepwalk when he felt anxious about anything.

I knew Jill was capable of reeling off similar personal knowledge about Jesse.

We'd loved each other's sons and so we definitely had things to say to each other.

I'd grasped the phone so tightly that day, my fingers hurt. My skin pulsed hot and damp, my mind swirling with a maelstrom of powerful emotions I didn't know what to do with. My entire body felt limp with hopelessness one moment, while the next, adrenaline coursed through my veins so forcefully I struggled to control my rage.

Over the years, Jill had always seemed to have lots of acquaintances, friends and neighbours – people who I knew would rally round to support her. She had Robert. For all his faults – and she had always talked as though there were many – he was there for her. And most important of all, she still had Tom. He was still alive and they would be together again one day.

'I just need to talk to you,' I'd whispered. 'I'm going mad, stuck in the house on my own. I need to make sense of it all, and you're the only person who knows what I'm going through.'

'I warned you about the danger for years. I told you Jesse was out of control, that it was going to end badly, but you refused do anything about it.' Even now, after all this time, just thinking about how coolly she'd said those words made me shiver. 'This might have all been avoided if you'd listened.'

'Hang on! I—'

'He was your son, Bridget, your *son*. Not your best friend, or someone to have a laugh with or hang around with.' The bitterness in her voice gave her words a tinny, harsh edge. 'You had a responsibility to Jesse, and to the people around him, to rein him in. And you failed on every single count.'

'Please don't tell me how I failed as a mother when it's *your* son that's charged with—'

'Jesse had a knife that night and he threatened my son …' Jill's voice cracked, and I imagined her closing her eyes and clutching her hands into fists the way she did when she got angry. 'Tom only lashed out because he'd felt forced to defend himself. And now his life is in ruins and Jesse is dead.' And then she'd put the phone down.

I'd called her back immediately, ten, twenty times, but of course she didn't pick up.

I'd rampaged around the house like a banshee. Smashing, tearing, breaking things.

Finally I'd folded myself up into a small ball and sobbed until my throat felt raw, until my limbs ached and my chest burned.

Her cruel words had taken root in my head. The way she'd spoken about Jesse as if he'd brought his death on himself. I tried to speak to her about it a few months later. I went to the house but Jill shut the door in my face.

And now, ten years later, here we were.

In a matter of hours, I'd be starting a new life with my young husband. The man who had loved Jesse like a brother but also taken his life. Tom and I had agreed that his parents would pick him up on his release and he would tell them when they got back to the house.

We were under no illusions. Getting Robert and Jill Billinghurst to understand the decision Tom and I had made felt like an impossibility.

But they had two choices.

They would accept that we were a married couple and we'd all try to get along; or they'd refuse to do so. And if that was the case, then so be it.

Tom and I were in full agreement. They would forfeit being part of our lives at all.

6

Jill

'You shouldn't be here this morning!' Audrey scolded me lightly when I got to the shop just fifteen minutes after she'd opened. 'I'm sure you've got enough on your mind with Tom being released.'

'I'm not stopping,' I said. 'I've got all morning to kill and I just came to get away from Robert's negativity. I feel better popping by just to check you're coping OK with the new deliveries.'

'Listen to me.' She enunciated her words with comical exaggeration. 'I can manage fine without you!'

'I'll make you a coffee before I leave; at least let me do that. It'll help allay my guilt.'

Audrey laughed. 'Fine, if it makes you feel better. Make yourself one too and we can have a quick chat while it's still quiet.'

Second Chances charity shop was situated right in the middle of town on a busy side street off the main pedestrian shopping drag, West Gate. We enjoyed a steady buzz of custom most days. Audrey was a choosier manager than most, and I laughingly collected her worst opinions about stock. 'We don't want any old rubbish,' she'd tell people shortly if their donations fell short of her expectations. Last month there'd been a toe-curling rebuttal for a customer trying to offload a well-worn mac: 'If *you* think it's too tatty to wear any more, what makes you think our customers would want it?'

Cringeworthy comments aside, the obvious advantage of her candour was that our stock was of consistently good quality, always keenly priced, and we now had a small army of regular customers who came from far and wide to browse, hoping to grab a bargain. Audrey was at the stage where she knew some of our regular buyers' tastes and would even call them if we had something come in she thought they might be interested in.

At that moment, a customer entered the shop, so I went through to put the kettle on. There were three rooms back here: a kitchenette, the staff office and a small cloakroom. I filled the kettle and set it boiling, then went into the office. It surprised me to see the lights already on in there, with the computer monitor displaying a spreadsheet and paperwork spread all over the desk. Audrey had an inherent dislike of admin, particularly anything involving numbers, and usually left any updating of the stock inventory or maintenance of our simple accounting software to me.

I leaned forward to peer at the monitor. I couldn't see properly without my reading glasses but I hoped she wasn't making a mess of the inventory. That job had taken me weeks to get ready to submit to head office.

'Oh there you are!' Her voice rang out directly behind me, making me jump back from the desk. 'Everything OK in here?'

'Fine,' I said with a grin. 'Just making sure you're not messing up my hard work.'

'Kettle's just boiled.' She inched past me and pressed a few buttons on the keyboard. The monitor instantly went black. 'I was just checking we had everything up to date. My contact at head office tipped me off the auditors are visiting various premises, and I didn't want us to be caught out.'

'Was it the stock sheet?' I said as she quickly scooped up the paperwork. 'I finished updating it last Monday.'

'Yes, I remember you saying now.' Audrey slid the papers into a folder and headed for the office door.

'Is … is anything wrong?' I said faintly, noting the harassed look on her face.

'What? No, no, nothing's wrong,' she said quickly. 'Now, where's that coffee you promised me?'

I shrugged off an uncomfortable churning in my stomach. Had I done something I shouldn't have? Maybe I'd made a costly mistake and Audrey didn't want to worry me. She was definitely being evasive.

I took our coffees through to the shop.

'So,' she said. 'How are you feeling? Goodness knows you've been waiting for this moment for long enough.'

'I'm … OK. I think.'

She peered at me. 'You look a bit peaky. Nerves, that's all it'll be. Perfectly normal.'

I took a sip of my coffee. 'I'm the world's best worrier, you know that. I keep fretting whether I've done the right thing.'

'In what way?'

'You know, getting everything organised so Tom can hit the ground running. So he doesn't have to worry about a job and money.' I let out a sigh. 'You know what I'm like, planning the hell out of everything. Robert's already had a go at me.' I grinned, but it was only to stop the emotion getting hold of me.

'Just go easy on yourself, love. You've moved mountains finding Tom a job and a flat. You can ease up now.'

'Thanks, Audrey. I just have to feel in control. Getting things ready for him is the only way I can handle the stress of it all. Robert thinks I'm overkill, but then he always does.'

'Well forgive me for saying, but what you've done for Tom is a hell of a lot more than Robert ever has. Is he still acting a bit weird? I know you said he'd been distant lately.'

'He seems fine now,' I said, thinking about Robert's odd behaviour. Shutting himself away in his office until late and going for long walks alone. I suspected he was worried about money but I didn't know why. We'd always been comfortable financially with modest savings. 'I think it might be Tom's release that's on his mind. Robert detests anything affecting his routine, but for all his bluster and snide comments, he may have actually been fretting that everything would work out, you know?' I didn't realise until I'd said the words that this might be a valid observation. 'He likes to play the hard man when it comes to feelings, but if you go deep enough, he has got a soft centre.'

'Hmm, well I'll take your word for that, Jill. I don't know much about deep mining,' Audrey quipped, and I couldn't help laughing.

But I knew she got it. We'd met on the first day of college, where we were both studying English and sociology A levels, and had been firm friends ever since.

Audrey put her mug down on the cash desk. 'Right, I don't mean to rush you but I really must get on. Sorry.'

'No problem,' I said, ignoring the grumbling worry that something might be happening behind the scenes she wasn't sharing with me. 'We can catch up soon.'

'Good luck and enjoy your two weeks off.'

I felt like she was rushing me to leave and I had another compulsion to ask her if everything was OK but instead I moved towards the door.

I'd got enough to deal with right now. I didn't need another crisis on my hands.

7

Tom

After lunch, Tom pushed his small toiletries bag into his rucksack and buckled it up.

For a long time he'd imagined this moment over and over, like Groundhog Day, and he'd assumed that when it finally arrived, he'd be bouncing off the walls, sick with nerves but desperate to get out and taste sweet freedom.

Now it was actually here, he didn't feel any of that – except perhaps the nerves bit. The whole experience seemed completely surreal. He felt as though some pompous official might arrive at any moment and inform him there had been a terrible administrative error and that he had a few more years to serve before they were able to release him.

They'd brought him down from his cell late morning and into this small holding space, the exact spot he'd arrived with a vast ten-year stretch ahead of him. He turned in a slow circle to take in his surroundings one last time, staring at the stark white walls and the minuscule window set high to give tantalising glimpses of the sky.

He wouldn't miss a single thing about this hole.

From the moment he'd arrived, every day had been virtually identical with nothing to set them apart. For the first few weeks, time ran on one unbroken linear track with nothing to distinguish one hour from the next. He'd never felt desperation like it.

As someone who'd always regarded suicide as a selfish choice and the coward's way out, he'd quickly come to understand how people might feel hopeless enough to take their own life. In here, at least.

With each sunset and subsequent sunrise, every fibre of him believed he couldn't physically withstand another day, that his heart would surely stop of its own accord. And, when he *did* survive, he truly believed he wouldn't make it through the next twenty-four hours.

But slowly, very slowly, he came to learn another lesson: how tenacious and indomitable the human spirit was.

From a place deep within him, a place he'd been completely unaware of, he'd felt a change gradually come. A quelling of the fire of injustice that raged in his heart, giving way to patience and finally – most importantly – an acceptance of the situation he found himself in.

This process had taken years, but after that, things became more tolerable.

Life on the outside and the family he'd left behind seemed like a fiction to him, a good story he'd once read and enjoyed. He found comfort in the pastel-coloured memories of long ago. His mother and her home-made tiramisu; the bitter-sweet memory of the clock repair workshop his dad had set up in the garage when Tom was a kid. He missed the times way back when he and his father would sometimes do stuff together. Before things became difficult between them.

His mum had visited him like clockwork in prison, twice a month. His father, grudgingly, once or twice a year. There had been times he wished she'd come less often, because it was so difficult looking into her eyes and seeing the hurt, the denial and, more than anything, the pure desperation to have him home again. She couldn't accept that he had done the crime and must serve the time. Even now, ten years later, her viewpoint hadn't budged an inch.

In all that time, nothing had really changed in here aside from the language the officers used. Prisoners were no longer 'convicts' or 'inmates'. Now they often referred to them as 'residents'. The concrete box he'd been living in was apparently a 'room', not a 'cell', even though he'd never been in a room so bleak and soulless.

Prison had largely been a desolate, miserable experience – until the last couple of years of his sentence at least. And then, about twenty months ago, in this place where nothing new ever happened, something *had* happened. Something that changed his outlook, his life and his entire future, thanks to the love and forgiveness of Bridget Wilson.

The news of their marriage would be a terrible shock for his mother, and that worried him, as her health had suffered with him being inside. She was on medication to treat both anxiety and depression.

But he refused to let that stop him from making a stand and putting an end to certain things that had gone on so long he almost didn't notice them any more.

Like the way his mother talked to him as if he were a fifteen-year-old kid who needed her help, protection and care. What Tom *really* needed was to be given the space to build his own life again. During her last few visits, Jill hadn't once asked him what *he* wanted from life in the future. Instead, she'd talked incessantly about her plans for him on his release.

She meant well, he knew that. She was trying to help him, the only way she knew how. But it was still hell to just sit there saying nothing and nodding in all the right places. Bridget had told him how she'd telephoned Jill and even called at the house a few months after Jesse's death but his mother had put the phone down on her and shut the door in her face. Jill had never mentioned that on her regular visits; the only time she'd spoken Bridget's name was scornfully, berating her for the publicity she was courting as a grieving mother who ran a charity.

Bridget had already told Jesse's ex, Coral, and his son, Ellis, about the wedding.

'How did they take it?' Tom had ventured, almost not wanting to know.

Bridget had shrugged and said simply, 'They'll get used to it. They just need time.'

Telling his parents the news on the day of his release had seemed the obvious choice a few weeks ago, but now it was upon him, he felt apprehensive. A small part of him hoped that if he explained everything to his mother, she'd somehow find it within herself to give their marriage her blessing.

The visitors' hall had definitely not been the place to tell her what he'd done. It had to take place outside the prison. He'd look her in the eye and explain why he wouldn't be needing her help after all.

His life had transformed in ways he could never have imagined, and it was all thanks to Bridget and her unconditional love.

The door to the room opened and a security officer he hadn't seen before appeared.

'Ready, Mr Billinghurst? Your parents have arrived to take you home.'

It was the moment he'd dreamed of for so long. The moment he'd envisaged himself punching the air and yelling out in pure ecstasy at regaining his freedom.

Instead, with a fluttering sensation in his stomach, he picked up his rucksack and walked out of the door.

It was time to put the past behind him.

8

1994

It was the third week Bridget had attended the playgroup with three-year-old Jesse, and in that time, she'd been spoken to just twice. There had been the mum who mumbled 'Sorry!' as she'd dragged her small daughter away when the child ventured too close to Jesse, then the mother who told her when she arrived that the seat she was about to sit on wasn't free because she was saving it for her friend.

Today, the playgroup seemed busier and noisier than ever. The venue was a large, carpeted room at the back of the library in Berry Hill, a desirable residential area on the south side of Mansfield. There was a £1 entry fee and the bus fare, which Bridget really had to think about seeing as she was on her uppers after being laid off recently from the supermarket. But Jesse got a glass of juice and a biscuit, and there was a cup of tea or coffee provided for her, too. And most importantly, it was nice here. Nice surroundings and people with safe, clean toys.

She looked around her at the quality clothing worn by the other parents. Bridget had on the only coat she owned, a frayed, thin beige mac she'd bought in the Debenhams sale three years ago. Underneath she'd dressed in two T-shirts and a polyester sweater to help keep the cold from sinking into her bones. Her right ankle boot had a small split where the man-made upper met the sole, and so, after the walk over here in the rain and sleet this morning, the bottom of her foot was soaking. She found a seat and reached down, pulling her foot halfway out of the boot to give the sock chance to dry out a little.

Despite the weather, she'd made the twenty-minute trek through the snowy streets from the nearest bus stop because Jesse loved it here so much. Interactions with other kids were a treat when you lived in a crumbling terraced house with mouldy walls on the wrong side of town. And there weren't any other small children on the street for him to play with.

Bridget watched Jesse now and felt a swell of pride and affection. He had beautiful thick, naturally wavy hair that she liked to keep long in the neck. Today, though, it was damp and frizzy from the weather, and his elasticated-waist trousers were too short for his growing legs. Her heart sank when she realised he bore more than a passing resemblance to a little scarecrow – a cute one admittedly – amongst the well-dressed girls and boys in this middle-class enclave. She'd had to come here, had to escape their grim reality just for a short time. The boost that being part of another world, a better life, gave her – even if it was just for a couple of hours – was priceless to her state of mind.

Settled at last, with Jesse happily running off to play, she looked around for a friendly face. The two women sitting on either side had discreetly turned away from her to talk to other people. Their own sort.

Bridget sat quietly in her soggy coat and boots with her hands folded in her lap and closed her eyes briefly. She hadn't slept well because the neighbours had had another drink-induced row. Something had smashed against the wall in the early hours and woken her up, but luckily, Jesse had slept through it. Bridget knew that Sandra next door was the self-confessed 'thrower' in that relationship, so she had no fear that the other woman was in danger. Living there often made her glad she was single.

She opened her eyes in time to catch the sideways glances being directed her way. She noticed the discreet, almost invisible ushering away of well-dressed sons and daughters from little Jesse, as if being slightly scruffy and obviously poor might be catching.

There was another playgroup, a free one, run by the local council in a draughty, musty-smelling church hall a couple of streets away from their house. All the kids looked like Jesse there; all the mums dressed the same as Bridget. They were people with identical problems and challenges to the ones she had in her own life. She would not have felt judged there.

But she didn't want that for her son. She wanted him to grow up able to feel at home with different kinds of people. To never feel inferior like she herself had as a child when her troubled mother had dumped her at Aunt Brenda's house and never returned for her.

She understood now how resentful her aunt must've felt, but she'd had a fearsome temper and frequently unleashed her fury on a young, impressionable Bridget for even a minor misdemeanour.

The words Brenda had uttered on the day of Bridget's mum's funeral were forever seared into her mind: 'You're useless. You'll never make anything of yourself; you'll end up just like her. A dirty slut, too old and ugly to be loved.' That was the last thing her aunt had said before she'd put Bridget into foster care. At fifteen years old she had silently vowed she'd make something of her life. And if only to prove Aunt Brenda wrong, she would start by never growing old and ugly.

Something had clicked into place when she'd made herself that promise, because since that day, Bridget had possessed a kind of conviction that however bleak life looked, she would eventually claw her way up to a better existence for herself and her son. They would enjoy comfort, warmth and security and a nice place to live. She would find a career she loved and work hard at it, and she would eventually find a partner who respected and supported her, instead of settling for one of the local lowlifes, who would only drag her further down.

One day she would have a wardrobe full of the best clothes and look after herself. Most important of all, she'd work hard to stay youthful and never let herself go like her mother had.

Exactly how and when this miraculous shift would occur, she had no idea yet, but the mechanics of it really didn't matter. For now, trips away from the swamp to nice places like this helped her to keep believing in the dream.

An angry yell broke her out of her reverie, and she turned just in time to catch Jesse tussling with another little boy over a big blue truck. The other boy was shorter than Jesse, but he was stocky and confident and gave as good as he got. Before Bridget had a chance to intervene, the other boy's mother rushed over.

Unlike most of the other parents here, who looked like they might have lunch plans straight after the playgroup, this woman was what Bridget would call functional. She had unfussy short brown hair and minimal make-up, and she wore well-cut jeans paired with a simple beige cashmere sweater, a navy blazer and tan leather loafers.

Bridget braced herself for the boy being pulled away from Jesse and an angry look directed her way. She felt her hackles rising in readiness.

But the woman didn't pull her son away. Instead, she crouched down between the boys and spoke to them encouragingly. Both children stopped tugging at the toy and looked at her, nodding. She took the truck and placed it on the floor between them. Jesse grabbed some brightly coloured blocks from behind him, and the other boy helped him load the bed of the truck with them.

Bridget left her bag on the chair and walked over.

'Hi.' She smiled as the woman stood up. 'Sorry about that. Jesse can be possessive about toys, he doesn't see many other children.'

'No worries, Tom is just as bad. People here like to bicker about which kid is right, but it's part of playing, isn't it? Sorting out their problems with a bit of help.' The woman grinned. 'I'm Jill, by the way. Jill Billinghurst. I think I saw you here last week too.'

'It's my third week coming here. Jesse loves it, so I trek across town. I'm Bridget Wilson.'

'Across town? Where is it you live?'

Bridget's smile faltered and a vague reply danced on her tongue. But what was the use in trying to be something she wasn't? Jill and the rest of the parents here would tell a mile off that she and Jesse weren't from Berry Hill.

'Just off Sherwood Hall Road,' she said simply, a vision of the damp, shabby accommodation they called home spoiling her optimism for a moment. The area's biggest achievement in recent years was its ranking in the country's most deprived neighbourhoods.

With a heavy heart, she prepared herself for Jill to remember she had something pressing to take care of and to haul Jesse's new playmate away to find a more suitable friend.

Jill hesitated. 'I was going to get myself a coffee. If you don't mind watching the children, I could get you one too.'

'That would be lovely, thanks,' Bridget said, trying to cover up her surprise.

She sat back down as Jill made her way over to the refreshment hatch, acknowledging other mums as she walked. Bridget felt brighter, somehow validated. Jill was obviously very much part of the in-crowd here, and had taken the time to be kind to her and Jesse. It was a nice feeling. Bridget wasn't the sort of woman to feel intimidated. She'd brazened it out here for three weeks with no one offering so much as a friendly smile until today. But it still felt good to have a chat with another human being. She did a low-paid job from home, collating and folding assembly instructions into envelopes, and some days she and Jesse didn't see another soul.

She watched as Jesse and his little friend worked together to load the truck with coloured bricks. They took turns to push it round in a big circle and then worked as a team to offload the bricks before the process started again.

Jill returned with their coffees, plus juice and biscuits for the boys on a small tray. The woman on the seat to Bridget's right had moved away, so Jill sat down on the vacant chair.

As the boys devoured their juice and biscuits, the two women chatted. Bridget learned that she and Jill were nearly the same age, and that Jill's husband, Robert, worked as an architect in Mansfield.

'You know, Tom hasn't played this nicely with anyone for a long time. He's an only child, so it's lovely to see him sharing,' Jill said as they watched the boys move away from the truck to a colourful cloth Wendy house. 'Would you like to come over to our house one afternoon next week? We can have a coffee while the boys play. We've got lots of space for them to run around.'

'Thank you, Jill,' Bridget said, hardly believing her ears. 'That would be really lovely.'

9

Jill

October 2019

We drove out of the prison gates and suddenly the car seemed too small to contain the three of us. All the things I'd been so desperate to say to Tom bounced silently round my head because I didn't want to expose myself to Robert's scathing criticism.

'I've got crisps, and Fanta or water if you want them,' I said brightly. 'I even got a bag of Haribo, your favourite.' Tom was sitting behind his father and I turned to face him.

'I try to watch my sugar and saturated fat intake these days, Mum,' Tom said, looking out of the window at the buildings, the people. 'I'm fine, please don't worry.'

His head twisted this way and that, tracking something or someone outside the window as the car moved past. He seemed fascinated, as if it surprised him that the world outside had continued to prosper while he'd been serving his time.

He looked clean and handsome wearing the new clothes I'd taken in for him on my last visit. I'd selected a navy bomber jacket with black denim jeans and a simple white T-shirt. He wore no jewellery, not even a watch, but when I kissed his cheek he was clean-shaven and smelled pleasingly of shampoo and soap.

I twisted around in my seat. 'Did they give you lunch before you left?'

'It's a prison, not a hotel, Jill.' Robert's fingertips tapped a disjointed beat on the steering wheel.

'I'm not hungry, Mum,' Tom said, and I saw him meet his father's cold eyes in the rear-view mirror. I looked away as the air in the car seemed to thicken. The old animosities were still alive and kicking.

Driving as a family like this felt like going back in time twenty years. One weekend a month, Robert would load up the car with roughly double the amount of stuff we needed and we'd set off to our static caravan on a small rural site in Northumberland. Me and Robert in the front, Tom and Jesse in the back like nodding dogs in time with the music they listened to through their sponge Walkman headphones. I felt a yearning inside me when I thought about those times.

I tolerated a minute of two of the silence before I felt moved to fill it.

'It's hard to know what to talk about, isn't it?' I turned my upper body to face Tom again. 'I mean, it's not like we're picking you up from a holiday or you've been living somewhere else all this time.'

Tom gave me a weak smile but said nothing.

'It must have felt like you were existing in a whole different world in there, like a parallel universe.'

On his lap, his phone lit up and he opened a text message. Vaguely, without looking at me, he said, 'Yes, that's sort of how it feels.'

'How did you get the phone?' I asked casually.

'There's a scheme at the prison. If you qualify, support services provide you with one on release together with your discharge grant.'

'All funded by the taxpayer, no doubt,' Robert said disapprovingly.

'I'm surprised anyone knows your new number,' I remarked. 'Who's texting you?'

'It's a message about my data allowance,' he said easily.

He tapped at the screen and I thought it seemed odd that he was texting back to an automated service. He noticed me watching and stuffed the phone into his jacket pocket.

'I thought there might be delays at the prison, or on the road,' I said, rustling the bag of goodies at my feet. 'That's why I brought plenty of snacks and drinks, in case we needed them.'

'Your problem is, you plan for every eventuality,' Robert said scornfully. 'Why not try going with the flow for once? You never know, you might even enjoy it and cut down those new tablets you keep popping.'

Tom frowned. 'Tablets for what?'

'To calm me down when I need it,' I said, glaring at Robert. 'Nothing to worry about.'

'She can't sleep at night, hasn't done for years,' Robert said with some satisfaction. 'The ripples of what you did travelled far and wide, Tom, you'd do well to remember that.'

'How can I forget with you around to remind me?' Tom clamped his mouth closed and continued to stare out as we passed through the outskirts of the city.

The car fell quiet again. Only twenty minutes to go and we'd be home.

'I almost forgot. Put the playlist on, Robert.'

'Honestly, I'm fine, Mum, I don't—'

'But it's Oasis, you've always loved them. I found a greatest hits playlist.'

'I'd rather sit quietly for now.'

I felt the tension rolling off him in waves. I'd almost forgotten how on edge it made me when he and his father were in close proximity, sniping relentlessly at one another. I had imagined the journey back home being light with pleasant conversation and everyone glad that the moment had finally arrived. Even Robert.

Tom took his phone out again and glanced at the screen before sliding it back into his pocket. Something was bothering him.

I rooted around in the passenger footwell for my handbag and pulled out a folded piece of paper.

'If you're sitting there fretting about what your life is going to look like now, there's no need.' I glanced at Robert, who kept his eyes on the road ahead. 'I was waiting until we got home to tell you all this, but we might as well use the time we're stuck in the car.'

'Tell me what?' Tom sounded tired.

I unfolded the sheet. 'So, I started off by googling *difficulties people face when leaving prison*, and lots of stuff came up. I also found some super resources on the Prisoners' Families website. Have you heard of them? They even have a helpline you can ring.'

'No. I haven't,' Tom said, his voice a monotone.

'I addressed some of the biggest worries I found, so you'd get the best fresh start possible. First thing, accommodation. I've found a lovely little two-bedroom apartment near the park that's come up for rent. If we move fast you might get it.' Tom opened his mouth to say something but I instantly filled the gap. It was important he had all the facts before deciding. 'When you went away, there was nothing around that area of town, I know. But now there are quite a few nice little shops, and a lovely café at the end of the road. They put a chalkboard outside most days, specials for lunch and breakfast. I met Audrey there last week and we had coffee and a croissant for a fiver. Can't grumble at that!'

'But I—'

'It's overwhelming to think about living on your own so soon, I know, and there's absolutely no rush, but I felt sure you'd want space after living in such cramped conditions for so long. It's going to take some adjusting to.' I waited for Tom to respond, but he stayed quiet. 'Anyway, we can view it and you can make your own mind up.'

'He wants to thank his lucky stars he's not headed straight for some grubby hostel,' Robert added unhelpfully, as if Tom wasn't sitting in the car with us.

'Next one on the list was getting a job. I called on one of my old contacts in the library service, and you'll never guess what … I've only managed to set up an opportunity for you!'

Tom looked incredulous. 'What kind of opportunity?'

I held up a hand. 'Before you panic, nothing is set in stone, so there's no need to feel pressured. I thought you might even fancy retraining in something completely different, and that's fine, too. I read that finding a job is one of the most difficult things for someone with a criminal record, and so I thought I'd give you the option if you wanted to get some normality back quickly.'

'I'll be fine sorting myself out,' Tom said, leaning his head against the glass. 'My probation officer can help with all that. I'll be meeting with him soon enough.'

'Well, mind that you get it sorted out sooner rather than later,' Robert interjected. 'We don't want a replay of where you left off.'

Tom had gone to college to study for A levels when he left school, but he found he didn't enjoy the subjects he'd chosen. The principal wrote to us to say he was falling behind with his studies. Then he got into his boxing and was excited when he found out that another local college did a year-long sports science foundation degree. He'd applied and was waiting for an interview when that terrible night changed the course of his life.

'We can talk about it all when we get home,' I said, deflated. I refolded the piece of paper and pushed it back into my handbag.

'Your mum has worked really hard for months and months getting all this stuff set up for you.' Robert lifted his flinty eyes to the mirror. 'You might show a bit of gratitude.'

'It's fine, Robert. He's tired, that's all it is.'

Tom sighed. 'Thanks, Mum, I appreciate it, but I have some plans of my own I want to follow up on, too.'

'What sort of plans?' I said carefully.

'I thought we might discuss it later.' His voice sounded strained. He must be under tremendous pressure with this new, intimidating world bearing down on him. This was when he most needed our reassurance.

'If it's money that's worrying you, Tom, there's no need. I don't want you to be embarrassed to talk about finances and I've put something in place for that too,' I said with renewed vigour. 'I know all this must seem immense so soon after your release and I won't go into all the details right now, but I wanted to set your mind at rest.'

'He'll have to earn his own money at some stage,' Robert said coldly. 'The last time I looked, there was no money tree growing in the garden.'

I'd noticed he kept sniping about money. There certainly never seemed to be much of a balance in our current account any more. I knew we had modest savings to fall back on, but that wasn't the point. I barely went out, so if money was being squandered, it was Robert's doing.

'I've every intention of earning my own money,' Tom said, and I felt surprised at how resolved he sounded.

'I very much look forward to hearing how you intend doing that,' Robert said with a smirk.

I set the Oasis soundtrack playing at a low volume. I saw Tom had closed his eyes, but he was feigning sleep, because his face was too still and tense. He'd done the same thing as a small child when he didn't like the way a conversation was going.

I sat back in my seat and folded my arms. He'd been through such a lot, I couldn't blame him for shutting us out. It didn't matter because at last I had my son back home. We had all the time in the world to discuss his plans, and I felt confident, if they turned out to be a bit too ambitious, he'd be open to some gentle encouragement.

He'd always been the same. If he had his heart set on something inappropriate, I had only to pick my moment to distract him and set him on a different path.

That was one thing about my boy. He always saw sense in the end.

10

Bridget

Tom texted to say they were leaving the prison and I'd quickly sent a message back.

Can't wait to see you. Can't wait for us to be together.

Three hours to go and it would be time.

There were many people that were going to struggle to accept our decision to be together but that was their lookout. We were a couple in the eyes of the law. We'd been through too much to let anyone get in our way now.

Following Jesse's death, there was an explosion of unexpected press attention when Tom was charged with the assault. The dubious glamour of Tom being a professional boxer, that he was Jesse's best friend and a good-looking young man from a respectable family seemed to feed the media's appetite for a sensationalist story.

But even in the midst of debilitating grief, I noticed a subtle change in the reports in newspapers and online. They began to refer to Jesse as a known troublemaker and the fact that he had a knife on him that night supported this image. Nobody mentioned that the weapon was a legal Swiss Army penknife that he kept on him for any impromptu repairs to his unreliable old motorbike. The obvious subtext of it all was that he had somehow contributed to his own demise.

I was the first to admit my son hadn't been perfect, but did those spells of laddish behaviour cancel out his life completely? Did they render what had happened to him unimportant, as if he'd somehow deserved to die? No, they did not.

The anger at the injustice of the media's reporting of the incident engaged the thread of steel I'd always had inside me. It had provided the inner strength I'd clung to as a young person in foster care, the resolve that had kept me going for years bringing Jesse up on my own and working two jobs to pay the bills.

I fought against the inequality of being different. Of being poor. Of being a single parent with a son who'd died in a violent situation. I clung on to my resolve like a life jacket.

Inside I was breaking into pieces, but I didn't let them see that. When the older kids at the children's home slapped my face and called me ugly, I stood tall and swallowed down the hurt until it was nothing but a little hard knot in the bottom of my stomach.

I remember feeling that fighting for my boy's memory was the final thing I could do for him.

I didn't have to look far to find examples of young working-class men who had died in tragic circumstances over the last ten years. Men subconsciously labelled failures, perhaps because they were not university-educated or did not have high-flying careers.

I made some noise, online, offline, anywhere I could. As the incident was still fairly new, several newspapers and women's magazines were happy to talk to me. I gave them some of what they wanted; that was, to talk openly about my grief. To have my picture taken against a grey sky with tear-filled eyes. But I also got in a line or two about the derisory attitude I'd noticed towards Jesse in the popular press.

Some newspapers changed their tone, talking about the attitude of the media as if they themselves had never been guilty of it.

Incredibly, people sat up and listened. Thanks to the tracing skills of the Royal Mail, I received letters vaguely addressed in the style of 'Bridget Wilson, Notts. (Mother of Jesse)' from parents who'd lost their own sons in similar circumstances, thanking me for speaking out. They wanted to share how they had experienced the same attitude from the press and public. More magazines asked for interviews. As time went on, I received invitations to speak in public by various organisations such as bereavement groups and support networks for victims of crime.

My simple, genuine message about kindness and equality quickly garnered more attention, and within a few months I was receiving messages of support from Europe and even the US.

Responding to a public need and with support and funding from sympathetic organisations, I set up the Young Men Matter charity. It grew quickly and prospered. The funding paid for my salary as CEO, and enabled us to operate as a charitable business, accepting payment for events and attracting donations. It had been my full-time job now for the last five years, giving me a good standard of living and no need to work two jobs at minimum wage any longer. But I'd give it all up in a heartbeat to go back to those days with Jesse, when we'd feasted on beans on toast like kings.

After work, through the long evenings at home, I felt so lonely.

Jesse's father had been nothing more than a one-night stand after a boozy night out. The guy was from out of town and I'd never set eyes on him again. Had no telephone number or address. I didn't even know his surname. I had lots of contact with Coral, of course. She had gone to school with Jesse and obviously knew him well but she hadn't had what I'd call a 'meaningful' relationship with him. I doubted they'd have stayed together if she hadn't fallen pregnant with Ellis.

There was literally no one who missed Jesse like I did.

Too much water had gone under the bridge to reinstate my friendship with Jill Billinghurst. Coral had heard on the local gossip grapevine that Jill was a virtual recluse these days, living in a stupor of misery. She'd given up her job at the library, and apart from helping at a local charity shop, she barely left the house. The thought of such self-pity lit a furnace inside me. Jill should be ashamed of herself. Her son was still alive, wasn't he? He was the one responsible for Jesse's death, whether or not by accident. *He* would start a new life in a couple of years' time, while my boy languished underground in a cold sleep that would never end.

About two years ago, I received a letter from the prison inviting me to take part in a restorative justice programme designed to bring closure to the families of victims of crime. They enclosed a booklet explaining how it worked, that it would begin with a visit to the prison.

For the first twelve months of his sentence, Tom had written to me with alarming regularity. I hadn't opened a single one of the letters. Instead, I'd bought a shredder and kept it by the front door. Within seconds of the prison-franked mail hitting the mat, I'd churned what I assumed were his meaningless platitudes and pleas for forgiveness into satisfyingly insubstantial paper strips.

Back then, to open those letters would have felt so disloyal to Jesse's memory. But in later years, I'd wished I hadn't destroyed them. Whatever I thought of Tom, he was the only other person who shared my closest memories of Jesse. Memories that were still as vibrant as ever, like beautiful living blooms, far too precious to be buried under a blanket of grief as I'd been trying so hard to do.

It was that realisation that prompted me to complete the enclosed visiting order. Impulsively I took it to the postbox at the end of the street before I changed my mind.

Three days later, I received emailed confirmation of my first visit to see Prisoner #A1756TF Tom Billinghurst at HMP Nottingham the following week.

The morning of the visit I felt queasy, and mooched around the house in my dressing gown, unable to eat any breakfast or lunch.

The visit was at two o'clock. Still debating whether I should follow through with it, I forced myself to shower and get ready, opting for jeans, roll-neck sweater and a leather jacket. I smoothed my hair back into a simple ponytail and applied minimal make-up. Dabbed enough concealer to help disguise the shadows under my eyes and a couple of sweeps from the bronzer brush to brighten the pallor of my skin.

The prison was in the Sherwood area of Nottingham, about a thirty-minute drive from Mansfield. The roads were quieter than I'd expected and I arrived early. I waited in the car park for twenty minutes, reclining the seat a little and closing my eyes to listen to a playlist on Spotify.

Once I got inside the building, the security checks I had to undergo along with hordes of other people took another fifteen minutes.

The visiting hall was large and echoing and filled with grim little square tables and plastic chairs with bowed metal legs. With the other visitors, I filed past bored-looking prison officers standing like sentries around the room and took my seat at the next available table.

The wait for Tom to emerge from the inner door seemed to last forever. More than once, I thought I might be sick right there in front of everyone. I contemplated cutting my losses and going back home when I looked up and he was suddenly there. He filled the doorway, dwarfing the other men who were filing in and the diminutive officer who escorted them.

My breath caught in my throat, my eyes widening with shock. He was so much taller and broader across the shoulders than I'd remembered. His short dark hair had grown longer, wavier, and framed his thick brows and serious dark eyes. He had a couple of days' worth of stubble on his well-defined jaw and his features looked chiselled and angular.

This mature, brooding man barely resembled the slightly hesitant, polite boy I'd seen grow up. I held up my hand in case he had failed to spot me, but he'd already fixed his eyes on mine as he headed straight for me.

'Bridget.' His voice emerged throaty and deep as he took his seat opposite. 'Thanks for coming. Even after I saw you'd scheduled a visit, I didn't know if you'd turn up.'

'I didn't know whether I would until the last moment either.' I felt ridiculously shaken by his presence.

What had I expected? I wasn't sure, but it hadn't been this. During the past eight years, Tom Billinghurst had clearly grown into his own skin. But there was no trace of arrogance, he was just … mature Tom. A self-assured but still humble man.

He'd linked his fingers and placed his clasped hands on the table. His nails were short and clean, and there was a scattering of fine dark hairs on the top of each hand, thickening as they traced up to his muscled forearms.

'I've been waiting a long, long time for this,' he'd said, his voice low and level as he looked into my eyes. 'I want to say that I'm sorry, Bridget. I'm so, so sorry that Jesse died because of me. Because of how I reacted that night.' His voice cracked. 'I never, *ever* meant for that to happen. I should have stepped back, I should have left instead of reacting.'

That had been the start of it. I looked down at my left hand, at the simple gold wedding band.

Later today, we'd begin our new life together.

11

Jill

I was first out of the car when Robert parked up on the drive. I'd visualised this moment a thousand times in my head, imagining Tom trying to control his emotions when he saw his family home again after all this time.

I'd hung winter flowering baskets either side of the porch and filled a wooden trough with cheerful pansies and violas in front of the window. I'd cleaned the glossy green front door and bought a nice new woven doormat that read *Home Sweet Home*.

I stood back and watched as Tom unfolded his broad frame from the back seat. He took a moment to look at the house and I watched with growing anxiety as his dark brows beetled. His mouth tightened and he walked around to the boot and retrieved his holdall and rucksack.

'Welcome back, son,' I said and pressed his old front door key into his hand. He pocketed it without even glancing at it.

'Thanks, Mum,' he said and we walked to the house together, tears blurring my vision. I opened up and Robert strode past us, down the hallway and disappeared into his downstairs office.

'Tom?' I said faintly as he stepped inside the hall. 'What is it? What's wrong?'

'Nothing,' he said, pasting a small smile on his face. 'I'm tired, I guess.'

I waited a moment or two for him to comment on the brighter hallway. I'd had the ugly old flooring ripped up and replaced with a smart light oak. Over the past twelve months, Joel, our decorator, had freshened up all the downstairs rooms ready for the big day. Our new start.

'Anyone would think we were expecting a visit from royalty,' Robert had grumbled. 'We've had to live with it long enough, I don't see why you've done it for his benefit.'

'It's not really for Tom,' I'd said, practising tolerance. 'It's marking a new chapter in all of our lives.'

Robert had snorted and made himself scarce. Even so, I kept the vision of our new family life together alive. I admit I felt deflated when Tom appeared not to have noticed my efforts at all. He didn't even seem happy to be home.

'Come on through to the kitchen. I'll make you a cup of tea and a sandwich.'

He pulled a regretful face. 'I need a lie-down, if that's OK. Try to get my head around everything.'

'Take as much time as you need,' I said, although I wasn't quite sure what he meant by 'everything'. After ten years of being without his family, I felt a little concerned that he immediately wanted to be alone in his bedroom. 'I'll make our tea for about four thirty.'

I imagined what Audrey would say to reassure me. 'Of course he wants some time alone, Jill, it's what he's been used to!' She'd roll her eyes and give me a hug. 'Nothing at all to do with how he feels about being home.'

Tom lugged his bags upstairs. I followed him up and watched as he hovered in the open doorway of his bedroom. My heart swelled as his head turned slowly, taking it all in. The Manchester United poster still above his bed, his model Star Wars memorabilia still displayed on his desk, the boxing trophies on the windowsill. I'd cleaned his room every week, dusted his collections, and last month, I'd cleared out his wardrobe and drawers ready for his new clothes.

'I kept everything the same as the day you went away,' I said softly behind him.

He turned around to face me. 'But why? I mean, I didn't expect you to do that. You and Dad could've used this room.'

I laughed. 'Used it for what, exactly? This is *your* bedroom, Tom. It'll always be your bedroom even when you're eventually married and settled down with your own young family.'

'I'll be down in good time for tea,' he said, his expression unreadable. He stepped fully into the room and gently closed the door, leaving me on the landing.

Coming back to the family home and his own bedroom must be fraught with emotion. His reaction wasn't what I'd expected, but I felt sure it was nothing to worry about. It was completely normal … wasn't it?

With Robert ensconced in his office as usual and Tom up in his bedroom, I found myself, as on so many other occasions, alone in the kitchen.

I poured myself a glass of water from the fridge cooler and sat at the breakfast bar. I hadn't expected the dull, heavy sensation in my chest. Of course, I'd known realistically that Tom's homecoming would probably be different to how I'd imagined it, but this … well, despite me telling myself it was normal, the situation was not what I'd hoped for at all.

I knew now that I'd been overly romantic and optimistic in my imaginings. Coming out of a ten-year prison lockdown would never be easy for Tom, and the biggest shock of all was how much I'd forgotten: the tensions, the moody undertone that had been the everyday backdrop to our family life, the crushing pressure I'd felt to keep the peace between Robert and Tom, to defuse arguments before they even started. I'd run myself ragged trying to absorb the resentment and negativity that had buzzed between them like an electric current, like I'd tried to do as a child with my mother and father.

After we'd lost the business and the house and had to move into a rented one-bed flat when I was ten years old, I'd somehow convinced myself that if I behaved perfectly, Dad would stop drinking, Mum would stop screaming at him and they wouldn't get divorced. Then everything would be fine again. Things would soon get back to normal.

Now, on the day of Tom's release, I'd forgotten the price I'd paid all those years in an effort to keep up the charade that we were a close, happy family. I didn't know whether I had the resolve to start all over again, and yet, on another level, I felt compelled to do so.

At 4.30 sharp, I called Tom downstairs. He appeared five minutes later in the kitchen, his hair still damp from the shower. He'd changed into grey sweatpants and a white T-shirt. He didn't look very rested, standing there biting his thumbnail while his eyes darted around the room.

Robert ambled in without saying a word.

'Sit down, son,' I said brightly. 'I made your favourite and there's my tiramisu for dessert.'

I carried the still-bubbling home-made lasagne to the table, where Tom and Robert now sat waiting in stony silence. Tom's first day at home was always going to feel strange. I'd prepared the meal yesterday and I'd hoped for a relaxed tea together, perhaps chatting about when Tom might go to view the flat I'd found, or his plans to catch up with his old friends at the boxing club.

I placed the earthenware dish on the heat mat and returned a moment later with the large flat round of rosemary focaccia and a bowl of chopped green salad.

Tom took his phone out of his pocket and placed it screen down on the table next to his plate. I saw Robert's eyes narrow – he hated phones at the table – and breathed a sigh of relief when he looked away again without comment.

I divided the lasagne into thirds and loaded a portion onto the serving scoop. When I lifted it towards Tom's plate, he put up a hand. 'Only half of that for me, Mum.'

I returned the scoop to the dish. 'But this is one of your favourite meals; you always used to have seconds.' It sounded ridiculous, but I felt like crying.

He glanced anxiously at me. 'I know. I'm sorry, but ... I'm not hungry.'

'A sandwich would have done for me,' Robert announced, opening his newspaper and shaking it out noisily above the table. 'I'll be asking for another dose of gout if I eat all that.'

'You shouldn't have cooked all this for me, Mum.' Tom picked at the salad. 'Looks good, though.'

'I shall be glad when things get back to normal around here,' Robert muttered, his eyes glued to the newspaper. 'Can't come soon enough, in fact.'

Tom put down his fork and stared at his plate. He'd had enough experience with his father to know that the best policy was to ignore his jibes. But this new Tom had waves of resentment rolling off him. I realised how he'd been like a coiled spring ever since getting into the car. And now he was behaving like he didn't want to be here with us at all.

'Robert, please don't make Tom feel like he's an inconvenience.' I dropped the piece of bread and charred rosemary needles showered the table like tiny dead insects. 'I wanted everything to be perfect for our first family meal together. Please don't spoil it.'

'How can everything be perfect?' Robert's nose and mouth screwed together in a tight knot. 'He's finished a ten-year stretch at Her Majesty's pleasure for killing his best friend, and you're trying to pretend we're the perfect reality TV family.' He threw the crumpled newspaper on the floor and stood up. 'Forget tea. I've remembered there's somewhere I'd rather be.'

'Stay where you are! Just for a minute!' Tom pushed his chair back and stood up. My cutlery clattered down onto my plate, and even Robert looked taken aback. 'Mum, Dad, there's something I need to tell you both. Something really important.'

The air in the room grew dense and still. I held my breath, waiting for what was obviously going to be a critical moment. I instinctively knew I was about to find out what it was my son had been holding back since we'd picked him up, and that it would be momentous.

My eyes met his and I saw dread there, a silent pleading. His face looked thinner, paler, and I knew whatever he was about to tell us would change everything.

Finally I let go of the breath I'd been holding and Robert sat back down. 'Well all right, if it can't wait. Lord knows, I haven't missed this sort of drama in the house.'

'Look, I want to say thanks. For everything you've both done. Especially you, Mum.' Tom spoke as if he'd rehearsed the words. 'Whatever you think of me when you hear what's coming next, I do appreciate your efforts and I'm sorry for bringing shame on the family.'

Was he talking about the night Jesse died, or was it to do with what he was about to say?

His voice sounded so thin and shaky, I squeezed my thighs together under the table, trying to give myself some fortitude. 'You've never brought shame on us,' I said faintly.

A thick silence fell over the three of us then like a blanket of snow arriving without warning. Tom stared down at the table as if he'd forgotten we were there at all, and Robert sat perfectly still, staring ahead.

'You don't know this, Mum, but about two years ago, I started to take part in a programme at the prison. Have either of you heard of restorative justice?'

He looked up. At me and then at Robert.

'I have, yes,' Robert said shortly. 'All about making amends for your crime, isn't it?'

'That's part of it.' Tom turned to me. 'The programme focuses on reconciliation with victims and their families, Mum.'

I frowned. 'But Jesse isn't here to reconcile with any more.' The smell of the lasagne, the burned rosemary scattered on the table, was making me feel nauseous.

Tom looked down and knotted his fingers together. I became aware of Robert's breathing growing heavier.

'Bridget joined the programme too,' Tom said carefully.

'What? How do you know that?' I was failing to make sense of the information. I knew I was missing something big, but the connection wouldn't come.

Tom continued. 'We both agreed to give the programme a go. Once a fortnight we met up and with the help of the programme leaders we—'

'You've been meeting up with *Bridget*?' I whispered. 'How is that allowed in prison?'

'That's what this programme is all about, Mum. Recognising the harm I did and trying to put it right with Jesse's family – his mum.'

'Well now I've heard it all,' Robert snorted.

My entire body felt rigid. Frozen. 'I can't believe they've had you going cap in hand to that woman.' I had to force the words out and swallow down the fire that burned in my chest and throat.

'It was voluntary. Nobody forced me to do anything.'

'What happened to Jesse, it was an accident. You said so yourself! You didn't mean for him to die.'

'But he *did* die,' Tom said simply, turning his palms upward as if he wanted to show me he wasn't hiding anything. 'Accident or not, Jesse isn't here any more because of *me*. Don't you see that?'

'He came at you with a knife and so it was self-defence! You should never have received such a long sentence.'

'The jury decided it was my fault that Jesse died that night and found me guilty.' Tom chanted the words sing-song style, clearly fed up with telling me the same thing again and again. 'I had the choice to walk away when things became heated outside the nightclub, but I didn't. I take full responsibility for that and I'll never forgive myself for it.'

I stared at the wall. I'd visited Tom twice a month for the duration of his sentence, and I knew nothing about this ridiculous programme. I knew nothing of Bridget secretly attending the sessions. I had noticed a change in him, though. He'd been more upbeat in a way I couldn't put my finger on. He'd looked brighter, sat up a bit straighter, though I'd put it down to his release date drawing closer. I'd assumed it was because he was finally coming home to us.

When Tom was sixteen, he'd started training at a local boxing club. It quickly became clear to the coach there – a local man called Kenny – that he had the skills and dexterity to become an excellent amateur boxer. He started training several times a week, but the thing was, he never told us. He'd taken part in his first two amateur fights before someone asked Robert if the hot young boxer beating everyone he fought was his son.

Robert seemed impressed, said he hadn't thought Tom had it in him, but I'd disapproved. I found boxing a barbaric sport, but more to the point, why on earth hadn't he told us what he was doing? I'd felt perplexed why he would enter into something so serious without consulting us. I never got an answer.

'You're finally seeing what I've known all along, that our son has a sly, secretive side,' Robert had said.

Tom had continued to box and had been successful, but it had ultimately been his downfall. The court treated the single punch he'd administered to Jesse as an intentionally lethal blow, and he'd received a far tougher sentence because of it.

Tom was still looking at me, his cheeks flushed. 'There's something else, Mum,' he said, falteringly. 'Something that's going to come as quite a shock. I'm sorry about that, but I—'

'What's that?' Robert tipped his head, listening, and Tom stopped speaking, swallowing hard.

Then I heard it too. A tentative knock.

'Someone's at the door,' I said, standing up, my hands flat on the table. 'I'll go. I'll get rid of them.'

'No, no … I'll go. Let me.' Tom moved quickly into the hallway. 'Wait there, both of you. I'll be back in a moment.'

Robert gave a derisory sniff and threw me his 'I told you so' look.

We sat in silence as the front door opened and closed. I heard Tom's voice, speaking softly but urgently, and then a woman's voice, faint, and … was that a giggle?

Robert looked at me and my mouth fell open.

Footsteps, and then Tom walked back into the kitchen, followed by Bridget Wilson. A waft of air filled my nostrils with the smell of congealing lasagne, and I covered my mouth and nose with my hand.

'Good God!' Robert thundered. 'What on earth is *she* doing here?'

A sickly knot pressed at my throat. I wasn't able to speak, could barely breathe. I wanted to be sick.

'Mum, Dad,' Tom said slowly, keeping his voice level, 'Bridget and I are in love. We got married in prison six months ago and today, we're starting a new life together as husband and wife.'

12

I looked at Robert and he looked back at me, his mouth hanging open. Bizarrely, I had a mad urge to burst out laughing, so surreal was the situation.

Bridget Wilson was *here*. In this very room with us, breathing the same air as we were! Standing in the doorway of *my* kitchen with *my* son looming behind her protectively, his hand resting on her shoulder.

'Hello, Jill,' she said warmly, then looked at my husband. 'Robert.'

She'd lost weight since I'd last seen her in the flesh, which was when she'd come to the house a few months after Jesse died. She'd been slim then, but she'd looked scraggy and worn out. Now she was lean and toned. Her hair was blonder, her skin smoother, glowing with health. Her eyes looked brighter and more energised.

She walked further into the room and the two of them stood side by side. A couple. My breath caught in my throat.

'What kind of programme was it that encouraged you to do this?' Robert demanded. 'I can see the headlines now: *Mother marries her son's killer.*'

'Dad, that's enough!' Tom snapped, his expression dark.

Bridget spoke up in a quiet, humble voice that didn't suit her go-getting attitude. 'I understand it must be a shock, but the programme has been amazing. It's enabled us to forgive each other and move on. Together.'

Together? Even though I knew the facts, I struggled to accept that word. It was like poison entering my ears, invading my body. It revolted me. A high-pitched ringing started in my head, trapping me behind a sheet of invisible glass. I heard everything that was being said, and yet felt completely removed from it all.

'Tom,' Robert said firmly, 'it's clear to me they've somehow brainwashed you. This programme, what's happened ... it can't be right. You must see that. She's old enough to be your mother, for God's sake!'

'I know my own mind, stay out of it,' Tom said, as if there was no sense in trying to reason with his father. 'I know it must be a shock, Mum, but this isn't a sudden thing. Bridget began visiting me a couple of years ago, and when we did the programme together, we fell in love.'

'Christ Almighty!' Robert pushed his chair back and stood up. 'I'm not listening to this crap any more. I've never heard such nonsense in my life.'

'Why is it nonsense, Robert?' Bridget said, folding her arms. 'It's unexpected, it's unusual, but it's most definitely not nonsense. Our love for each other is perfectly real.'

'There's a twenty-year age gap between you!' I heard myself cry. 'It's not right.'

Tom looked straight at me and I saw shadows underneath his eyes. His secret had clearly been weighing on his mind, but I saw something else in his face now, too. A glow that came from the inside. A glow he'd been keeping hidden all this time.

It was why he'd wanted to be alone in his bedroom as soon as we arrived home. Not because he felt overwhelmed or tired, but because he'd been safeguarding his secret. Their secret.

I closed my eyes against the thought of her being with my son, being his *wife*. I fought the obvious thought.

She'll be making love to him tonight.

A noise escaped my throat.

'Mum, please just hear us out.' Tom looked pained but resolved. They stood there together, strong and united. Determined to declare their undying, *ridiculous* love.

But my son *was* in love! It radiated from his pores, surrounded him like a halo. It was in the way his eyes softened when he glanced at her, the tender touch of his hand on hers.

It was hard to tell if Bridget felt the same way. She was cool and collected, fully in charge of the situation. Tom was like a lamb to the slaughter.

Robert and Tom were talking in low voices now, both trying not to get angry, whilst Bridget chipped in here and there. Nobody spoke to me, nobody looked at me. The buzz of their conversation filled the room, but I didn't hear any of the detail. I was too busy trying to filter out the horror of the situation and prepare myself for what was to come.

What would people say? Our neighbours, the press … the entire town?

More to the point, how would Tom possibly make the most of his life with this woman twenty years older than him and who had blamed him so publicly when Jesse died?

I knew he hadn't yet grasped the full extent of it. He'd only just returned to the real world. And then I realised what had happened here.

In a nutshell, Tom was vulnerable after being in prison for so long, and she'd taken full advantage of that. He had clearly forgotten how he'd played at Jesse's house, under Bridget's care, since he was a toddler. How she'd changed his nappies, as I had once done for Jesse. He'd forgotten that when he was five or six, he'd sometimes called her 'Auntie Bridget'. When the boys were older, they'd enjoyed sleepovers at each other's houses. I would pack up Jesse's lunch and iron his school uniform for the following day, and Bridget would do the same for Tom.

And now she had married him. The little boy she'd cared for like a second mum. Although Tom was now nearly thirty years old, it was impossible to wipe the past out.

It was – and there was no other word for it – *obscene*. I felt empty inside. Hollow.

My fingers touched my cheek and it was wet.

'It's disgusting,' I whispered. 'Vile.' And then I realised I wasn't whispering at all, I was shouting. Tom looked alarmed and Robert's mouth moved as he glared at me, but I couldn't stop. Couldn't hold it back. 'You lost your son and so you waited and waited and then you took mine. Is that it?' I shrieked, my voice hoarse. 'You came to steal his future, to ruin him and get your revenge!'

I shrugged off the concerned hands that were placed lightly on my shoulders. I knocked away a proffered glass of water. Faces loomed above me and merged into one blurry mess.

I felt something split inside me, and the panic rose, pushed its way up into my chest.

'For God's sake get out of here. Go!' I heard Robert yell at Tom. 'Do you realise this will kill your mother? She'll never get over it. It will kill her and it will all be your fault.'

13

Bridget

We said little on the journey back. We'd bolted from his parents' house. Tom belted upstairs, grabbed his holdall and rucksack and rushed back out to me like a young runaway.

He'd fallen quiet and sat still in the passenger seat, his fingers fused together. I steered the Mercedes on to Main Road as Tom continued to stare vacantly out of the window.

'You shouldn't feel bad, you know.' I kept one hand on the steering wheel while leaning across to pat his firm thigh. 'You did the right thing in telling them as soon as you could. It's not your fault they don't agree with what we've done.'

He didn't answer.

Halfway along the long, wide street, I pulled over and parked the car on the road behind a silver BMW. I turned off the engine.

'Nice Beamer,' Tom remarked. He'd told me he'd loved the brand since being a boy.

'So here we are,' I said. 'This is home.'

Tom looked at me and then glanced at the three-storey red-brick house. It felt slightly bizarre that this was the first time he'd seen the place where we were going to start our married life together.

'This is your house?' he gasped.

'Yep, all mine,' I said, pleased with his reaction. I'd played the place down on purpose so it would be a pleasant surprise. 'Or it will be mine once I've paid the mortgage.' I hesitated. 'Actually, ours. It's *our* house, Tom.'

I watched with pleasure as he got out of the car and stared up at the house. His eyes were wide, his mouth slightly open in disbelief. It was one thing I loved about him, and something that hadn't changed since he was a boy. He wore his heart on his sleeve, and it was easy to see it impressed him. Jesse had been far more crafty and able to cover up how he felt, but Tom was always the more innocent one.

Ten years ago, when he used to come over to the house to hang out with Jesse in the den – the name Jesse coined for our third bedroom, so poky it wouldn't accommodate a double bed – I had lived somewhere very different. He knew I'd recently moved, but despite that, he'd probably been expecting something more modest.

'It's amazing,' he said, still not moving. '*You're* amazing, Brid, how far you've come.'

Thanks to money I'd invested from the GoFundMe community campaign when Jesse died, plus my substantial salary from the charity, I'd been able to buy the property off plan two years ago. I'd put down a hefty deposit and mortgaged the rest. It was in an exclusive cluster of brand-new three-storey detached houses on the outskirts of Ravenshead, a well-regarded residential area in Nottinghamshire and only about three miles from the house where Tom had grown up.

The gardens of these new-builds weren't huge. They stood tightly packed together, because land was at a premium in the area, but the outlook from the front aspect was a rare one of space. The master bedroom, on the third floor, was high enough to enjoy unhampered views over open fields and woodland.

But I had another surprise waiting for my new husband. I took the car keys out of my handbag and held them in front of him.

'What's this?' he said, grinning. 'Are you gonna let me drive your motor, too?'

'No need,' I said, nodding to the BMW. 'You've got your own little runaround now.'

'What?' His mouth dropped open as he looked at the keys and then the car.

'Someone at work was selling it. I knew it was a good buy so … consider it my coming-home gift to you.'

'No way!' He took the keys and rushed over to the car. Then rushed back and kissed me. 'Thank you! Thanks so much, Brid. This is unreal. To think I was driving Mum's little Fiesta when I went away.'

I suggested we made a move inside the house.

'Unless you're planning on staying out here all day admiring the dashboard, we'd better get you inside.' I grinned and led him up the short path through shared frontage to the glossy black front door. 'We can get your stuff out of the car later once I've shown you around.'

I guided him across the ground floor, a big open-plan sweep of gleaming black and white kitchen units, a dining and living space, and pristine white ceilings dotted every few inches with silver spotlights. Outsize bifold doors led to a spacious decked patio complete with a built-in fire pit, and beyond that, a modest but reasonably sized lawn.

I pointed to a row of spindly trees. 'Another year and the conifers will be mature, and then we'll have great privacy here.' There were houses behind, a couple of which had upper floors that overlooked the patio area. 'Long summer nights and BBQs on the terrace. What do you think?'

Tom grabbed me as I headed for the glass-sided staircase, and caught unawares, I squealed.

'I think that sounds incredible.' He nuzzled into my neck and I shivered, the thrill of his touch sending shock waves way down into the core of my aching body. I'd purposely worn the perfume he loved when I visited that he said smelled like burned sugar. 'I can't wait.'

'Everything we talked about and longed for is a reality now,' I reminded him. 'That's why you have to be brave and push through the next few weeks with your parents. Jill will come round, I know it.'

He bit his lip and took a step back from me. 'I know,' he said, but I didn't think he did. Not really.

Jill had totally bucked against our marriage like I'd known she would. That was why Tom wanted to get married before his release. It had seemed like the perfect solution.

'We can have a party for family and friends once they come around to the idea, but like the prison officer's suggested, if we're already man and wife on the day you're released, there's nothing anyone can do about it,' he'd said and I'd agreed.

What he really meant was that there was nothing his mother could do about it.

I'd been prepared fully for a showdown when I went to their house, but her reaction had been totally over-the-top. While the rest of us were calmly discussing things, she'd begun making strange wailing noises, and finally losing it. Robert had ushered us out of the house in a panic.

She'd looked awful – old way beyond her years. Her neat brown bob was longer now, ragged at the ends and shot through with grey. And her clothes looked like she'd got her entire wardrobe from that grubby charity shop she worked in. She didn't seem too fussy if the garments actually fitted or not. Her mud-coloured skirt, round-neck sweater and cardigan all bagged and hung off her scrawny frame. If she hadn't acted like a crazy witch and upset Tom, I'd have almost felt sorry for her.

Robert had aged too, but in that infuriatingly craggy way that some men did, almost rendering them more attractive than when they were younger. I'd wanted to take Jill aside, warn her what might happen. She knew the story of how my dad had left Mum for a woman half her age once she'd hit her forties. You had to keep yourself tip-top, stay youthful and fresh. That was why I loved to be in the company of young people; it made me feel safe from getting older.

'Brid?' Tom said, waving his hand in front of me. 'Ground Control speaking.'

'Sorry.' I smiled. 'I'm thinking about how long I've waited for you to be here, for us to be together in our new home. Upstairs next.'

'Music to my ears.' He winked cheekily and my stomach lurched with delight like it hadn't done since I was a teenager.

He climbed the stairs, his powerful thighs taking them two at a time. God, he looked fit from behind. Halfway up, I saw him hesitate and I swallowed. He'd spotted the photographs.

'They don't bother you, do they?' I came up behind him and put a hand on the small of his back. 'The photographs, I mean?'

'No! I mean, I'd expect you to have photographs up.' He did a double-take and peered closer. 'Oh! You cut me out of that one?'

I'd taken this picture of the boys myself. We'd been on a trip to a local park during the school holidays when Jill had been working at the library. Jesse and Tom had played on the climbing frames while I'd dozed on a blanket in the sun. While the boys fished for sticklebacks with brightly coloured rod nets and jam jars, I crept up behind them with the camera. I'd loved the vitality in Jesse's face and called out their names so they both looked straight at the camera before I snapped the shot.

'After Jesse died, I couldn't bear to see you up there. Not for a long time.'

'It's OK, you don't have to explain,' Tom said softly, and I loved him for that.

I showed him the two bedrooms on the first floor and the family bathroom with the free-standing white tub and the TV set into the silver marbled wall tiles.

'Awesome.' He gave a low whistle. 'A beer, a bath and Man United. What more could a man want?'

'Charming!' I mimed a slap, and he dodged my hand like a boxer. Jesse's face flashed into my mind and I pushed it gently away.

Tom winked and bent down to kiss my forehead. 'Tub's big enough for two, gorgeous, so no worries there. Footie won't even come close.'

I headed to the next staircase and began climbing up to the second floor. Tom followed me this time, lingering again as he passed the collage I'd compiled as a visual representation of the eighteen years of Jesse's life. From his first baby picture in hospital the day he was born to one I'd taken of him blowing me a kiss from the garden gate the week before he died.

Tom had been in many of the original photographs, but back then, in the maelstrom of raw grief, I'd taken each one and carefully snipped out his image. Excised him from my son's life like a malignant tumour. It had felt like the right thing to do.

He didn't comment, and I was glad.

When we reached the top landing, I led him into the large master bedroom, the *pièce de résistance* of the house. It featured an expansive floor-to-ceiling window that overlooked the open countryside beyond the road, including what was a spectacular wildflower meadow in the summer months.

'Wow!' His voice sounded strange, and I saw his eyes were glistening.

'Oh Tom, that's so sweet.' I wrapped my arms around his waist.

'Ignore me, I'm turning soft,' he said gruffly. He wiped his eyes with the back of a hand before hugging me closer. 'After everything that's happened, I guess I never thought I'd feel happy again. I've *never* felt this happy.'

I snuggled into him, laying my cheek on his chest, feeling his steady heartbeat. Jesse's face fluttered in front of my mind's eye yet again, and I took a moment to remember my strong, beautiful boy, whose heart would never beat again.

'I like to think Jesse is here now, looking down on us,' I said softly. 'Watching us, you know?'

Tom coughed. 'I suppose I've never thought of it like that.'

'Oh, I've always felt his presence,' I said easily, walking to the window and scanning the vista. 'I feel him with me all the time. Even here, in this bedroom.'

Tom looked away, shuffled his feet. 'Well, he would've loved it here, I'm sure. All that open countryside for his motocross.'

'Look at the bed.' I sat on the edge, smoothed the black and silver throw. 'I got us a super-king. I thought you'd appreciate the extra room.'

'You bet I do.' He walked over and kissed me lightly on the top of my head. 'I think you've done amazingly, Brid, going from your life as it was before to this. You've worked so hard, and now it's time for you to enjoy the fruits of ...' His voice trailed off as he became distracted by something on the other side of the room. 'Is that ...'

He peered at the far wall, where I'd hung the framed order of service from Jesse's funeral.

'Yes, it's such a wonderful memento of his life. Too beautiful to pack away in the attic.' I stood up and pressed my fingers to his cheek, gently guiding his gaze back to me. 'We'll be so happy here, Tom. Here with each other and, as you've always said, our shared precious memories of Jesse.'

I slid my hands under his fitted T-shirt and pressed them into the smooth warmth of his muscular torso.

Our lips met, barely touching at first, and I felt an electric jolt shoot through me. He pulled me towards him, over to the bed, peeling off his T-shirt. He smelled clean and fresh and I buried my fingers in his thick dark hair. The bulk of him hovered over me, his weight anchoring me in bliss as he lowered himself gently on top of me.

'We belong together, Tom,' I whispered in his ear. 'Nobody can come between us now.'

14

Jill

When Tom and Bridget had left, I sat down on the comfy sofa by the French doors in the kitchen.

Comfy was a polite word we used to avoid facing the fact that the furniture had seen better days. When we were younger, with Tom growing up and me changing to part-time hours, it had seemed a constant struggle to keep renewing things, tweaking the house and the accommodation within to make it fit for our growing family. We'd splashed out on this kitchen extension, and the stylish French doors that made the most of the view of the garden. 'To bring the outside in,' I remembered the kitchen planner saying to good effect as Robert willingly handed over the deposit.

We'd taken to enjoying a cup of tea there – and the odd gin – while we kept an eye on Tom and, more often than not, Jesse as they played out in the garden. We'd relish letting off steam about the day we'd had, Robert grumbling about his colleagues at the architect's office where he'd worked then, while I'd tell him about some rude or noisy customer I'd had to tolerate in the library.

Now, it only ever seemed to be me on my own, sitting there staring out at the patchy lawn and the tired, colourless borders.

When I first sat down, I'd felt light-headed and slightly confused, Tom's words whirling around in my mind and still not making any sense.

'Now do you see why we can't trust him?' Robert kept saying until I yelled at him to stop.

I watched as he moved back and forth making the tea. Nearly thirty years ago, we'd met at our high school dance. He'd been in the sixth-form, a couple of years older than me which I'd found very attractive. At fifty-two he had a bit more padding around the middle than he did then. His jeans bagged slightly around his bottom and his hair had grown a little thinner. But he was still a good-looking man and when he wore his blue and white striped scarf from his Birmingham university days, it gave him that college student air again.

He opened the cutlery drawer and selected a teaspoon, humming something tuneless and unidentifiable as he took two tea bags out of the canister. He didn't seem gutted about what had happened with Tom. In fact, he didn't seem concerned at all but then Robert always thought he knew best.

Life had held little excitement for the two of us for many years now. Over the years he'd become increasingly selfish, only interested in serving his own needs. For instance, when Robert began his counsellor training back in 2007, he took over the small office down the hall which I'd used as a little reading room. Nothing fancy, a squashy armchair, a lamp and a blanket. A quiet space to sit in, surrounded by my books.

When my mother died and we cleared the house, I found a set of my gran's Charles Dickens books in an unmarked box amongst piles of old greetings cards and mildewed clothes in Mum's cluttered attic.

Robert, whom I'd never seen read a book, looked on disparagingly when I asked him to put the books in the car. 'Surely you don't want these fusty old volumes? I'll buy you a new set,' he'd said airily.

'I don't want a new set!' I'd removed one volume and carefully leafed through. 'Look, published in 1930 and they're illustrated.'

They weren't quite first editions but were still pretty old – their fading red leather covers still replete with gold leaf lettering. The memories had come flooding back when, as a child of only seven or eight, Gran would let me sit next to the bookshelf and run my fingertips across their spines. I'd take one out at a time to leaf gently through the illustrations.

Despite Robert's disapproval, I'd folded down the box lid and carefully taped it up again. 'If I take nothing else, I want these.'

When I fell pregnant with Tom, I attended a night school course on book repair, intending to restore Gran's books to their former glory and display them. Time passed and I'd begun the lengthy process when Robert took over my reading room. One day I came back from work to find he'd packed up all my books without asking, including the Dickens set, and dumped them in a dusty corner of the garage.

When I complained, he looked at me with an astonished expression. 'It's a few old books, for goodness' sake! I'll cart them all back in again when you can find a good place for storage,' he'd said from behind his newspaper. 'Preferably somewhere I won't be tripping over them.'

He'd never got around to hauling the books back out again and when Tom went to prison, I forgot about them all together.

'Why are you scowling?' Robert said curtly, bringing my tea over. 'Let me guess. Your precious son upsets you and yours truly is about to take the rap for it.'

'I'm thinking back. Seeing things in a different light,' I said in a tone that made it clear I wouldn't be sharing my thoughts.

I pushed thoughts of the books out of my mind and opened up Facebook on my phone, searching for Bridget's profile page. I'd viewed it many times over the past few years, but she had a high privacy setting so there had been nothing new to see in terms of public posts for ages.

'Oh no,' I whispered as the page opened up.

'What is it?' Robert said, straining to see. 'What's wrong?'

I held my phone screen up to show him Bridget's new profile picture. A full-length photo of her and Tom captured as they walked down a makeshift aisle scattered with rose petals. Bridget looked elegant and youthfully slim in a cream silk sheath, clutching a neat bouquet. They were both smiling, gazing into each other's eyes as they moved. They looked extraordinarily happy.

Robert huffed. 'There's no surprise there, is there? You already know they're married.'

I glanced at the photograph. Posted an hour ago. 'She obviously waited until Tom had told us, then immediately posted it for everyone to see.'

Robert shrugged. 'That's Facebook for you. I don't know why you bother torturing yourself. I've got some work to do in the office.'

Robert detested social media, partly because he had to deal with the fallout when it went wrong for the students he counselled. 'I've seen too many young lives ruined by Facebook and Twitter and worst of all, Instagram,' he'd always claimed.

'I've texted Audrey and she's on her way over,' I said as he headed into the hallway.

He threw his hands up in the air. 'Why are you involving Audrey in this? The whole of Mansfield will know about it once she gets all the gory details. I don't want her here.'

'That's not fair.' I pulled him up. 'Audrey's a good friend to me and that's what matters. Not the fact that you can't stand her. Besides, now Bridget has pasted their business all over Facebook, everyone's going to know about it anyway.'

Robert mumbled something I didn't quite catch and headed out of the kitchen door. There'd never been much love lost between him and Audrey, he seemed to sense she had a low opinion of him. In recent years, the animosity had somehow seemed to flourish in

Tom's absence. Audrey could be scathing about the way Robert ran me down all the time, adamant I'd be better off without him. Robert called Audrey 'an interfering battleaxe who hasn't got a life of her own so sticks her nose into other people's'. Which was completely groundless, of course.

I drank my tea and stared at the wedding picture, then took a screenshot of it in case Bridget applied a higher security setting to her account. I'd already scrolled down her profile page, but there was nothing new on there.

She looked good in the photograph, even though it pained me to admit it. You could tell she was older than him, but you'd have said there was a lot less than twenty years between them.

Bridget had always been skilled at making the best of herself, but ten years ago I remembered she'd looked drawn. Crow's feet around her eyes and tiny lines radiating out from the corners of her mouth. She'd come over to the house in the months after Tom had received his sentencing and gone to prison. It was an episode I'd rather forget. She had been desperate, seemed almost on the edge of madness, and I'd sent her away. Closed the front door in her face. Although I'd felt she deserved it, it hadn't been my finest hour, but then I'd also been suffering. When I looked in the mirror, I knew that I'd aged because I'd been grieving the loss of my son, too.

Now, Bridget looked like she'd been through a time tunnel. She appeared much younger. There was a telltale frozen quality around her eyes, and her strangely puffed-up cheeks were probably due to a syringe full of filler. With freshly highlighted hair and understated make-up, her dress style was classy but contemporary.

This was a woman who'd done a lot of work on herself both mentally and physically. I'd felt about a hundred years old next to her, frumpy and definitely past my best.

Mansfield was a big town, and living in different areas as we did, there was never any danger we'd bump into each other. In all these years I hadn't seen her out once, though that was probably on account of me barely going into the main shopping area. I shopped online or at local stores in Berry Hill.

The front door opened and I heard Audrey's voice call out, 'Only me!'

'I'm in the kitchen,' I called back. Robert often wore headphones as he worked, listening to music, but it was typical of him to pretend he hadn't heard the door.

'Here you are, love.' Audrey walked over and handed me a bunch of glorious orange chrysanthemums, their stems wrapped in a floral paper bag. 'From my garden, with love.'

'They're beautiful.' I sniffed at the flowers. 'Just what I need to cheer me up. Thank you, Audrey. Look at this.' I pushed my phone screen towards her. 'She's crowing about it already.'

I thought Audrey would gasp in horror, but she didn't seem fazed. She wrinkled her nose at the wedding photograph, then slipped off her jacket, draping it over a bar stool, and reached for my empty mug. 'Right, first things first, let's get you a fresh cup of tea and then you can tell me all about it.'

My heart sank as I placed the flowers down beside me. Even though my head was full of it all and I'd turned to Audrey for a sympathetic ear, it was a different thing altogether to repeat it word for word. It was traumatic.

Audrey bustled around the kitchen, opening drawers and cupboards.

'So the gist of it is that Tom and Bridget have got married in prison and now he's gone to live with her, yes?'

I gave a half-hearted laugh. 'You make it sound so simple.'

She brought the drinks over on a tray with a plate of shortbread fingers I'd had in the cupboard since Christmas.

'Are these still in date?' I picked one up.

She rolled her eyes. 'You've got a family crisis on your hands and you're *still* trying to control every meaningless detail. For heaven's sake, relax!'

'Yes, Mother.' I took a bite of the biscuit.

'What's Robert think about it all?'

I shrugged. 'Doesn't seem to give a toss, he's back in his office at usual.'

'Maybe he's got other stuff on his mind,' Audrey remarked, looking at the biscuits but not taking one.

'Like what?'

'I don't know. You're the one who said he'd been quiet lately!' She sighed. 'Look, I know this is the last news you wanted or expected from Tom, but trust me, the best thing you can do now is to accept it's happened.'

So easy for Audrey to say. She didn't even seem surprised about what Tom had done! Though we were the same age, she had got no children. She'd had a couple of long-term relationships over the years, but she'd never married. When her elderly mother died, she'd left Audrey a bit of money so she was, in anyone's book, in a comfortable position.

'He's my son, Audrey. I can't pretend this isn't happening.'

'That's not what I said.' She took a sip of her tea and leaned towards me. 'You've got to realise that Tom is not the same boy who went into prison. He's a man now and he's entitled to make important life decisions.' She tipped her head and regarded me. 'Don't for a moment think I'm agreeing with what he's done. Frankly, I think it's appalling. But maybe give him a little space. He'll soon get fed up of life with a woman old enough to be his mother.'

I reached for my tea.

When Tom had been around five or six, we'd made edible gingerbread decorations for the Christmas tree. We had different-coloured icing, tiny silver balls, glacé cherries in red and green, and even striped ribbon to hang them on the tree. I remembered hovering over his red and green mess, the frayed ribbon, and as I reached out to help him, he'd turned to me and said, 'No, I can do it, Mummy. I want to do it on my own.' So I had let him make a mess, and somehow the gingerbread men had still looked cute and festive and everything was perfectly OK.

Now Audrey was suggesting I should do the same thing again. Leave Tom alone to get on with his life, make his own mistakes. But there was something bigger at stake here than broken ginger biscuits. There was a real danger Bridget was playing a much darker game and he wouldn't realise it until it was too late.

Audrey studied my expression. 'What is it?'

My hand flew up to my face and clamped over my mouth. I pressed hard and suppressed the wail that had risen suddenly in my throat. 'It's not the marriage, it's not because I want to control him, it's that I think she's out to ruin him,' I said in one long sentence before drawing breath.

Saying the words out loud didn't bring relief, it only seemed to emphasise my fears, make them appear more real than ever.

'Ruin him how, love?' Audrey looked at me pityingly. 'Remember they're both adults. She can't make him do anything he doesn't want to.'

'She hated him, Audrey. For years she hated Tom, and me too. When they left the house earlier, she turned and looked at me from the door. She didn't say a word, just smiled in a loaded sort of way, if you know what I mean. It was a smile filled with triumph, with accomplishment. All of which seemed invisible to my husband and my son.'

'Hmm. I think it's easy to read things into non-verbal signals. Sometimes things that aren't really there,' Audrey said gently. 'But one thing is for sure. If you want to maintain a relationship with Tom, you're going to have to accept that they're together.'

I knew then that my worst fears were already realised. Bridget Wilson had pulled off a masterstroke, probably years in the making. She had successfully manipulated events to put herself in control of my son, and nobody realised it but me. Nobody *suspected* it but me.

Worse still, I could do precisely nothing about it if I wanted to keep the lines of communication open between us.

15

Audrey

Later, Audrey fed Soames, her ten-year-old Burmese, then settled down to watch an episode of *Virgin River* on Netflix. She turned on the gas log burner, which looked just like the real thing without any of the mess or the invasive toxic fumes she kept reading about, and settled back with her glass of white wine.

She looked around the small living room. It was nothing special, this house. Semi-detached, two bedrooms, with a small, narrow garden that she'd had fully decked for convenience three years ago. But it was paid for and it belonged to her and her alone.

On reflection, her life hadn't turned out quite how she'd expected, but then as far back as college when her friends – including Jill – would chatter on about getting married and having kids, Audrey never joined in. She'd never imagined herself as a sort of mother hen figure, organising her husband and kids and perhaps a family dog.

And now here she was, at almost fifty. Never married and forever hearing how women of her age were unable to find partners because the men all wanted younger women. Well good luck to them! What would she want a grunting, moaning old bloke in her life for, anyway?

She pointed the remote control at the television and watched the beautiful scenery roll by in the show's opening credits. The series was supposed to be set in California but Audrey had read that they'd done all the filming in Vancouver.

Interesting that, when you believed one thing and then found out another. Quite different but sort of the same was the position she'd found herself in. She'd had to make some uncomfortable decisions but, if push came to shove, she'd stand by them.

The truth would not go down well with her old friend. Audrey had done her best to wake Jill up to reality but she was blind to anything other than what she wanted to believe.

Currently, Jill was as infuriated by the age difference between Tom and his new wife almost as much as she was worried about Bridget's possibly sinister intentions. Audrey had heard whispers of gossip already around town. People who'd sent her a message or text, asking her if it was true that this middle-aged woman had married Jill's son, a man who'd not yet turned thirty.

The glossy magazines Audrey had a weakness for were always full of photographs and shallow articles about young women and their much older partners. George Clooney was seventeen years older than his wife, Leonardo DiCaprio was twenty-three years older than his current beau, and nobody seemed to care a jot about it. The vicious comments and wave of negative responses had been saved for Brigitte Macron, twenty-four years older than her husband, the French president.

It annoyed Audrey that Jill subscribed to the same annoying double standards. Of course, she understood her friend's worries and her resentment of the situation. Bridget and Jill were once good friends and the fact Tom had gone to prison for the manslaughter of Bridget's son would traumatise anyone.

Still, as an older woman herself, Jill should have known better, been able to separate the age issue from the family issue. Jill had married Robert in her early twenties, and her beloved full-time career in the library service had instantly taken a back seat when she'd had Tom but she'd picked it up again later, taken part-time hours.

Books had been everything to Jill when she'd been younger, and now she barely mentioned them. When he'd been booted out of the architect's firm and retrained as a student counsellor, Robert had packed Jill's collection of Charles Dickens and Jane Austen away in boxes and relocated them 'temporarily' to the garage to give him space to work. He'd converted the room into his own office and it had been that way for years now.

'It's not right that everything you care about is constantly pushed back,' Audrey had fumed when Jill told her about the books she'd been in the middle of restoring. She'd tried her best to rekindle a bit of inner fire in her old friend, but it had fallen on deaf ears. Like everything else did.

'I don't mind,' Jill had said placidly. 'I haven't the heart for reading or repairing them any more.'

Audrey had been forced to accept that Jill had chosen a gentler path in life, conducive to what Robert's idea of a good wife was. When Tom had gone to prison, Jill had rapidly faded to a shadow of her former self. She'd quit her job and had begun to rely more and more on their friendship, looking to Audrey for guidance and advice although never wanting to take heed of any of it when it came to Robert.

Jill had been too soft for years, allowing Robert – who Audrey had always felt disapproved of their friendship – and Tom to dictate her every move.

It was time for Audrey to even up the playing field a bit. She knew a lot more about the people in her friend's life than Jill thought she did. More than Jill herself, in fact. The Billinghurst family weren't quite the wonderful, innocent bunch Jill would lead her to believe, and they had trodden on other people they considered beneath them for long enough.

The last thing Audrey wanted to do was to hurt Jill needlessly. But that was an impossibility now because things had gone too far. One day soon she'd explain to Jill exactly what she'd done and hope she'd somehow understand.

Audrey turned up the volume and settled back into her cushions, cradling her wine while Soames purred on her lap.

She had the distinct feeling that life was about to get very interesting indeed.

16

1995

Jill had made a Mediterranean vegetable tortilla and a tomato salad for tea. Bridget and Jesse were coming over for their regular Wednesday-afternoon visit to the house.

Jill looked forward to their company. She liked to make a bit of an event of it, set the table properly. Pretty paper napkins, nice cutlery, new water glasses she'd bought in the House of Fraser sale last week. She always asked the cleaner to work an extra hour on Tuesdays, and the woman had done an excellent job. The heated ceramic tiles in the kitchen sparkled and looked clean enough to eat lunch off, but Jill thought she spied a smear and took a cloth to it before her friend arrived.

Bridget Wilson wasn't like most of the other women around here, and she wasn't like Jill herself, either. She didn't appear to expect or want anything fancy and elaborate. But then Jill setting the table and cleaning the floor wasn't really about Bridget. It was about trying to satisfy the almost constant niggle inside herself, wanting everything to be perfect. Which it invariably never was.

She suspected it came from having parents who fostered high expectations. Then she'd left home and married Robert, who had similar aspirations of striving for perfection in all things. But she'd lived enough life by now to know that almost nothing was perfect, no matter how hard you tried.

She stood at the kitchen island and watched Tom running around the garden excitedly in his little padded coat and mittens, waiting for Jesse to arrive. It was early March, but it had been a bleak winter and there had been snow on and off for what seemed like months.

After meeting at playgroup a year ago, the women had become firm friends. Bridget had had the opportunity to take up an evening cleaning job twice a week but had nobody to look after Jesse. Jill invited him to stay at their house. As Bridget didn't have a car and didn't finish work until eight, it made sense for Jesse to stop over on Wednesdays and Fridays.

'She's certainly fallen on her feet,' Robert had grumbled. 'You providing free overnight childcare.'

But Jill didn't mind at all, and Tom loved it. She'd swapped his single bed for bunk beds painted to look like Thomas the Tank Engine, which both boys adored. They played so well together, hardly a cross word between the two of them.

Bridget repaid the favour and regularly took the boys to the park, and Tom would sometimes stay over at hers at the weekend. Jill worried about the area, about crime, but she'd learned to push that out of her mind. She trusted Bridget to look after Tom and that was what mattered.

In any case, with the extra income, Bridget was soon able to move and rent something nicer just a twenty-minute walk from Jill's house. Unbeknown to Robert, Jill paid for the removals service as a housewarming present. She had a contact at the school and, although Bridget's address didn't fall into their catchment area, she put Bridget and her friend in touch and Jesse was able to get a place from the waiting list. Now, the two women saw even more of each other, meeting up for coffee, and Jill often popped over to Bridget's for a chat.

Tom was changing from being a shy, clingy boy when other people were around to seeming completely comfortable when he was with Jesse. And more than that, Jill really liked Bridget. She liked her transparent manner, the way she never tried to impress anyone. She didn't try to convey an image different to her reality. She seemed to be saying, 'This is me, and if you don't like it then that's your lookout.' Surrounded by neighbours who seemed obsessed with keeping up with the Joneses, Jill appreciated that.

She didn't feel judged by Bridget like she did with a lot of the other women in the area, acquaintances she met at playgroup and coffee mornings. There was an expectation to look a certain way, do the right things – like volunteer for mind-numbing community events and the school fete, for instance, or host people you didn't overly know for dinner because you wanted to show off your new kitchen, as neighbours down the street had done only last week. Jill had never been as concerned with the latest fashions and status symbols as most of the women around here were, and it set her apart.

Bridget was the first one to admit she was poor and living a life she hated. Yet Jill found it endearing she would often speak, with astonishing conviction, of her plans and ambitions for the future for both herself and Jesse.

She was a free spirit all right, and Jesse had that in him too, even at this young age. Jill saw it in his sense of adventure. Where Tom held back in new situations, Jesse would charge in head-first without a thought. More often than not, after a few moments of caution, Tom would follow his lead and end up enjoying himself.

Jill wondered if Tom liked the fact that Jesse seemed a little wild. Last time they were here, she had run out alarmed when she spotted Jesse chasing a terrified Tom around the garden armed with a big stick – a tree branch, it turned out to be. But when she got out there, Tom was laughing so hard he was unable to catch his breath, and before Jill reached the end of the garden, they'd swapped and he was doing the chasing.

Jesse was a little boisterous at times, for sure. But Jill felt sure he'd grow out of that in time. They always did.

17

Bridget

October 2019

We lay there entwined after making love on waking up in our big new bed. I felt satiated, calm. For the first time since Jesse died, I felt truly loved.

'I was thinking,' I said tentatively. 'About asking your parents around here for a meal next weekend. You know, to try and break the ice a bit.'

Tom sucked air in through his teeth. 'I don't know about that.'

'But why?' I turned on my side, hitched up onto an elbow and looked down at him. 'The worst is over. You've told them the situation now and your mum has to accept we're a couple.'

'That may be so, but she's taken it badly, and Mum lets stuff fester.'

'I doubt she was that upset,' I pointed out gently. 'Once she'd got over the hysterics, I mean.'

'I'm not convinced,' Tom sighed. 'You know Mum as well as I do, and she's a determined woman. She was not happy at all.'

I lay down flat again and stared up at the ceiling, my guts twisting in annoyance. 'I'm a determined woman too. If she wants to lock horns over this, I'm ready for it.'

'There's no need for you to get into any spats with her,' Tom said, a little sternly. I bristled at his patronising tone, the same one I'd heard Jill use on many occasions, and opened my mouth to retaliate, but then decided against it. I didn't want an argument in our first few hours of married life together. 'I know she has no choice but to accept we're married now, but I still worry about her well-being. She's stuck in that house with Dad and his snide comments. I don't want to do anything to make things worse for her.'

I swallowed down the bitter laugh that rose in my throat. If we started doing everything for Jill's benefit, there would be no point in being together in the first place.

'Me and your mum have known each other a long time and I thought a little gathering would help our families heal together.'

He thought for a moment and I felt his arm soften slightly next to me. I pursed my lips towards him and he kissed them.

'If you think she'd go for it, then I'll trust your judgement. You're a generous person, Mrs Billinghurst, I'll give you that.'

I laughed. 'Mrs Billinghurst, I love it! Will I ever get used to it, I wonder?'

'You'd better.' He made a grab for me. 'Because it will be your name for life.'

I pushed him away playfully. 'No time for more hanky-panky yet, Romeo. Coral and my grandson will be here in half an hour. Let's get sorted for the next mountain to climb.'

I sat up and slid my legs over the side of the bed but there was no movement from Tom. I looked back at him over my shoulder. His eyes were closed, his brow furrowed.

I knew he was nervous about meeting Ellis and also Coral for the first time since Jesse's death. I felt nervous too, because there was nobody more important in my life than my grandson. No one at all.

It was imperative the two of them got along, even if it took a while.

*

I got dressed and went downstairs to make some coffee. I sprang back from the kitchen window when two familiar figures appeared in front of the house, fifteen minutes earlier than I'd expected. 'They're here,' I called upstairs.

Tom came down immediately and walked with me to the front door, brushing down his jeans with his hands and smoothing back his hair after his shower. I opened the door and we waited together in the hallway, watching their hesitant approach.

'Hi, Coral.' I greeted her and stood aside while she stepped into the hallway. Ellis hung back and stood on the path, scuffing up the gravel with the toes of the new Converse trainers I'd bought him last week. Tom and Coral had attended the same school, so they knew each other well enough. I figured there was no need for introductions.

'Hello, Coral,' Tom said, taking the lead.

Turning her back on him, Coral shrugged off a short cream padded coat. Underneath she wore a pink velour lounge suit with diamanté detail on a feature pocket. It didn't suit her; she'd got so skinny lately. She was short in stature and liked to wear her blonde hair with the dark roots purposely on show. Her eyebrows were too thick and dark for her thin, pale face, and when I saw her like this, I always wondered what Jesse had seen in her.

Tom held out his hand. 'Long time no see.'

Coral's whole face seemed to sag for a moment before she collected herself.

'Hello,' she said stiffly, but she ignored his proffered hand.

She had made no secret of the fact that she didn't approve of my decision to marry Tom. I'd told her about a week ago, before the two of us sat Ellis down together to explain it to him. I'd known she would probably find my decision difficult, but I'd been shocked at the look of horror on her face when I broke the news.

'How could you?' she'd hissed. 'After what Tom Billinghurst did to Jesse? After what he did to me and to Ellis!'

I hadn't expected her blessing straight away. She was bound to feel resentful of the man who'd taken her partner and Ellis's father away. But she wasn't the brightest spark, and wouldn't have grasped the reasoning behind my marrying him. There had seemed no real point in bothering to fully explain it to her, nor had I attempted to explain the restorative justice programme I'd been involved in with Tom.

Now, she was being hostile to my new husband, and I felt my face tighten.

I watched as Tom shifted uncomfortably and pressed his back against the wall. Before they'd arrived, he had asked me if he should apologise to Coral for his actions on the night Jesse died, but I'd said that wasn't necessary. 'I'm Jesse's mother and you've apologised to me. That's all that matters. Coral might have been pregnant with Jesse's child, but they weren't that close. Not really.'

'Go through and sit down, Coral, I'll bring you a coffee,' I said, trying not to sound dismissive but she wasn't my priority. I turned at a noise on the doorstep and instantly brightened. 'Here he is, the light of my life! Ellis, this is Tom. Tom, this is my grandson, Ellis.'

Ellis stood very still in the doorway, sullen and silent. His shoulders were hunched, his expression dark and dangerous. He looked so much like Jesse when he was in this mood, my heart squeezed in on itself.

When I'd sat down with Coral to tell Ellis about marrying Tom, he'd barely said a word.

'How do you feel about what I've just told you?' I'd pressed him for a response, but he had simply shrugged.

'Your nan has married Tom and that means he'll be coming to live here.' Coral had spelled it out to him. 'When you visit the house, he'll probably be around.'

'Nobody is going to force you to spend any time with him,' I'd added, slightly annoyed that Coral seemed to be painting the worst picture possible to Ellis. 'But I hope in time you two will find a way to get on.'

Ellis had wriggled in his seat. But I took the fact that he hadn't had a meltdown or ranted and raved as a positive. Seeing his face now, though, I wondered if I'd been naïve to think that.

'Hello, Ellis,' Tom said, again offering his hand.

Ellis instantly sneered at the gesture and turned his whole body away from Tom.

'Ellis! Shake Tom's hand,' I snapped without thinking. Softer then, I added, 'We talked about this, remember?'

'It's fine,' Tom said. He nodded to the Nintendo Switch in Ellis's hand. 'I see you're a bit of a gamer, Ellis.'

Ellis glared at me. 'I'm going through to Mum. There's a funny smell out here.' He wrinkled his nose at Tom and pushed past, purposely knocking him with his shoulder.

'Ellis!' My face burned.

'Let him go, it's fine.' Tom laid a calming hand on my shoulder. 'It's no big deal. We just have to give it time.'

I pressed the heel of my hand to my forehead. 'When I told him about us, he seemed OK about it.'

'It's one thing talking about it, another thing to actually face it,' Tom said gently. 'He's young, Brid, cut him some slack. You can't expect him to be all jolly, that's unrealistic.'

'You're very wise.' I rested my head on his shoulder. 'And kind, too. Coral's probably been bad-mouthing us for Ellis to openly be such a little shit like this.'

We both looked up sharply at a muffled noise. Ellis hadn't gone through to the living room after all. Instead, he'd lingered by the door and had heard everything we'd said.

'I might be a little shit,' he shouted, his features twisted, his eyes wet, 'but at least I'm not a murderer like *him*.' His head swivelled towards Tom, his eyes burning like lasers. 'He killed my dad and I HATE HIM!'

'Ellis, stop. Please … wait!' I rushed towards him, but he ran into the living room and slammed the door behind him, his yelling still ringing in my ears.

Tom laid his hand on my arm. 'He'll soon calm down,' he said.

Coral appeared a few moments later, her pale mouth set in a tight line.

'I think it's best I take Ellis home,' she said in a tone that smacked of 'I knew this would happen'.

'What?' I said, instantly alarmed. 'No, you can't do that! We have to work through this, Coral. It's important.'

'He needs time to get his head around this, Bridget. We both do.' She glanced at Tom's feet, unable to acknowledge any more of him.

I stared at her, speechless. I'd never seen her take a stance like this before. Not against me, at least. Coral *needed* me. Everything she had was because of me.

I came to my senses. 'He's my grandson and I want him to stay. He needs to get to know who Tom is, see he's not the monster you've probably made him out to be.'

Coral laughed. A hard, hacking sound. 'I think he's got a good grasp of that already, without my interference. Tom killed his father, for God's sake! Don't you see, it's cruel to do this to him? Our lives will never be the same because of *him*.' She spat out the word, unable to keep the hatred from her eyes. Tom faltered, didn't know where to look.

'Coral!' I grabbed her arm and she instantly shook me off.

'No, Bridget. This is wrong. What you've done, marrying *him*, it's wrong and you're completely blind to it.' She looked over her shoulder and called, 'Ellis?'

Ellis slouched in the doorway, his shoulders relaxed. He was looking at the floor, seemingly more contrite now.

'Come on, let's get you home,' Coral said. 'Say bye to your nan.'

'Bye, Nan,' Ellis mumbled, his eyes still firmly trained on the carpet.

I steeled myself. 'I'm warning you, Coral, you do this and—'

'And what? What will you do? You can't hurt us more than you already have, bringing *him* back into our lives.' She bustled Ellis to the door and then they were gone and I was left standing in the echoing hallway with Tom.

I looked down at my hands and saw they were shaking. 'I can't believe she just spoke to me like that.'

'Come on, let's sit you down,' Tom said, leading me into the living room. 'This is supposed to be a happy time for us. She had no right to have a go at you like that, especially in front of Ellis.'

'She wouldn't have survived without me, do you know that? She was pregnant and had nothing but her benefits and a nasty damp bedsit. I won't let her take my grandson away from me. He's all I have left, he's—'

'Bridget, calm down. It's OK. Nobody's going to take Ellis away.' He wrapped his arms around me. 'This is a knee-jerk reaction, Coral will calm down when she gets home and reflects on the things she's said.'

I didn't answer for a moment. When I did speak, my voice was devoid of emotion, as if it belonged to someone else.

'She'd better calm down, because she's got a whole load of trouble coming if she tries to keep Ellis away from me.'

I forced myself to breathe and wiggled my clenched jaw to release it. When I looked up, I saw Tom watching me with a strange look on his face.

'What?' I said, feeling heat in my face.

'Nothing.' He laced his fingers and looked down at his hands. 'I can see how much she winds you up.'

'She'll live to regret it if she keeps this attitude up.' I took a breath and tried to calm down a little. 'If she tries to keep me away from Ellis, she's heading for a very dark place. She'll wish she never crossed me.'

18

Jill

Three days later, I stood in the kitchen making myself an omelette. Robert said he'd grab something later because he had counselling appointments booked in until 6.30.

I cracked the eggs into a jug, added salt and pepper and a dash of milk. I picked up a fork intending to whisk the mixture but found myself instead staring out of the kitchen window at the silver birch at the bottom of the garden. It was a sapling when Robert had planted it twenty-odd years ago. Now it towered there, regal and strong. Almost as tall as the house itself.

Tom had always loved that tree. When there was a full moon, the spot where it stood in the garden was a magnet for the ethereal light. Tom would sometimes wrap a quilt around himself and sit on the back doorstep, entranced and slightly terrified by the luminous trunk that Robert had once told him was made of bone. I'd threaten, beg and finally manage to coerce him back inside to bed with the promise of cocoa and a biscuit.

Those were the days when I still had influence in his life. Still had the power to protect him.

I glanced at my phone, feeling a compulsion to check Bridget's social media accounts again. There had been nothing else since the Facebook photograph of their wedding, and I felt desperate to see more of that day. At the same time, I dreaded seeing my son's handsome face plastered all over social media.

We'd heard nothing from Tom all weekend. I didn't have his mobile phone number and I hadn't a clue where they were living. I'd thought about contacting Bridget directly on Messenger. Asking to meet up and speak to her, find out more about the wedding. See the photos. Ask questions and find out what was in her head.

I tore my eyes away from the phone. I'd been checking it all morning and it was making me feel sick inside. Still, I'd used my time well this past couple of days. I'd had a bit of a brainwave and researched something online. I'd made comprehensive notes to discuss with Tom when I got a chance.

All at once, my throat felt swollen, clogged up with all the things I wanted to say, wanted to *scream*. I wanted Tom to see what she was doing, to shatter the spell she seemed to have cast on him.

When he was growing up, she'd always had this way of turning his head – in an innocent way back then, of course. We ran a more ordered house here, and whenever Tom was challenged about his behaviour, we got the retort 'Bridget lets Jesse do this' or 'Bridget doesn't moan at Jesse about that'. Tidying his room, doing his homework, eating and drinking at the table rather than in front of the television – the list went on. He wasn't exaggerating. I'd seen Bridget's non-existent parenting for myself. Treating the two boys like her mates when they were round there, letting them scoff crisps and biscuits before tea, the sort of thing most parents tried to avoid.

One time I'd forgotten to pack Tom's pyjamas in his rucksack, so I popped around there to drop them off. The living room curtains were open and I pecked in before ringing the bell. The three of them were sitting together on the sofa, howling with laughter at some childish cartoon they were watching. *South Park*, I remember it was called. I'd never heard of it at the time, but Bridget obviously had and was laughing just as hard as the boys she was supposed to be in charge of.

Now, she was acting as if she was in her late twenties too. Marrying a boy young enough to be her son, dressing inappropriately for her age.

What did Tom see in her? Did he look at her and see that young mum who used to be so much fun when his own mother was a bit stuffy?

It was embarrassing and stomach-churning. Most of all, it was terrifying. She'd already somehow convinced him to marry her – what might she convince him to do next? How easy would it be for her to lead him astray and end up ruining him?

I forced my attention back to the eggs.

Robert thought I was in denial, I knew that. I accepted Tom was a grown man and that I couldn't run his life any more, but I also knew something else. I knew Bridget Wilson had the power and, I feared, the intention to devastate my son's second chance at life.

Nobody knew her like I did. Only I understood that she'd stop at nothing to achieve her goals. It was *what* she had in mind that I had to somehow figure out.

To give her credit, when Jesse was young, she had always worked two or more cleaning or shop jobs to try and make ends meet. It wouldn't be unreasonable to say that at that point in time, when we met, she was a struggling single mother with zero sign of a rosy future ahead of her.

Yet within a short time of getting to know her, I'd seen glimpses of her iron will, an unshakeable belief in the future. I think that deep down I knew, even back then, she would make something of herself in order to carve out a better future for her and Jesse.

I was in a different position when our boys were young. I never really gave it much thought at the time, but now I can see I had an altogether more comfortable life that I largely took for granted. A nice house bought prior to a property boom in a respected part of town, an architect husband back then who worked hard and reaped the benefits of a very good salary, usually with the welcome addition of a juicy annual bonus. For myself, a career I'd happily reduced to part-time hours while Tom was young but that I fully intended returning to full-time at some point when he got to senior school.

In those days, I kept busy. I always seemed to be rushing around, ferrying Tom and Jesse to their various sports clubs and classes whilst Bridget worked her long and often unsociable hours.

When Tom began his lengthy sentence, it blew a very big hole in my life. An all-consuming black hole that swallowed up anything I tried to do to fill it. Nothing held my attention any more. I finished work and for the first couple of years, nothing distracted me from the horror of what had happened. I found it impossible to sit still long enough to watch a programme on television or read more than a few pages of a book.

Robert was scathing about my inability to cope. I'd never anticipated losing my confidence as quickly, allowing my self-esteem to be eroded by my husband in a clever sort of way. It didn't seem like he was doing anything at all. The seemingly innocent comments about the way I looked, the programmes I watched on television. At the time, I chastised myself for being over-sensitive. And yet, compounded over years, those remarks and spiteful observations somehow gathered a sort of dreadful power that undermined and belittled me in a way that was hard to describe. I suppose it amounted to a feeling of not being worthy, not being good enough. Of falling short on every single level.

On better days, I flirted with the idea that I might get myself a little job, much to Robert's concern.

'The thing is, Jill, things move on. Systems, procedures … they're likely to be unrecognisable to you after all this time. Think of the work involved in getting up to speed again! I think your anxiety would be sky high in no time at all. I really do,' he'd say regretfully and I'd agree with him. The thought of starting again in a completely new environment, of having some impatient young person straight out of university having to show me what to do felt like the ultimate humiliation. It was far safer and more comfortable to stay at home.

But Robert still wasn't happy when I considered going back to the library service.

'These days, libraries are full of technology rather than the books you love. They'll spot you're a bag of nerves a mile off. You'll end up making some dreadful error and crashing the whole IT system or something equally horrendous.'

His careless comments hit home. I would probably do something just like that. Pressing a button that would have devastating consequences, or managing to lose some historic tome through my dated and incompetent indexing skills.

In the end, I ditched the idea of returning to my career and visited the doctor instead to explain the anxiousness and the black moods that constantly hovered above me. He'd glanced at his watch and prescribed a list of medication that I'd been taking ever since.

Audrey was my saviour. She eventually persuaded me to work a few hours at the shop, and slowly, things started to improve slightly. Years before Tom was due to be released, I began planning the ways I might help him when he eventually came home.

'It's a bit early to start all this, if you ask me,' Audrey said.

Now, I understood she had a point. She was trying to save me from a crushing disappointment. 'You have to live in the moment rather than constantly looking to the future' was one of her regular pieces of advice.

But what she didn't realise, what *nobody* seemed to realise, was that obsessively planning for Tom's homecoming was my antidote to the raw hopelessness I felt every hour of the day.

Half-heartedly, I began to whisk the eggs again. A couple of days ago, we were preparing to collect Tom and bring him home. I'd expected my life to look and feel very different by now. But this new situation felt like a fresh sort of hell.

I should have been preparing a family meal, not an omelette for one. I'd imagined people popping by to say hi. Me joking I hadn't a moment to spare. Instead, I'd made an appointment with the doctor because I felt like my tablets weren't helping.

I drizzled olive oil into the small frying pan and turned up the heat. Some people might say my disappointment was selfish. But it wasn't myself I wanted to cry for; my concern was for Tom, and the future he was putting in such grave jeopardy.

When he went to prison, he had a lot of local support. People around here knew the circumstances of Jesse's death. Our neighbours all asked about him when they found out it was close to his release date. They knew that Tom was an honest, steady sort of guy whereas Jesse was always more volatile. Given time, Tom would have easily fitted in again and begun to build a new life. Was it too much to ask to think he might've got married and had a couple of children in the coming years? It was hardly an outlandish fantasy.

When it came down to it, I just wanted my son back home. I wanted Tom here where he belonged. I wanted to look after him, be useful ... have a worthwhile function again. An old-fashioned view maybe, but was that such a terrible crime?

I heard the front door open and rushed out, thinking that Robert had gone out without saying anything. I stopped dead in my tracks as my son walked in, clutching the front door key I'd given him. He was alone.

'Tom!' I whispered as he closed the door behind him. It felt as though I had conjured him up with the strength of my thoughts. Our bond was still so strong.

'We need to talk, Mum,' he said in an ominous tone. 'There are important things I need to discuss with you.'

I looked at his face, his serious expression, his furrowed brow. I felt my burst of hope drain away from me. I dreaded what might come next.

19

Tom

Jill offered to make a hot drink, but Tom asked for a glass of water. They sat on the kitchen sofa and Jill stared wordlessly out at the garden.

His father must have heard him in the hallway but he never came out of the office to say hello. Typical.

Tom felt suddenly desperate to fill the awful silence.

'I hope you're OK, Mum. I know it was a shock.'

'I was thinking earlier about your silver birch nights,' she said. 'Can you remember? You'd sit on the step and stare at the moonlight shining on the tree trunk. You really believed it was made of bone.'

'I do remember,' he said softly.

'I actually spoke to your dad a couple of months ago about the garden. I said we should get someone in to give us ideas on what to do with it. You know, put some borders in and get more colour in there. The lawn's lush now but it was always scrappy because you and Jesse would play so many ball games on there and—'

'Mum.' He kept his voice calm and gentle.

Jill clamped her mouth closed. Urgently, she pressed her hand to her chest as if her heart might be mere seconds away from bursting out of it.

'I know you had a massive shock last night, but I hope you'll accept that Bridget and I are married and—'

'I *have* accepted it. I have to, don't I?' The tendons in her neck bulged dangerously. 'The way I see it, I have little choice in the matter.'

'Please let me speak, Mum, I know you're incredibly upset. Bridget understands, you know. She says it's natural you'll be devastated.'

'Of course I'm upset, it was a shock.' She bristled at the mention of his wife. 'It's your choice, I know that. I do wish you'd found it in your heart to tell me on one of my visits.' He hung his head but didn't comment. 'I can't help wondering how it happened, though, how you came to marry the mother of your victim. Because regardless of the fact that you acted in self-defence, you do realise that's what people will say? That she's the mother of the best friend you killed.'

'Mum. I accept it must be almost impossible for you to understand how we came to fall in love. But it didn't happen overnight, Bridget has been visiting me for the last couple of years. The only way I can describe it is that Bridget my wife feels like someone completely different and separate to Bridget the mum of Jesse all those years ago. That seems like another life for both of us. We feel brand new to each other, if that makes sense.'

Judging by the look on his mother's face, it didn't make any sense to her at all.

'I see,' she said finally, touching her face with the back of a hand. Her cheeks looked flushed and hot.

Tom dipped his chin down and looked up at her. 'I'm not sure you do see.'

'If the tables were turned and I'd married Jesse, how do you think you'd be feeling about it?'

For a moment or two Tom felt nonplussed. Then he said, honestly, 'I'd be shocked. In denial for a while, I expect.'

His words hung in the air for a few moments before Jill spoke again.

'There's only two years in age between Bridget and myself. I assume you know that, right? Two years between your mother and your new wife.'

'Of course I know that, but it's different somehow. Bridget, she's so … I don't know, *young* in her ways, her outlook. Do you know what I mean?'

'Yes,' Jill said shortly. 'But someone closer to your own age might have given you children, for a start. Bridget is a grandmother!'

She'd told Tom on one of her earliest visits that her friend, Audrey, had heard the news that Coral had given birth to Jesse's son.

'I don't want anyone else, I'm in love with Bridget, Mum. The fact that there won't be children is a far less important consideration for me. Anyway, we have Ellis.'

'Ellis isn't your son, though, he's Jesse's!' Jill bit her lip. 'What I can't understand is why you had to get married before your release. In prison, of all places! Why would you rush into marrying her instead of dating for a while … did she force your hand?'

'Of course she didn't, it was my idea.'

'Did you know she's posted a picture on Facebook of your wedding?'

Tom frowned. 'No, I didn't know, but … well, that's OK, isn't it?'

Tom hadn't got a Facebook account yet, what with being in prison but Jill seemed to think it was a big deal.

'I can't understand why you had to get married in secret,' she said again, petulantly.

Tom sighed. 'Because of exactly this. The way you're behaving. We knew people would disapprove. We knew you'd try and stop us.'

'Just me?'

'Everyone. Ellis's mum, Coral … she's giving Bridget a hard time about it too, and the boy won't even look at me yet.'

'Well, I can understand that. Jesse was Coral's partner and Ellis's father, after all. The lad is young to have to deal with you being in his face all of a sudden.'

Tom swept a hand towards her. 'This is exactly it, you see. Everybody has an opinion about us, about what we've done. But we're married now. We made our commitment to each other because against the odds, we fell in love. I don't want some clueless girl my own age. I want Bridget. Someone strong, who has a bit of life experience. Someone who understands everything I've been through.'

Tom had never possessed Jesse's confidence when it came to girls. He'd been on a handful of dates but had found them torturous because he'd been so nervous and tongue-tied. Instead, he'd immersed himself in boxing. 'I've no time for dating,' had been his stock reply if anyone asked.

His mother tried another angle. 'I worry that Bridget comes with a lot of baggage. If Jesse had gone to prison for causing *your* death, I'd never want to see him again, never mind marry him!'

'Well, you and Bridget are very different people, Mum,' he said mildly. 'Bridget found it in her heart to forgive me before we even fell in love, and that shows what an amazing person she is.'

Jill fell silent for a few moments and looked away, as if she was deciding whether to say something. When she looked back at him, she sounded resolved.

'Don't take this the wrong way, Tom, but it needs saying. You've been in prison for ten years, living a very limited life. Bridget has been out in the big wide world, building her charity, achieving a lot of things, it seems. How easy do you think it would be for her to convince you that you have a future together while underneath she still despises you for the fact that Jesse isn't here any more?'

'We've been totally open and honest with each other.' Tom ran his hand through his hair, wondering how long he had to keep saying the same things in a different way to try and get through.

'Bridget admitted she felt like she hated me for a long time, but now she understands I never meant to hurt Jesse. That what happened almost destroyed me too.'

'What if Bridget's only motive is to ruin you, to get revenge for Jesse's death? If she poured all her efforts into that, how would you know until it was too late?'

The idea was so ludicrous he wanted to laugh, but he managed to keep his face straight. 'Thanks to the restorative justice programme, we've done far more talking than if we'd just dated. I know Bridget inside out, Mum, and she knows me. Our love is strong and deep. All this rubbish about revenge, it's not real. It's only in your head. Bridget's already shown her commitment and faith in me in other ways. One of the things I came here to tell you is that I'm going to be working at the charity, making new contacts and bringing in donations.'

'You've never expressed any interest in that sort of work before.'

Tom shrugged, irked that she was unimpressed. 'I've never had the opportunity before, and it beats some crummy job working in a library.'

He instantly regretted the snipe as her face fell.

'Sorry, Mum. I shouldn't have—'

'It's fine.' Jill waved his comment away. 'I'm only going to say this once, but it has to be done. I have to be sure you understand.'

'Huh?'

'This marriage can be annulled, Tom. I've googled it, you've only to say the word and we can go and see a solicitor. If you'd felt forced into marrying her, they'd have to—'

He stood up. 'Right. I'm going now, I—'

'No, please!' Jill shot up and grabbed his arms. 'I had to say it, I had to. I won't repeat it, I promise. I do want you to be happy. It's just … I honestly worry that you've made a huge mistake.'

He sighed and sat back down again.

'You'll see, Mum. Everyone will see how happy we are together, I'm asking you to give it time.' He reached for Jill's hand and she let him take it. Her fingers felt warm and dry. 'I know you only want the best for me, but you can have your own life back now. You and Dad can do all the things you've been wanting to do together.'

'But—'

'Please, Mum. Don't make this harder than it needs to be.' Being in this house was squeezing the life out of him. He needed to go home. 'Bridget wants you to come over for dinner on Friday night if you're free.'

Her face froze and he imagined her throat tightening. 'That's … unexpected.'

'It was all her idea.' He smiled. 'She's asking Coral and Ellis if they'll come too. She desperately wants us to all get on. Please come.'

'I'll speak to your dad,' she said lightly and he imagined Robert instantly looking for a way out. 'I'm not sure he'll be able to make it if he's working late.'

Tom pulled a face. 'I'd rather you came alone anyway. I don't want him there.'

'Tom!'

'He doesn't deserve you, Mum.' He let go of her hand, battled to keep the sadness off his face. 'I'll tell Bridget you'll come, anyway. She'll be so thrilled. The house is amazing. She's only been living there six months, I can't wait for you to see it.'

Jill gave a small nod, seemingly unable to answer.

He gave her his mobile number and his new address before kissing her at the front door. At the bottom of the drive he turned and looked back at the house. His memories were largely unhappy here, at the mercy of his bullying father for so much of his childhood and teenage years.

His mother truly wanted the best for him and that pulled at his heartstrings. But she was wrong about Bridget. They'd been friends for many years and yet she refused to accept what a decent person his new wife was.

He and Bridget loved each other and, despite his mother's fears, she'd never do anything to hurt him.

Tom felt certain of that.

20

Bridget

Mid-week, we decided to go food shopping for Friday night's dinner to give me plenty of time to prepare. Jill had already contacted Tom to say both she and Robert would be gracing us with their presence and I saw he was both surprised and delighted.

I'd called Coral and held out the olive branch and she'd agreed to try again and bring Ellis to the meal. I hadn't mentioned Tom's parents would be there. No need to complicate matters and give her an excuse to refuse my request.

Tom drove to get some practice in and when we got back to the house, he carried in the bags. He had a spring in his step. Before going shopping, we'd called in at the charity's offices in Nottingham city centre. A year ago we'd rented refurbished premises in a building that afforded great views over the historical market square and council house.

We didn't stay long as I was supposed to be on annual leave for two weeks. Still, Tom was able to meet the staff and get a better overview of the work he'd be doing as our new development manager.

'It's a key role in our five-year business strategy,' I explained to him as we admired the urban vista from what would be Tom's own small but smart office. 'Your work will make a huge difference to the business.'

He wasn't to know I'd created the role for him and besides, it was true it would make a big difference. If he was successful at it.

He'd turned and embraced me. 'I can't thank you enough for the faith you've shown in me, Brid,' he'd said, his voice tight with emotion. 'Nobody's ever really believed in me like you do and I won't let you down.'

How I wished Jill had heard him say that. She'd always been supportive of Tom provided his goals and activities hadn't taken him too far away from her apron strings. Anything too ambitious had been swiftly discounted without him having much of a say.

I overtook Tom on the path leading up to the house. 'Let me get the door, you've got your hands full.'

'Anyone would think we were feeding the five thousand with the amount we've bought,' he laughed, grappling with the numerous bags.

'Well, nutritious meals are complicated to prepare,' I told him. 'Lots of ingredients when you cook from scratch.'

Tom had told me about Jill's home-made lasagne and garlic bread on the day of his release, and I'd decided to pull out all the stops to show her how a meal should be done. This was the first time my culinary skills had been properly on show to Tom. I knew how health-conscious he'd become in prison, training at the gym and eating only vegetarian food in an effort to preserve the fitness he'd worked so hard to build as a boxer before he began his sentence. He was also interested in converting to a plant-based diet, so I was hoping to wow him with my vegan menu. If nothing else, Jill would realise she wasn't the only person capable of keeping her precious son happy!

In front of me, Tom stopped dead in the hallway. Ellis sat in the living room, next to the windows that overlooked the garden. His profile, the way the light fell on his face … for a moment he looked just like Jesse, and I felt a stinging pang of loss. Ellis glanced up, saw Tom staring and went back to his game.

My heart soared. I'd telephoned Coral earlier and although it rankled, I'd swallowed my pride and asked if she'd consider letting me see Ellis before the weekend. Now he was here.

'I suppose Ellis could come over for his tea today,' she'd said craftily. 'I'm a bit tight this month and there's not much in.' Stupid she was not when it came to money.

'Bring him over after school,' I'd said. 'And I'll put a hundred quid in your account to tide you over.' If money was what it took to have Ellis around more then so be it.

'Hello, Ellis,' Tom said, putting down the bags in the hall and walking over to him. 'I didn't know you were coming over.'

Ellis didn't look up.

'Hello you,' I said, hoping to smooth over our recent snappy little exchange. 'How long have you been here on your own?' He was earlier than I'd expected, but I didn't care.

'Dunno,' he said. 'About thirty minutes, I think. Mum let me in and went into town to meet her friend for a drink.'

So much for counting the pennies! I thought. And the last time I'd looked, she didn't *have* any friends. I walked into the kitchen and tossed the car keys on the side. Tom followed me.

'Coral has a key?' he asked in a hushed voice. 'Sounds like she comes and goes as she pleases.'

It had slipped my mind, but I did give her a spare key when I first moved in. We'd always done that with each other for ease of access. It had seemed a good idea at the time, but that was going to have to be reviewed now Tom was living here.

'Can I have some juice, Nan?' Ellis called.

'One second.' I kicked off my shoes and slid my feet into my Ugg slippers before heading for the fridge. 'Ellis, say hi to Tom.'

'It's fine.' Tom shook his head and dropped his voice. 'Don't make a thing of it.' He took the carton of juice from me and poured some into a glass, then took it over to Ellis.

'There we go, buddy. Playing anything good?'

Calling Ellis 'buddy' like that wasn't going to go down well. I held my breath.

'*Animal Crossing,*' Ellis replied shortly, taking the glass.

'Never heard of that one,' Tom said. 'You know, I was thinking of getting a PlayStation and connecting it to the big TV here.'

Ellis looked up. 'Really?'

'Yeah. Trouble is, I'm totally out of touch with the games that are out now. I don't suppose you … Nah, doesn't matter.'

Ellis put his glass on the coffee table and sat up a bit straighter. 'What?'

I leaned forward on the worktop, listening.

'I wondered if you'd be interested in helping choose some games and then maybe playing a few together. You know, to get me into it again.'

'I know all the good games,' Ellis said, putting the device down on the seat cushion next to him. 'I mean, *Call of Duty's* the obvious choice, but there are loads of other good games, too. *Marvel, FIFA,* stuff like that.'

'*Call of Duty*? That's an 18 rating, isn't it?' I chipped in.

'It's 17,' Ellis said quickly. 'But Mum lets me watch films that are 18. I'm not a baby.'

'I bet a good action film has about the same amount of blood and gore in it,' Tom remarked.

Ellis nodded. 'It's not real life, Nan. I'm not going to suddenly go out and kill someone …' His voice petered out as he realised what he'd said.

Tom jumped in right away. 'Tell you what, then. I've promised your nan I'll put some flat-pack shelves up now, but next time you're over, we'll look at the PlayStation stuff online together. OK?'

'OK.' Ellis picked up his game again. Then he looked up at Tom and said grudgingly, 'Thanks for the juice.'

Tom looked over and winked at me. This man was certainly full of surprises.

21

Jill

On the day of the dinner at Tom and Bridget's house, I was completely incapable of concentrating on my book or watching daytime television. I'd already checked Bridget's social media half a dozen times and there was nothing new. I was going to drive myself crazy, so I decided to start weeding the borders in the garden.

I used to garden regularly, loving the birds, the different seasons, the fresh air. When Tom was small, he'd sit with a sketchpad and pencil and painstakingly draw a flower or a ladybird. He'd focus and apply himself without me having to coerce him.

It had been a long time since I'd taken pleasure in the garden. Robert tended to put off the mowing until the lawn was an inch off resembling a jungle, but I didn't have the drive for it these days.

For the first ten minutes of tidying the borders, I wanted to go back inside. It was bright but cold and I hadn't really dressed warmly enough, but I kept at it. My back made its discomfort known, but I felt freer out here then I had felt for ages. I began to wish I'd turned to the garden, rather than away from it, during my most difficult times.

For the first five or six years of Tom's sentence, I had found it virtually impossible to avoid scrolling through Bridget's social media. Her Young Men Matter Facebook feed and the regular reposts of newspaper articles and magazine interviews she'd done, headlines such as:

When beauty dies – a mother's meditation on the loss of her son
Learning to live without Jesse – Bridget Wilson reflects, five years after the manslaughter of her son

Jesse. Jesse. Jesse. Thrill-seeker, boy racer and promiscuous risk-taker. That had been the truth that had never made the headlines, the unpalatable facts that no one ever spoke about, least of all Bridget.

Startled by a noise behind me, I turned around to see Robert hovering.

'Keeping busy, are we?' he said in that patronising way of his that I'd made excuses for during most of our married life.

'Somebody's got to tackle this mess,' I said coldly. 'Might as well be me.'

'Seeing as I'm working and struggling to pay the bills, I'll let you take over the Monty Don mantle, if that's all right.'

I stopped weeding and straightened up, massaging my lower back as it twinged in protest. 'And why *is* that? Why are we short of money and struggling to pay the bills?'

'The bills are high. It's a big house and—'

'But it's always been a big house,' I said, shaking clods of clammy dark earth from the trowel. 'I can't recall there being a problem before.'

He laughed. 'I can't recall you ever asking.'

'You know, if you can't think of anything constructive to say, may I suggest you bugger off back inside?'

'There's no need for that!' he said, taken aback. 'Look, Jill, this is not the outcome you expected, I know that. It's not the fresh start you'd planned for Tom.'

Not *we*, but *you*. I was done skirting around the issue.

'He's your son too, or have you forgotten that?' I knocked over the bucket as I stepped back, and the limp, dying weeds spilled out onto the grass. 'You're probably just glad he'll be out of your hair.'

'That's hardly fair,' Robert said, his eyes widening with surprise.

I bent forward and righted the bucket. 'The prison service is to blame for this as much as anyone. Filling his head with this retentive justice nonsense when he's so vulnerable.'

'It's called *restorative* justice,' Robert remarked, stepping forward and surveying my handiwork. 'Very fashionable in liberal circles at the moment, I understand.'

'How can anything ever be restored to what it was?' I demanded. 'What happened happened. Sadly, Jesse died and Tom paid the price. The past can't be airbrushed away or moulded into something else. It can't be *restored* in any way at all.'

'I'm not entirely sure that's the concept behind it,' Robert said, amused. 'It's more about forgiveness, about both sides moving on and healing.'

'I keep coming back to the same question. What does a forty-eight-year-old woman want with a twenty-eight-year-old man?'

'Aside from the obvious, you mean?'

'The obvious?'

'He's fit, good-looking, ripe for the picking, or hadn't you noticed that?' Robert smirked. 'Caged for all those years, I'm sure he must be like a frustrated stallion in the sack.'

'Stop it.' Bile rose in my throat. 'I'm not talking about anything as simple or crude as that, Robert. I'm talking about something much darker.'

He looked baffled. 'Such as?'

'Revenge for Jesse's death, for goodness' sake! Think about it. Jesse's gone for good, but Tom has done his time and now has a chance at building a good life. She can't stand that and she's planned to get close to him so that she's well placed to destroy him.'

'Honestly.' Robert snorted and turned back to the house. 'This is all getting a bit "TV thriller", Jill. I'll leave you to it.'

'OK, so answer this. Why would Tom want *her*? That's what I really don't get.'

'Well, he's never had much luck with girls his own age, has he?'

'You mean he was a bit shy?'

Robert pulled a face.

'People around here know that what happened that night. It wasn't straightforward and in time, they'd forgive him.'

'Nevertheless, Jesse *did* die,' Robert said smoothly. 'The judge sent him down for ten years for manslaughter, and that's what you still can't accept.'

22

Nottinghamshire Police

2009

Aside from the usual teenage antisocial behaviour at the park and the odd drunkard causing trouble in a late bar, it was rare that anything really serious happened in Mansfield or the surrounding area.

So when DS Irma Barrington got the call from her boss, DI Marcus Fernwood, at 2.45 a.m., she was surprised to say the least.

'Hope I've not caught you at a bad time,' he said drily. 'Serious assault outside Movers nightclub in town. Victim unconscious with suspect still at the scene.'

Irma's interest was instantly piqued. 'Sounds interesting.'

'You can drive. Pick me up on the way through.'

Irma said, 'See you in ten.'

She'd fallen asleep on the sofa for the third night running, and the single advantage of that was that she was still fully dressed. She popped her head around the spare bedroom door and saw that her dad was still out for the count. She'd be back home in a couple of hours and he'd be none the wiser. It was the second time this month he'd turned up just before midnight ratted out of his skull, and it couldn't keep happening. But she'd worry about that later.

She grabbed a bottle of water from the fridge and, closing the front door quietly behind her, padded out to the car. The street light outside the small front garden lit her path. She pointed the fob at the car, and the corresponding beep seemed loud enough to wake the whole street.

It was cold, and she wished she'd grabbed her warmer coat before leaving the house, but once the car heater had got going and started to belt out a bit of warmth, she instantly felt better.

She picked up Marcus from his smart townhouse in Oak Tree Lane and they drove towards the centre of town via Nottingham Road. Marcus wasn't very talkative; in fact, when she glanced over, she saw his head was slumped against the window and his eyes were closed.

She navigated around the one-way system, passing the Four Seasons shopping centre, and turned into a side street that would lead her to Movers nightclub. In contrast to the deserted roads she'd driven through, the area outside the club was rammed with a large crowd of people.

'Bloody hell,' she said. 'Haven't folks got beds to go to?'

Marcus shook himself and looked around. 'This lot have obviously piled out of the club and found themselves some late-night entertainment.'

They got out of the car and pushed their way through the clamour of bodies, walking down the side of the building to the back entrance. It was a particularly cold night, and most of the crowd were underdressed. Irma pulled her jacket tighter and cursed herself for not remembering her scarf.

A man of around twenty lay prostrate in the quiet road that ran behind the club. He wore jeans and a white Lacoste T-shirt. His arms were wiry and his head had twisted at an awkward angle, his eyes closed. There was no obvious injury and Irma spotted shallow movement from his chest.

Marcus held up his ID and addressed the uniformed officer.

'What's the situation?'

'His name is Jesse Wilson, sir,' the young officer said, standing a little straighter. 'He's a local lad. The guy who punched him is over there. Says he's his best friend.' He handed Irma the victim's ID.

'With friends like that …' Marcus murmured.

The detectives turned to see a stocky young man standing with a female police officer. He had dark hair and wore black jeans and a black T-shirt, the short sleeves straining around his muscular biceps. He stared at his boots and did not glance up.

'Sounds like they had some kind of disagreement outside the club,' the officer continued. 'His mate over there reckoned he only punched the victim once, but Jesse slipped and fell, hit his head on the concrete. Ambulance is on its … Ah, looks like it's just arrived.'

The crowd parted and fell away to let the emergency vehicle through. Irma glanced at the details on the ID in her hand, then dropped to her haunches and studied the face of Jesse Wilson, eighteen years old. He was a good-looking lad, in a rocker sort of way. The kind of bad boy her teenage niece would no doubt go weak at the knees for.

With the absence of any visible injuries, he looked deeply asleep, as if he'd simply had too much to drink and had passed out in the road.

She stood up and met the eyes of the young man the officer had said was Jesse's best friend. She took in his naturally assertive stance, the look of dread on his face, and let out a small sigh.

He looked like a decent young man who'd come out for a good night and found himself in a whole lot of trouble.

23

Tom Billinghurst sat quietly in the back of the car as Irma drove him to the station with Marcus.

She watched him in the rear-view mirror but he would not meet her eyes. He stared out of the window at the deserted streets. It was almost 4 a.m. now; soon daybreak would arrive. Another day would start, very different to the one this young man – an amateur boxer, Marcus had since told her – had experienced yesterday.

Today, with a single, solitary punch, his whole life had taken a hairpin bend.

Before they'd got into the car, the paramedics had informed Marcus that Jesse's prognosis did not look good. 'They said there were signs of internal brain trauma when they got him into the ambulance,' he told her. 'They'll be sending him directly for a CT scan when he gets to hospital.'

Irma had heard of one-punch deaths before. Freak accidents. Particularly lethal when administered by a trained boxer, as seemed to have happened in this case.

'The doorman insists there was nobody else involved,' Irma had reported after she'd spoken briefly with the security manager. 'He told me they were arguing about something inside the club. One minute they were nice and relaxed, talking over a pint, the next he said Jesse was acting weird and there was some pushing and shoving taking place.'

'CCTV?'

Irma shook her head. 'Went on the blink last week.'

Luckily, Tom Billinghurst had been the epitome of helpful, summoning an ambulance himself. 'Strangely, the operator told him that one was already on its way, so we need to follow up on exactly who called the emergency services when there appear to be no witnesses.' Marcus had frowned. 'When uniformed officers arrived, he immediately admitted to hitting Jesse, and was arrested at the scene.'

At the station, while Billinghurst got booked in by the desk clerk, Irma and Marcus grabbed a coffee and had a quick chat about how they intended to handle the interview.

'It looks fairly straightforward. On the face of it, he's taking full responsibility,' Marcus said. 'Let's not overcomplicate matters. Billinghurst hit him, the victim slipped and hit his head. He may not realise it, but because he's a trained boxer, the CPS will come down on him like a ton of bricks if Wilson has serious brain trauma.'

When the interview room was ready, one of the uniformed officers provided Billinghurst with some water and he sat quietly opposite the two detectives. Irma explained the proceedings to him for the benefit of the recording, and Marcus kicked proceedings off.

'Tom, can you tell us in your own words exactly what happened tonight? Start with how you happened to be in the club and take us through how things escalated.'

Irma was struck by how tired and anxious the young man looked. It was difficult to believe he had an ounce of aggression in him.

'It was Jesse's idea to go out, as usual,' he said.

'As usual?'

'He always wants to go out. Hates a night stuck in.'

'I'd guess you are both out a lot then?' Irma asked.

He nodded. 'Yeah, but not every night. Usually once or twice in the week and definitely all weekend if Jesse's funds stretch to it.'

'Had you been to Movers before?'

'Oh yeah. Loads of times. With it being midweek, I suggested we went to the pub for a quiet drink.' He hesitated. 'I'm supposed to be attending an early training session today at the boxing gym. I wish I'd insisted on the quiet drink now, but Jesse, he's not easy to put off once he gets something in his head.'

Marcus nodded. 'So on balance, would you say you were in a bit of a bad mood?'

Tom shook his head. 'Not at all, but I admit I was slightly irritated. Everything always has to be done the way he wants, you know? After a while, it gets …'

'Annoying?' Irma offered.

'Yeah, it can get very annoying,' he confirmed. 'Is there any news on how he is? Has he regained consciousness yet?'

'No news yet, I'm afraid,' Irma said, referring to her notes. 'Back to earlier in the evening. Did you go for drinks before the club?'

'Only one, in the Mayflower bar. We don't go out until late, ten o'clock usually. We had a few beers at home, played some *FIFA*. Then we got a cab straight into town.'

'What kind of mood was Jesse in?'

'He was OK at first, in the bar, although I sensed he was a bit on edge.'

'Did you ask him if anything was wrong?' Irma said.

'Not at that point, because I assumed that was why he'd wanted to come out, to loosen up a bit, you know?'

'You said he was OK "at first",' Marcus said. 'What about later on in the night?'

'He was drinking heavily. I stuck to beers but he started getting a couple of shots with each pint. Called me a wuss when I said I wanted to take it easy for my early-morning training session.'

'Did that make you angry?'

'No, I'm used to him. He doesn't mean anything by it. Usually.'

'But this time he did mean something by it?'

'I don't know what got into him. He started acting really strange. I asked him what was wrong, but he got crazier, dancing like a madman and then sort of mime-attacking me with kung fu style moves. He got that close I had to push him back.'

'And he did this for no apparent reason?' Irma frowned.

'For no reason. The doorman came over and told him to leave, that aggressive behaviour wasn't permitted. Jesse pushed into him sort of accidentally on purpose, and then started giving it the usual.' Tom used his hand like an opening and closing mouth. 'When we got away from the dance floor, another security guy grabbed me and they pushed us both out of the fire exit, the rear doors.'

'Then what happened?' Marcus prompted him.

'I had a go at Jesse, asked him what the hell was wrong with him, and that was when he pulled the knife on me.'

Irma consulted her notes. 'There was a Swiss Army type penknife found tucked under him, the sort with small tools and gadgets attached. This is the knife you're referring to, yes?'

'Yes. Doesn't sound much when you describe it like that, but all I saw was a blade flashing in the street light. He jabbed it at me and I jumped back, told him not to be so stupid. I actually laughed, because I couldn't believe what he was doing.'

'How did that go down with Jesse?'

'He lost it. Lunged at me again with the knife. I sidestepped him and he came after me. He was like a man possessed.'

'Had Jesse taken any drugs that you know of during the night?'

'No. He can drink like a fish, we both can at times. Jesse has the odd joint, but that's it, nothing harder, and as a boxer, I'm strictly drugs-free.'

'So Jesse came at you a second time, then what?' Marcus said.

'It's a bit of a blur, but my instincts kicked in and I just threw a punch. Without even thinking about it. I had to stop him because he'd definitely have stabbed me. His eyes, they were wild.'

'And to clarify, you hit him just the once?' Irma said.

Tom nodded, looked down at the table. 'The punch landed on the side of his jaw and he went down. I saw his head smash into the pavement and then ... well, he lay very still and I panicked. I've seen enough boxing matches to know.'

'To know what, Tom?' Marcus pushed him.

'To know that there was a chance he'd suffered a brain injury when his head hit the concrete. I had this feeling that I was in serious trouble. Listen ... can you go and check if there's any news yet?'

Irma gave Tom a hard look. 'Not at this precise moment but rest assured, when we hear anything you'll be the first to know.'

24

Jill

October 2019

It was an hour before we were due to leave for the dinner party.

I'd already showered, scrubbed the soil from my fingernails and washed and dried my hair. After applying a little make-up, I stared into my dressing table mirror and tried to flatten my hairstyle.

Earlier, I'd dug out my heated rollers for the first time in years. My hair was longer than it used to be – through neglect rather than intention – and the effect had been a bigger and bouncier hairdo than I'd anticipated. I'd used extra-hold spray, and my hair felt voluminous but also very stiff, like cardboard.

With a light dusting of bronzer and blusher and a pink lipstick I'd found at the back of the drawer, I'd scrubbed up. I'd made an effort, at least.

Audrey rang. 'How are you feeling? Remember what we said. Head held high, don't let her get to you.'

When Tom left the house on Monday, I'd called her and poured out my heart and soul.

'I don't want to go for dinner because I can't stand the thought of her smug face watching me suffer, but if I don't go, I feel like I'm letting Tom down.' I paused. 'When I texted him to say we'd be there, he told me Coral and Ellis are going too. Awkward isn't the word for it. That poor boy.'

'You have to go and Robert must go too, whether he likes it or not,' Audrey said firmly. 'You have to show you're being reasonable – on the surface, at least. If they close down communications, you'll not find out a thing. At least if you play her at her own game, you can keep an eye on what's happening.'

It had sounded like common sense. The last thing I wanted was for my relationship with my son to end up the same way as his father's.

'I don't want to go any more than when we last spoke,' I said now, putting the phone on to loudspeaker. I turned my head this way and that, evaluating my big hair in the mirror. 'But I *am* going and I'm going to put on an act in the hope of getting up Bridget's nose.'

'Good girl,' Audrey said with approval. 'And what does Robert think about it all?'

'He's trying to squirm out of it again,' I said.

'Astonishing!' Audrey murmured. 'He finds it the easiest thing in the world to run away from responsibility, doesn't he? Well, good luck. Let me know how it goes.'

We said our goodbyes and I ended the call. I stood up and straightened my knitted dress. It didn't look as good on as when I'd bought it ten years ago. I was the same weight as back then, but my body shape had changed. The bits that used to go in stuck out a bit more now, with a thickening around the middle I could do little about.

I'd decided to wear opaque black tights, and on a whim, I slipped on a pair of barely worn red patent loafers I'd found at the bottom of the wardrobe. I hoped they added a touch of quirkiness against the dull grey of the dress. With Bridget flouncing around and looking half her age, I felt a growing determination to give myself a bit of an overhaul.

'Cab's here,' Robert called up as I reached the top of the stairs. He'd decided he'd have a drink after all and leave the car at home. 'Good Lord, what have you done to your hair? Looks like you've had a fright.'

I didn't give him the courtesy of a reply. He opened the front door and I followed him out.

It was a fifteen-minute cab ride to Bridget's house. While Robert paid the driver, I stood outside and looked at the brightly lit front of the three-storey house. So much illuminated glass! It must have cost a fortune to heat.

The front door opened and Tom appeared, waving.

'Welcome, guys!' He stood aside as we entered the house. He looked so happy, glowing from within, and was effortlessly smart and handsome in a paisley-print long-sleeved shirt that he wore loose outside his black trousers.

'Dad.' He nodded as Robert walked by him and left me standing inside the doorway, still trying to pat down the volume in my hair. I glanced around. Everything was so open and white and shiny and clean. And so modern! It made our house look like a mausoleum.

Tom moved sideways and my breath caught in my throat as a large, framed headshot of Tom and Bridget on their wedding day revealed itself on the wall behind him. It was a different one to the picture she'd put on Facebook, and I stepped forward and studied it. Her hair pinned up, delicate little flowers dotted throughout. Tom looked his usual handsome self, but Bridget's skin, eyes, teeth were perfect, not a blemish or a wrinkle to be found. *Filters*. That was what all the celebrities used on their pictures these days. Filters that made them look wonderful, even on close-ups like this one.

'Hi, Mum,' Tom said, kissing my cheek. His eyes swept quickly from my hair down to my feet, where they fixed on the loafers for a couple of seconds before he looked back up at me and smiled. 'You look so ... different!'

I decided to take his comment as a compliment. 'Thank you! I love your shirt, Tom.'

'Paul Smith.' He winked and stroked the fabric of his sleeve. 'It's a gift from Bridget. She spoils me rotten!'

Bridget appeared, a forced smile stretched across her face. 'Well, we had to do something about those God-awful clothes you were wearing. Jill! How nice to see you.'

With tremendous effort I managed not to react, bristling from her thinly disguised jibe. Tom must have told her I'd bought him new clothes for his release.

She wore a cream chiffon top, nipped in at the waist, and skinny jeans with impossibly high ankle boots that made my knees ache just to look at them. Had I not known her, I'd probably have guessed her to be in her late thirties.

'You look very nice, Bridget,' Robert simpered, air-kissing her. 'So youthful!'

I felt like kicking him in the back of the knees. The creep. He was all Mr Nice Guy to her face, but it was a different story back at home when he was ranting about their age difference.

'Thank you, Robert. I think it helps working with young people,' Bridget said.

Helps bagging yourself a ridiculously young husband, too! I'd have loved to have added.

'I like to keep up with the latest fashion,' she continued. 'It's so easy to slide into dressing like a fuddy-duddy without noticing, isn't it?'

Suddenly my conspicuous red loafers felt clumsy and dated.

Tom and Robert started talking together in low voices, which put me on edge. It was difficult for those two to pass the time of day without a full-scale row ensuing.

I pushed away my troubled thoughts.

'Thanks for asking us over for dinner, Bridget,' I said.

'You're very welcome. I thought it might help seeing as we got off on the wrong foot last week.'

Said as though it was all my fault entirely!

'How are you feeling, Mum?' Tom looked at me with concern. 'Dad's told me you went to see the doctor yesterday.'

I glanced anxiously at Robert, but he'd made himself busy hanging up his coat.

'I'm fine. It was just a routine visit,' I said briskly.

The doctor had reviewed my prescription medication and made a couple of tweaks as I'd been so stressed recently but I wouldn't be sharing that with Bridget. That was Robert all over, talking about something so intensely personal at a dinner party.

'And who's this handsome young man?' Robert said.

I noticed a figure hovering behind Bridget, and then a skinny young woman wearing neon-pink lipstick stepped in front of him and blocked our view. I realised it was Coral. Ten years after I'd last seen her, she looked nervous and tired.

'Ellis, go into the other room,' Coral hissed, her face puce. Another person who obviously didn't want to be here.

Bridget either didn't hear or she purposely ignored her. 'This is Ellis, my grandson.' She turned to look at him. 'Say hi to Jill and Robert, Ellis.'

A surly boy dressed in a hoodie and clutching a portable games console shuffled forward. So this was the son Jesse had never got to meet. He stopped moving and pressed himself back against the wall as if he were trying to make himself invisible. Jesse's arrogance shone in him all too clearly.

'Hi,' he murmured.

'And this is Coral, who'll you know of course, Ellis's mum.'

Coral chewed the inside of her cheek and avoided eye contact with all of us.

'Hello, Coral,' I said. 'Nice to see you again after all this time.'

'Hello again, Coral,' Robert said, full of nervous energy. He was trying far too hard to fit in and say all the right things. 'I remember you from the dad taxi service I provided more times than I can remember.'

Coral had been to our house a few times when Tom had had friends over for a barbecue or a movie night, and Robert, when he was feeling generous, would sometimes ferry them to the cinema or pick them up from some bar or other.

Coral wasn't a very memorable sort of person, but she'd been Jesse's girlfriend and now she was the mother of young Ellis, so I guessed it suited Bridget to keep her around.

She pressed her lips together and glanced at my face for a split second. Her eyes flashed. 'Hello,' she said quietly, choosing to speak only to me, and that was when I realised with a jolt that she wasn't nervous at all, but quietly seething and trying her best to control it.

'Is that your black Mercedes parked outside, Bridget?' Robert turned his back on me. 'Very smart. Very *sexy*, I think the word is these days for something good, isn't it?'

I cringed. He thought he was so down with the kids, it was embarrassing. But I heard Bridget giggle and agree with him.

'And that's my "sexy" BMW right behind it,' Tom said, mocking his father. 'Another present from my generous wife. What do you think, Mum?'

I glanced out of the window at the silver car Tom was proudly pointing out. 'It's lovely, Tom. Very nice indeed,' I said.

Tom gave me a hug, pressed his cheek next to mine.

'I really appreciate you coming over, Mum,' he said. 'I know it can't be easy for you.'

I closed my eyes and breathed in his subtle cologne. My head filled with an image of him as a child, running excitedly into our house on the day Bridget picked him up from school because I worked late at the library. All the things I'd planned for us to do together when he was released from prison drifted through my thoughts like a thin trail of smoke that led to nothing.

Behind us, Robert's conversation with Bridget faded out. Tom's arms fell stiffly down by his sides and I realised I was still holding on to him.

'Jill,' Bridget said softly. 'It's been far too long. I hope this can be the start of us rebuilding our connection.'

I let go of my son, turned around and saw her slim, lightly tanned arms outstretched towards me. My instinct was to turn my back on her, but Robert and Tom were watching, so I allowed her to place her hands on my shoulders and kiss my cheek. Close up, she was heavily made up with foundation and powder and didn't look nearly as youthful as I'd initially thought. I guessed she was probably wearing eyelash extensions, and she'd outlined her lips in a nude shade the same colour as her lipstick so they appeared fuller than they actually were. Smoke and mirrors.

'Love your hair, Jill … very eighties!' She laughed a little cruelly, I felt, but nobody else seemed to notice. I pulled away.

'Come through,' she said to the others. 'We'll have a drink and I've got some nibbles. Dinner will be ready in about twenty minutes.'

I walked ahead, but within seconds Bridget was there at my side. 'How long is it since we spoke, Jill?'

My fingernails scraped at my palm. Was she goading me to refer to the time she came to our house after Jesse's death? I'd closed the door in her face back then.

'I can't remember,' I said, but of course I knew exactly when it was. 'Sorry, I need to use the bathroom.' She gave a little smirk as if she knew I wanted to get away from her and directed me to the small downstairs cloakroom.

Like the rest of the house, it was immaculate. Soft white porcelain and pale coffee walls. Very restful. It was such a relief to get away from Bridget's intense focus. I had the disturbing sensation that everything she said to me was loaded. That she was laughing at me in plain sight because she'd taken away my son. But she was too clever to overplay it and risk anyone else noticing.

Feeling a little hot and light-headed, I splashed some water on my face and pulled at the neck of the grey wool dress. It had been a mistake to wear it, I should have dressed in layers, easy to slip off if I felt too hot.

I turned from the sink and froze as my eye rested on something on the opposite wall. It was a colourful framed poster, prettily illustrated with flowers and fruits and scripted writing that read: *Karma has no menu. You get served what you deserve.* The bold black words sprang out and branded themselves in my mind. Their irony was not lost on me. I held on to the sink and waited for the dizziness to pass. Robert would say, 'It's just a poster, Jill. Stop seeing such drama in everything.'

But *was* it just a poster? Tom had said she'd only been living in the house for six months. So I had to ask myself why, given the circumstances of Tom's very recent release, she'd hung something so leading on the wall where every visitor would see it.

25

When I came out of the cloakroom, I walked slowly down the hall, listening to the hum of voices in the open-plan kitchen. This had to be the most unlikely of nightmare gatherings, and at the centre of it all, Bridget's laughter. She seemed to relish holding court.

I passed the bottom of the stairs and glanced up, my eyes led by the silver-grey carpet and stylish glass banister. I stood very still, the breath catching in my throat. The wall of the staircase was covered, floor to ceiling, with photographs of Jesse.

I climbed up a couple of steps and peered closer.

'Ah, I see you've found my memory wall.'

I jumped, and turned to see Bridget standing at the bottom of the stairs looking up, her hands on her hips as if she was ready for a challenge.

'There are … so many of them,' I said lightly.

'You must have as many of Tom, I'm sure,' she said nonchalantly. 'Framed and hung around the house, no doubt.'

'Yes, of course,' I said carefully, and then grabbed the opportunity. 'Have you got a photo album of the wedding? I saw the picture in the hallway, but—'

'All in good time.' She smiled. 'We're getting the shots sorted, but don't worry, you'll see them soon enough.'

I nodded, feeling a pang for the dream wedding I'd once visualised for my son, a dream that had now turned to dust. I regarded the stairwell again. It was less of a memory wall and more of a shrine to Jesse.

Bridget said something, but I didn't quite catch what it was, because at that exact moment I realised that Tom had been cut out of many of the photographs. I had some of them in my own collection, so I knew they had originally featured both boys.

'I have lots of these photos at home,' I said, looking at her pointedly. 'And Jesse is still present in all of mine.'

She smiled. 'How noble of you, Jill. But then Jesse didn't do anything wrong.'

'Seems strange that you couldn't stand to see Tom in the photographs, and yet you've married him,' I said, trying to match her boldness. 'I can't help thinking how conflicting that is.' *How screwed up* was what I really meant.

But Bridget wasn't fazed. 'Not really,' she said, placing one foot on the bottom step. I saw she'd removed her skyscraper heels. 'I trimmed the photographs when Jesse died. I found it difficult to cope with seeing Tom on there, plus I wanted a wall of pictures of only my son. That's all it was.'

'But now you *can* stand seeing Tom. You've recovered sufficiently to marry him!'

I knew I was pushing it, but felt unable to stop. None of this added up.

'Tom completely understands my thinking.'

'I see.' I stepped down. She didn't budge, so I hovered close to her on the first step.

'Good. I'm so glad you see.' She dropped her voice so low I had to strain to hear. 'Maybe you've forgotten how well I know you, Jill. You're a control freak at heart, but you need to understand that you're not in control of Tom any more. You'll have to learn to deal with that.'

'Tom is his own person,' I said, choked. 'He doesn't need you running his life either.'

'We'll see about that,' she hissed.

I felt suddenly winded. I folded my arms, hugged my hands close to me.

'I'll always be his mother,' I said. 'I'll be here long after you're sick of him, because you forget I know you too, Bridget.' I paused to take a breath. 'I know how you lose interest in things very quickly, how you're fond of idealising but struggle with the reality of situations. Just like your son.'

It was satisfying to see the false mocking smile instantly melt away.

'Don't you dare drag Jesse into this.' I glimpsed bared teeth through her painted lips, her eyes flashing with quiet fury. 'I can make your life a misery, remember that. We can be civil to each other for Tom's sake or you can make an enemy of me, Jill. It's your decision.'

'Hey! What're my two favourite girls talking about?' Tom walked casually down the hallway looking handsome and relaxed.

'Oh, we were reminiscing about the old days, darling.' Bridget moved away from the bottom of the stairs so that finally I was able to step down. She kissed him on the lips and pointed to the photographs. 'Your mum was admiring Jesse's memory wall.'

I watched his reaction carefully.

'She's done a fantastic job with it, hasn't she, Mum?'

'There are so many photographs,' I said simply.

'Yeah, and lots of great memories on here for me too.' He glanced at the wall and then lowered his eyes. 'I loved him like a brother. Miss him every day.'

Bridget grasped his hand and jiggled it. 'Come on. You know Jesse wouldn't have wanted us all moping around. Let's go and get our drinks. Dinner will be nearly ready to serve.'

And in a jiffy they were both headed back to the kitchen and I was alone in the hallway again. Tempted as I was to creep upstairs and have a bit of a snoop, I decided I'd wait until Tom offered to show me around. It would probably only end up making me feel sick, imagining my beautiful boy here with *her*.

I walked slowly towards the kitchen. Movement to my right caught my eye. It was Ellis, sitting alone in a comfortable snug lit with lamps. His gaming device was on, the glare of the screen lighting up the room, but he wasn't playing on it; he was staring vacantly ahead, looking lost. Even though he'd never met his father, his grandmother marrying the man who'd gone to prison for Jesse's death must be incredibly difficult for him to fathom.

'Hello, Ellis,' I said, hovering in the doorway. 'I'm glad we got to meet at last tonight.'

'Hi,' he mumbled, and snatched up his device. I wondered what was going through his head – the fact that I was the mother of the man who killed his dad? Probably.

I took a few steps inside the room, and he looked so alarmed, I stood still.

'It's OK, I'm going through to the kitchen in a moment. I wanted to say that I know all this must be very difficult for you, Ellis. I understand that, and if—'

'It's not difficult, it's unbearable.' I turned to see Coral behind me. 'For us both, if you must know.' I stepped back and she came properly into the room, pushing the door almost closed. 'I know you don't like her. I can tell. We feel trapped. She controls our lives, and Ellis … well, he says he hates Tom because of what happened.' She hesitated. 'Sorry to have to say that to you, Jill. But Bridget is forcing Ellis to spend time with him, and it's not fair.' She peered through the gap in the door nervously, her eyes wide. 'Please don't say anything to her. Not tonight when she's on a high. She'd never forgive me, and she's already threatening to withdraw my rent support.'

'I won't say a word.' I touched her arm. 'Look, I don't approve of this marriage any more than you do, Coral. And I completely understand that it must be incredibly hard for Ellis and for you to see Tom at such close quarters.'

Ellis sat very still, his eyes downcast, his face red.

I decided to say what I was thinking. 'If you ever want to talk, you only have to say. I'm happy to meet and ...'

She looked at me so strangely, the words died in my throat.

'Thank you for that, but I don't think it will work. None of this is your fault, I know that. In fact, I feel very sorry for you.'

'Don't feel sorry for me,' I said, far more blithely than I felt. 'I'll get through this like I've managed to get through everything else in life. Bridget doesn't scare me one bit.'

'Well, maybe she ought to.'

I frowned. 'What do you mean by that?'

'Nothing.' She turned away from me slightly.

'Coral, if there's something I need to know, please tell me. I'm as concerned about this sham marriage as you are.'

She looked at me as if she pitied me.

'It's just temper. I've nothing to tell you.'

But she did know something, I felt sure of it. She'd forgotten herself for a moment, been about to share something important and then thought better of it.

I wouldn't wait around for her to confide in me. I'd start to poke around a bit myself, use my librarian's research skills to find out what I could about Bridget.

If he was going to get this joke of a marriage annulled, there was no time to waste.

26

Bridget

It didn't escape my notice that Jill, Coral and Ellis all came back into the room together. Neither Jill nor Ellis would look at me, which was a big clue that they were feeling jumpy about something.

'Ready for dinner, Jill? I'm so looking forward to it,' I said brightly, though in reality I was counting the minutes until they'd be leaving. I'd forgotten what a scheming, sly personality she hid underneath that dull, humble exterior. I turned away from her to the collection of bottles on the countertop. 'I bought a couple of bottles of fizz for us.' I winked at her, the warmth of the alcohol relaxing me. 'You're already a glass behind me, let's put that right.'

I poured Jill a drink, aware of Coral standing over by the door, arms folded, her face pale and furious. I didn't offer her a drink on purpose, didn't want her in here listening to everything that was being said. But of course, she was intent on supervising Ellis, making the boy nervous and jumpy.

Tom and Robert were silent. They glanced at Coral's sour face and Jill's miserable expression. This had the makings of a really great party.

'Everything OK, Brid?' Tom said meaningfully. 'Need me to do anything?'

'Nope. Everything is under control, thanks for asking though.' Jill hadn't offered to do a thing. 'In fact, everyone can take their seats at the table.'

Everyone moved towards the table which I'd dressed simply with white linen napkins, candles and grey Portuguese stoneware plates. I watched as Jill picked up the Robert Welch cutlery and inspected it for smears.

'Something certainly smells delicious,' Robert remarked, inhaling deeply. 'What's on the menu, or is it a surprise?'

'Not at all,' I said, pleased he'd asked. 'We've got a super-green risotto to start and then butternut squash and spinach curry for main.'

'It's an all-vegan menu,' Tom said proudly. 'Bridget's got an amazing imagination when it comes to plant food.'

'I'm very much looking forward to sampling it, Bridget.' Robert beamed.

'Really?' Jill fixed him with a glare. 'I thought your opinion of vegan food was that you might as well eat dry cardboard?'

Robert laughed lightly, clearly embarrassed.

'Maybe it's the way you're cooking it, Mum,' Tom said and I wanted to kiss him.

'I can pass on the recipes if Robert enjoys them, Jill,' I said with relish. 'Tom can't get enough of my cooking.'

'No thank you,' Jill said shortly, nostrils flaring. 'I prefer to stick with classic food, I'm not one to follow fads.'

'Glass of cola, Ellis?' I called over, gleeful my comments had obviously hit home. 'Hungry?'

'I'm OK, thanks, Nan,' Ellis mumbled. 'I'm not hungry at all.'

I took pity on him. 'Tell you what, you go and sit in the snug and play your game for an hour while we eat, sweetheart. That's the best plan.'

Ellis immediately turned on his Nintendo Switch.

'He's had his gaming hour already today, Bridget,' Coral said tightly.

'Has he?' I smiled at him. 'Well let's give him an extension, shall we?'

'Ellis, turn it off now, please,' Coral said, ignoring my comment.

Jill took another swig of her Prosecco and perched on a stool, enjoying the show. Ellis didn't look up from his console.

'Ellis!' Coral said, her voice full of warning.

'In a minute!' he snapped at her.

'Hey, chill, buddy,' Tom said.

Ellis wheeled around. 'You're not my dad, you can't tell me what to do, and I'm not your buddy.'

'Wow, seems everyone's an expert here tonight on Ellis's behaviour.' Coral stood there challenging us all, holding court as if this was her house and her party.

'Coral, why don't you go home?' I turned to her. 'I wanted to include you tonight, but you obviously don't want to be here. Ellis can stay over.'

'I'll go with pleasure,' Coral said. 'But Ellis is coming home with me.'

I shook my head. 'He isn't going anywhere.'

'Yes he is! Ellis, get your coat.'

Reluctantly, my grandson shuffled forward a few steps.

'Go upstairs to your room if you like, Ellis,' I said, and, eyes darting between me and his mother, he suddenly rushed out of the kitchen. Coral stepped forward and I squared up to her, fury coursing through my veins. I felt so angry, but I forced myself to back off before I throttled her.

'Come on now,' Tom said smoothly. 'Let's all take a breath.'

'Please don't undermine me again in front of Ellis,' Coral told me, clearly trying to make a point in Jill's presence. 'You know he isn't allowed to—'

'For God's sake, Coral, pipe down!' I snapped. 'We're here to have a good time. Take a chill pill, will you?'

I turned away from her and saw that Jill's glass was empty. I picked up the bottle and topped her up. 'So what are you up to these days, Jill? Tom says you're working.'

My heart was racing but I'd be damned if I'd let Coral see she'd got the better of me.

'Yes, I'm in retail,' she said. 'In the centre of town.'

'She helps out for a few hours at the Second Chances charity shop,' Robert kindly provided. 'Do you know it?'

'Actually, yes,' I said, wanting to laugh out loud at Jill and Robert's differing descriptions of her job. 'I do.'

'Some super things in there. Last Christmas, Jill got her dress—'

'Robert, nobody wants the boring details of my wardrobe,' Jill interrupted, slugging back half of her drink in one gulp.

'On the contrary, it's fascinating,' I said, amused that nobody else seemed to notice her constant irritation with me. I topped up her glass again.

'I think there are far more important things to discuss.' She snatched up her drink. She was becoming careless and rude.

'I'm going up to check on Ellis,' Coral said. 'I really don't want him buried in that game for hours on end.' She left the room. I was heartily sick of her attitude. She was selfish and ungrateful and it was about time she heard some home truths about taking people for granted.

'She worries far too much about that boy,' I said as I carried the food over to the table. 'He's a sensible lad, he'll work it all out in his own time.'

'Some of us prefer to give our boys boundaries, Bridget,' Jill said tightly. 'Rather than treat them as adults before their time.'

'Mum!' Tom hissed.

Saying nothing, I placed the tureen of risotto on the heat mat and returned to the kitchen counter. An awkward silence descended before Jill spoke again, her words slightly blunted at the edges with the effects of the alcohol she'd consumed.

'I remember only too well, Bridget, how fond you were of leaving Jesse to *work it out*.' Tom and his father stared at her, mute and aghast. 'It usually ended up with school ringing you to threaten his exclusion, or even worse, the police knocking at your door.'

'That's enough!' Robert raised his voice and Jill froze on the spot, seeming suddenly to realise how badly she'd behaved.

I stood very still and looked at the floor. Tom flew across the room.

'Brid, are you OK? I'm so sorry, Mum wasn't thinking. She—'

'It's OK, Tom,' I said magnanimously, turning to meet Jill's basilisk stare. 'I understand we've a long way to go. I thought having dinner together tonight would help us bond a little, but I can see now that's probably not going to happen.'

Jill turned her entire body away from me and took an unsteady step towards Tom.

'You're making a big mistake, Tom, and I will prove it to you.' She started breathing heavily with her mouth open, her chest rising and falling. 'It's not too late to get this ridiculous marriage annulled. I won't stand by and see her ruin your life. I won't let that happen.'

Tom looked winded, as if she'd punched him in the stomach.

'Bridget, Tom, I'm so, so sorry.' Robert looked at his wife in disgust, clearly mortified. 'Jill, get your coat, I'll call a cab. It's time for us to go.'

'I'm not going anywhere until I have some answers about this farce of a marriage.'

'Jill! Coat ... now!'

She stood up, adjusting her terrible outfit. The shapeless dress hung on her frame, clinging in all the wrong places. But she didn't follow Robert to the door. Instead, she turned desperately to Tom.

'Is that what you want, Tom? For me to leave before we've talked about everything that's happened?'

She waited. I waited. Robert sighed and looked at his watch.

'I think it's for the best,' Tom said without meeting her eyes. 'We're married now whether you like it or not, and you knowing all the ins and outs of it isn't going to have any bearing on that. You need to accept it, Mum, like we talked about.'

Robert nodded and glared at her. 'What Tom's saying, Jill, is that you're going to have to like it or lump it.'

'I couldn't have put it better myself,' I said. 'Good night, Jill.'

27

2005

Tom stood outside the disused factory and glanced nervously down the track again. This place was not exactly remote, but it was out of the way, down a long dirt road off Little Carter Lane, a five-minute bike ride from Jesse's house.

Years ago, this place used to be a joinery, but now it was boarded up and disused.

Tom wasn't interested in drugs but there was no telling Jesse, who'd collect weed for older boys for a fee. Everything Tom said to try and reason with him fell on deaf ears, and so here they were yet again.

'I'm not asking you to come in with me, am I?' Jesse said scornfully. 'You can wait out here with the bikes. I'll only be five minutes.'

Before Tom offered any further warnings, Jesse had disappeared through a loosely boarded door at the front and was swiftly swallowed up into the shadows.

It was a long lane and there were several other working businesses down here. A scrapyard and some kind of car repair shop. It was nearly eight at night and all were in darkness.

Tom coughed and scraped the toe of his trainer into the broken concrete of the track. It was quite spooky, being out here on his own. Silly really, but there weren't that many places to go where it was this quiet. Where the leaves rustled behind you and the odd branch cracked as some small animal scurried invisibly through the bushes.

Like a far-off party, he heard faint voices and laughter from deep within the bowels of the building. Jesse had told Tom that infamous local drug dealer Jason Fletcher and his crew had taken over the basement, where the joinery workshop had once operated from.

'It's freaky, man, there's still some metal equipment down there. One machine had this big vice on the end and Jason told me they crushed some loser's fingers who didn't pay for his gear.'

Tom shivered. He wasn't a coward but these weren't the kind of people he wanted to associate with.

The sound of wheels on the loose gravel of the track, still some way off, made Tom jerk to attention. The lane was mainly long and straight, but there was a sharp bend about a hundred yards before the spot where Tom stood. There were no headlights yet, but it was easy to guess why they might be coming here.

Only people doing business with Jason Fletcher and his cronies came this way, and if they were driving, it meant they weren't kids like Tom and Jesse, but adults. Tom had watched enough movies to know about rival drugs gangs and the methods they used to extract information from people.

The back of his neck prickled and, almost as a knee-jerk reaction, he grabbed Jesse's bike and tossed it clumsily behind a cluster of gorse bushes. He did the same with his own, then, as the crunch of wheels on crumbling asphalt drew closer, he dashed to crouch behind another group of bushes nearby.

These people might be already high and looking for trouble …

He tried to stay calm, but his breathing became more and more erratic as he waited, the noise of the vehicle growing louder as it neared the bend. He drew in air, feeling queasy as he inhaled the sweet, rotting smell of the damp earth and leaves around him.

Headlights flooded the area in front of the old factory, exactly where he had been standing a few seconds ago, but he was wrong about it being rival drug dealers. He gasped as a marked police car emerged from the lane, parking up outside the front of the dilapidated building.

Tom held his breath for as long as possible. He was going to throw up, he knew it. He hadn't even got his phone with him – he'd left it on his bedside table because it was out of charge.

He watched the two police officers in the vehicle. The blue light flashed silently on the roof, casting its reflection onto the windows of the old factory and skimming the bushes where he had concealed himself. For a couple of minutes, the officers stared at the building and didn't move at all. To a clueless passer-by, the place would have looked completely empty. There were no signs at all that anyone was inside. Tom reckoned if the police had taken the trouble to come down here, they must have had a tip-off.

One of the officers began speaking on a phone or walkie-talkie. He nodded, never taking his eyes off the building.

Don't come out now, Tom screamed silently in his head in the vain hope that Jesse would receive the message telepathically, like in that *Buffy* episode he'd secretly watched in his bedroom last week because everyone knew *Buffy* was for girls. But Jesse had definitely said he'd only be in there for five minutes, and he'd been gone for at least ten.

Tom was quite close to the vehicle, although thanks to his dark clothing, he was completely camouflaged amongst the bushes. His cover would easily be blown if they came looking, though, particularly if they spotted the bikes glinting nearby.

Tom knew there was no way to make a run for it, the officers would see him immediately. Besides, he couldn't abandon his bike, because his dad would kill him. It had been his main birthday a few months ago when he'd turned fourteen. His dad hadn't wanted to fork out that much money, but his mum had managed to convince him.

He caught his breath again as both doors opened at once on the police car. The officers got out, fixing their hats, and in their thick-soled shoes moved stealthily towards the same boarded-up entrance Jesse had used to enter the building.

Tom grimaced as his left leg spasmed with pins and needles. He adjusted his posture slightly, and as he pulled his lower leg out from under his right thigh, a branch beneath him snapped, a loud noise in the otherwise unbroken silence.

Both officers turned and scanned the bushes and sparse trees.

'Hello?' the shorter one called, his hand hovering over his equipment belt. 'Who's there?'

Tom opened his mouth to make his breathing as quiet as possible. It felt as if his heartbeat had relocated into his throat. This was it. He was going to be arrested and his parents would be devastated. His mother would have a breakdown and his dad would take pleasure in grounding him for months.

At that moment he heard the far-off party sounds again, though this time the voices sounded urgent. Someone in the basement must have seen the blue lights flashing outside.

The police instantly lost interest in the area where he was hiding and began pushing at the boards on the ground-floor doors and windows. Within seconds they were inside.

Tom stood up, stretching his legs but careful to stay in the shadows. The blue lights were still flashing, but fortunately they didn't quite reach his hiding place. He tried to decide whether to grab his cycle and just make a run for it when he saw movement at the far left of the building. As the solitary figure darted forward, he saw the familiar light-grey sweatshirt with the Simpsons appliqué on the front ... Jesse!

He hurried to the gorse bushes and grabbed Jesse's bike.

'Quick,' he said breathlessly, pushing it towards his friend. 'Go! Go now.'

Jesse didn't speak, he grabbed the bike and jumped on it, pedalling for his life. Tom's bike had got tangled in long weeds, and he wrenched it out, jarring his shoulder in the process. Voices shouted and there were suddenly figures outside the building.

'Backup is on its way!' he heard one of the officers call out.

At last Tom managed to pull his bike free of the foliage. He jumped into the saddle, scooting towards the bend and then onto the straight part of the lane. He saw Jesse's rear reflector disc shimmering in the distance, and he kept his head down and his feet pumping the pedals.

A few minutes later, he emerged onto Sherwood Hall Road. Jesse was sitting outside the Ravensdale pub, still in the saddle but bent over his handlebars, wheezing. When Tom got close, he realised he was laughing deliriously.

'Oh man,' Jesse spluttered, clapping a hand on Tom's back. 'Now that's what I call a close shave.'

'Yeah. One I don't ever want to have again,' Tom said breathlessly. 'Let's get going.'

'It's fine, man.' Jesse laughed, pulling out a crumpled packet of cigarettes and lighting up. 'Just chill.'

If they'd kept pedalling, manoeuvred their bikes into the quieter side streets, they'd have probably been OK. But five minutes later the police car pulled up at the side of them and before they registered what was happening, an officer jumped out.

Jesse gave his address and phone number and said that Tom was his brother. The officer looked doubtfully from one boy to the other but he wrote down the details anyway. Then he rang Bridget in front of them.

*

Five minutes later, Bridget pulled up in her little battered Fiat.
Tom knew if it was his mum the police had rung, she'd have gone
absolutely mental. But Bridget was supercool and didn't even direct
a threatening glare in Jesse's direction.

The police radio burst into life in the car and, whilst the officers
briefly conferred about something, Bridget grabbed Tom's arm.

'I need you to take the rap for this, Tom,' she hissed. 'Jesse's
already got two cautions, he can't afford any more trouble. Say
it was you who wanted to go to the old factory, that you forced
Jesse to go with you, yeah?'

Tom looked wildly at the police officers as they approached
them again. He looked at Jesse, who winked at him, and at Bridget's
pale, worried face.

'Just this once … for me,' she whispered pleadingly.

And so Tom did as she asked.

28

Jill

October 2019

Saturday morning, I heard Robert leave the house and reverse the car off the drive. He tended to go into the college for two or three hours most Saturday mornings. Most of his clients were students and they often preferred a weekend counselling appointment, provided they hadn't been out partying the night before.

I knew how they felt. I drank far too much last night. I haven't got a clue how many glasses of fizz I knocked back but I remembered Bridget constantly topping up my glass.

I inched out of bed, visited the bathroom and then slunk downstairs for a badly needed cup of tea.

I hadn't got so drunk I couldn't remember crawling into bed and Robert snatching his folded pyjamas from the pillow and then stomping off to the spare bedroom, muttering to himself. I remembered most of what had been said last night, too. Sadly, that was all too clear in my mind. It wasn't that I regretted saying any of it, but I did feel slightly worried that Tom would be furious with me this morning.

It was too late for regrets. I'd had far too much to drink and it had loosened my tongue, releasing too many home truths.

I finished my tea then sat down at the kitchen table with a notepad, pen and my laptop. I tried to clear my mind of any preconceptions I had about Bridget. Not an easy task, but my aim was to regard her like a stranger might do, to assess her without fury and resentment marring my judgement.

A librarian's work is methodical and precise by nature. It had been so long since I'd called on those skills but I felt the reliable structure of a calm and thorough process returning to me.

Bridget's achievements were impressive. From very humble beginnings – a dysfunctional home life including time in foster care when her father left her alcoholic mother – she had struggled for many years while Jesse was growing up. I knew all this, of course, had been a witness to it, but looking at it dispassionately helped.

Over the next hour or so, I catalogued the articles that had been written about her and her son after Tom's trial and conviction. From the point, in fact, when Bridget had appeared to be courting attention from the press.

Jesse's death was the watershed. The awful moment when many parents would have slid so fast downhill it would be nigh on impossible to claw their way back again. Conversely, Bridget appeared to flourish.

In less than a year after his death, she had spoken to most of the national newspapers and magazines and begun her zealous campaign for the Young Men Matter movement. She'd provided carefully selected photographs to accompany her words. Jesse looked young and fresh and handsome in all of them. No images of him looking dazed and unwashed, the way he usually did when he'd visited our house. There were also photographs of Jesse with Tom, and in all of them, Tom looked a little shifty. He had dark stubble in one, his eyes half open in another, whereas Jesse looked bright and full of life next to him. Even if you hadn't read the article, you'd get the impression that Jesse was a shining star whose life had been cruelly snuffed out by his suspicious-looking friend.

I had to stay as detached as possible. I bookmarked the articles as I discovered them and saved the accompanying photographs to a folder on my laptop. It felt good to actually do something.

There were photographs of Bridget, as head of the charity she'd set up, with some pretty high-profile people, including one when she'd met Prince Harry on his visit to Nottingham in 2013 and gained his public approval for her work with grieving families.

Fascinated, I studied her appearance in these photographs compared to a year earlier. There was such a marked change, I wondered if she'd engaged the services of an image consultant. She'd clearly lost weight and, I suspected, had various minor cosmetic procedures: Botox, filler and possibly one of the non-surgical facelifts I'd seen in various magazines and online beauty articles.

She wore more make-up now, but it was skilfully applied, softer. Her nose looked slimmer, her cheekbones more defined, but on closer inspection, I realised she'd used shading and highlighting techniques to good effect. It was astonishing to see, remembering as I did the days not so long before when she had looked tired, hassled and without a smudge of cosmetics on her face. Even more incredible when you realised that this woman had lost her only son – had gone on record as saying that some days she didn't want to continue living herself.

Of course, there was no crime in pulling oneself up by the bootstraps and rising like a phoenix from the ashes. I'd seen it before: a mother or father, grief-stricken and bereft, who'd found a cause, started a charity or changed a law in the name of their lost child. The grief fuelled some kind of drive for change that helped not only them, but others too. I had nothing but admiration for it. But I'd also seen pictures of those people, and they still looked haunted, like husks of their former selves.

Bridget, though, looked rejuvenated, and that was when I realised what seemed so wrong. There was a *glamour* about the whole thing. A sort of satisfaction, an enjoyment of the attention she'd garnered in Jesse's name.

Yet again I tapped my phone screen and brought up their wedding photograph. The scene looked pleasant and celebratory, but that belied the awful truth of their 'special day'. The setting was a prison! The very place that must remind her what had happened to Jesse.

I zoned out for a moment while I pictured the scene I'd imagined for so long, the scene I had craved. Tom marrying a nice girl at our local church, the same church he'd been christened in as a baby. A dream wedding that would have taken place in a few years' time, when he was settled into a new career and had put the past firmly behind him. He'd have been surrounded by his friends and family, by the people who loved him, who wanted to celebrate this happy new stage in his life. Later there would be grandchildren I would adore and help to raise. Bridget had robbed me of all that and she had stolen Tom's chance of having a normal life like other men his age.

Following Jesse's death and long after I'd snubbed her invitation to talk on the phone, she'd called round at the house. I'd been so shocked to see her standing there and she'd looked me up and down, clearly startled at how dishevelled and exhausted I must have looked. I had a sudden urge to reach out but when I took a step towards her, she visibly shrank back from me, her eyes flashing.

'Why have you come here if you're still so angry? At the end of all this, we're still two mothers,' I'd told her. 'We're both grieving for our sons.'

'The difference,' Bridget had said, 'is that you're the mother of a boy who's alive and I am the mother of a boy who is dead. And I hope and pray with all my heart that one day you know how I'm feeling at this moment.'

I'd closed the door without answering. She'd hammered a few times, left her finger on the doorbell for what seemed an eternity, but I'd shrunk back into the depths of the house. I shouldn't have shut the door in her face but couldn't handle a doorstep argument and truthfully, I'd felt quite intimidated. Even though she'd lost Jesse, she seemed so much more pulled together than I was.

The memory, still fresh in my mind, made me uncomfortable, and suddenly I felt even more afraid for Tom. Bridget was so determined, so resolved.

What lengths might she be prepared to go to, in order to destroy him?

29

Audrey

Audrey didn't call at Jill's house as much as she used to do. At one time they were always popping in to see each other but that all changed when Tom went to prison. When Jill became a virtual recluse.

This had affected their friendship in that it introduced a distance that hadn't been there before. Their conversations lost a little depth. You only talked truthfully to people who understood you the most and you knew wouldn't judge. Sadly, Audrey didn't really feel this way with Jill any longer.

Once Audrey had convinced her to start working at the shop things had improved a bit. She'd given Jill a reason for getting up in the morning before she faded away. But gone were the days where they'd meet up out of work and regularly visit coffee shops or enjoy shopping trips.

Still, Audrey did still consider Jill to be a good friend and she felt it was her duty to support her, even if some of her actions were a form of tough love. She couldn't tell Jill *everything* that was happening behind the scenes but her discovery online was something that would be of interest to her friend.

'How was the dinner party?' Audrey asked brightly when Jill opened the front door on Sunday morning.

'Disastrous!' Jill answered immediately. 'But I'll tell you about all that later. How nice to see you – to what do I owe this honour? Is everything OK?'

Jill ushered her inside and waited while Audrey slipped off her coat and shoes in the hall. She heard Robert talking on the phone and felt glad when he didn't show his face.

'Everything is fine.' Audrey left her oversized handbag at the door, then reached down and plucked out her phone before hesitating. 'There's nothing wrong *per se*, but the reason I've called is that there's something I think you need to see.'

Jill sighed and massaged her temples. 'I'm not sure I can deal with more bad news. This is my first hangover for about fifteen years and it's in its second day now.'

'*That* good at Bridget's party, was it?'

Jill grimaced and led her into the living room where they both sat down. 'I'll make us a drink but first, tell me. What's wrong?'

'It's easiest to just take a look.'

Audrey passed her phone over and watched as Jill stared at the flattering photograph of Bridget and Tom looking into each other's eyes. The national newspaper headline read: *Grieving mother finds love with son's killer.*

'Oh no, I've been dreading something like this,' Jill whispered, her hand shaking. 'I've been checking Bridget's Facebook regularly to see if she's posted more wedding pictures, but it hadn't occurred to me to search the general press.'

Audrey held her hand out for her phone back but Jill didn't even notice she'd done so. She was unable to tear her eyes away from the photograph. Audrey understood. She herself had been shocked. Bridget looked about thirty-five years old in the picture, dressed in flattering colours of pale gold and honey. Tom was handsome and rugged in a navy open-necked shirt and with his hair swept back in a dashing style Audrey hadn't seen him sport before.

The camera had caught them at a magical moment. The buzz of electricity between them was almost tangible and almost made you want a piece of what they had … that transparent yearning for each other that not everyone got to experience.

Jill was stuck in some sort of trance staring at the photograph, so Audrey gently took the phone out of her hands and began to read the report out loud.

Ten years ago, Bridget Wilson thought her own life was over when her eighteen-year-old son, Jesse, was killed by a single punch issued by his best friend, Tom Billinghurst, also eighteen. Six months ago, Bridget and Tom secretly married in a special ceremony at HMP Nottingham, and now Jesse's killer is her husband.

How can a grieving mother travel so far from that place of devastation years earlier? How is it possible to fall in love with the man who ended your son's life so callously? 'Tom was a big part of it,' Bridget told the *Daily Mail*. 'We both entered the restorative justice programme at the prison and it was impossible not to be touched by his honesty, his remorse and, more than anything, his need for me, as Jesse's mum, to forgive him. Over time, we grew closer and fell in love. We never planned to get married, but it was a natural step to making a completely fresh start together when he was released.'

'I don't believe it,' Jill raged, suddenly snapping back to life. 'It's making Tom sound so … so guilty! It wasn't like that. He didn't mean to kill Jesse, he—'

'Jill, listen,' Audrey said gently. 'There's more.'

Billinghurst is now a quiet man of twenty-eight. Does the age gap between the couple bother him?

'As far as I'm concerned, age is just a number. I've never felt as close to anyone as I do to Bridget. She's such a generous, forgiving soul. I'll be forever grateful to her for giving me the chance to make amends. All I want now is to spend the rest of my life trying to redeem myself for the enormous loss I caused her.'

Bridget and Tom have bought a smart new home in an affluent area of Nottinghamshire.

So what about the future? What are the couple's immediate plans?

Bridget told us, 'Tom will soon take up a key position in my Young Men Matter charity. He'll be talking to groups of people about his own redemption and how he discovered the power of admitting his guilt – to himself as well as to me, Jesse's mother.'

Tom added, 'I'll be speaking to young people about the need to look at their own families and what they're told growing up, how they're raised. I never realised at the time, but my own upbringing contributed to my lack of empathy and failure to see beyond my own wants and needs.'

'I want to help Tom heal from his damaging childhood,' Bridget added. 'It's time for him to shine without the shadow of domineering family members to dim his light.'

Audrey pressed a tissue into her friend's hand and Jill looked surprised, as if she didn't realise her cheeks were wet with tears.

'It's so painful to see you suffer like this, Jill, but I had to let you know when I saw it. I knew it would kill you to hear it from someone else, or if you'd stumbled on the article yourself.'

'I don't know what to say.' Jill dabbed at her eyes. 'Have I really been such a terrible mother all these years?'

'No! This article is utter crap. It's clickbait, a lurid story designed to attract people to the news website.'

'So Tom didn't actually say those things about me ... about us?'

Audrey tucked her wavy chestnut hair behind her ears. 'Who knows? They probably twisted his words, exaggerated them, but I think you should speak to him about it.'

'And say what, exactly? You don't know the gory details yet but ... Friday night was not what you'd call a success. I said some things I don't regret but I haven't heard from Tom yet.' She sat up a little straighter. 'I'm glad you told me though.'

Audrey grabbed Jill's hand. 'My heart's breaking for you. You've given up everything to keep things stable and prepare for Tom coming home. I feel so angry with him for doing this. I feel like going over there and—'

'No, no. You mustn't do that, Audrey. This is not your fight.'

Audrey's eyes flashed. 'I can't believe they'd be so heartless, giving an interview like that without a thought for your feelings. What happened on Friday? What did you say?'

Jill closed her eyes as if she were trying to shut out the memory of the evening. 'It's a long story and I've got such a thumping head. Suffice to say, I'm even more convinced she's not genuine, Audrey. The house is covered in photographs of Jesse as a kid and Tom has been cut out of most of them.'

'What?'

Jill nodded. 'She's playing some kind of sick game, pretending to be the devoted wife when it's clear that underneath, she still blames Tom. I'll tell you in detail once I get rid of this hangover.'

'Are you going to tell Robert about the interview, or do you want me to have a word with him?'

'I'm not sure he's talking to me after how I showed him up at the party, either,' Jill said miserably. 'Put it out of your mind for now.'

'I think you should do the same,' Audrey said. 'I'll make us a drink.'

Jill followed her into the kitchen and Audrey glanced at her white knuckles. Her fists were coiled so tightly her fingernails must have been digging into her palms. There was no chance of Audrey putting it out of her mind. In setting up this article and the things she'd said in it, Bridget Wilson had basically declared war on Tom's family.

Audrey felt sick at the hidden betrayals Jill didn't even know about yet. She pushed the thought away as fast as it came into her head.

Jill would hate her when she found out what she'd done but Audrey was too far in to change her mind now.

30

Ellis

On Monday morning, from a sheltered spot at the far side of the playground, Ellis watched the new boy at break time.

He'd joined the school last week and he was in Year 4, a year below Ellis, who was now a Year 5 pupil. Next year he'd be going to the big comp in the next town. Compared to him, this new boy was a little kid.

His nan had insisted that Tom walk home from school with him last Friday, and it had made Ellis furious. He'd refuse to let Tom walk with him later today if he turned up, cramping his style. Ellis knew what she was up to, she was hoping that time spent together would mean they grew closer. How twisted was that? His nan expected Ellis to become friendly with the man who was responsible for murdering Jesse, his own dad?

Ellis hated Tom with all his heart. *Hated* him. He strutted about his nan's house as if he owned the place, and kept grabbing her and kissing her, jumping out like a big kid from round corners so she squealed like a young girl. It was gross and pathetic.

Ellis didn't really care if Tom had killed his dad by accident like his nan had told him. The fact was, he had punched him and his dad had fallen and hit his head and died. Whichever way you looked at it, the fact that he was dead was all Tom's doing.

Ellis had tried to talk to his mum about not wanting to see Tom, but she'd got stressed out about it.

'I don't want to go to Nan's any more,' he'd said decisively. 'Not if *he's* there.'

His mum had held her head as if she had a splitting pain.

'Can't you see, I'm between a rock and a hard place, Ellis. I'd like nothing more than to walk away from what your nan's doing, but I can't afford those gaming subscriptions, or that Jack Wills stuff you like to wear now. But it won't be for long, I promise. I'm working on it and soon things are going to get much better.'

Her hands had scrunched into tight fists, though, and Ellis knew she felt as angry as he did. Tom was affecting his mum's life in a bad way too. But she never mentioned the other thing about him. The thing Ellis wasn't allowed to talk about.

Everything had been so much better when Tom had still been in prison.

Ellis sometimes lay in bed at night planning how he might get revenge on Tom for what he'd done. His head used to be full of his gaming tactics before he dropped off to sleep, but now that had all changed. He'd lost count of the number of times he'd fallen asleep with a picture in his mind of Tom hanging by the neck from a tree or left a bloody mess in the middle of the road after Ellis had pushed him under a passing truck.

It had been horrible on Friday night, having to be with them all in the same house for that stupid dinner. His mum had ended up being upset, too. He loved his nan, but everything was messed up because she'd brought Tom Billinghurst into all their lives.

Ellis did feel a bit sorry for Tom's mum, Jill. It wasn't her fault that Tom had turned out to be a murderer. She was a nice lady and Ellis sensed from her dull eyes that she felt as sad as he was underneath. His mum said it was because Jill thought Nan would end up hurting Tom in some way.

Ellis hoped she did. If his nan made sure Tom got what he deserved for what he'd done, everything would be cool again, go back to normal.

The new boy leaned against a wall with one leg bent so that the heel of his shoe tapped against the brickwork. This was an attempt to look cool, as if he wasn't bothered he had no one to stand with. But Ellis knew the signs of feeling nervous. He remembered from his own first days in school.

The boy kept biting the inside of his cheek, inspecting his fingernails. The kid acted like he was too cool to get involved with the other boys' activities, but Ellis knew it was just a show. He recalled how rotten it felt.

Like the new boy putting on an act, Ellis had tried to do the same with his nan when Tom had first moved in. But it was so hard to pull it off. Tom Billinghurst was a convicted killer and nothing he did would ever change that. Not offering to set up a PlayStation on the TV or asking Ellis lame questions about his Nintendo Switch games. Ellis saw through his tricks.

Ellis's nan was a smart woman, everybody round here said so. When Jesse had died, instead of moping around, his nan had started the Young Men Matter charity in his dad's memory. Now she had a much better life. She lived in her big new house and Ellis had his own bedroom there. His nan also drove a really cool car. She'd let Ellis play his favourite rap music loud in the summer when they had the roof down.

Ellis loved his nan but it was impossible to understand why she'd married Tom. His mum said she didn't know, either.

'Maybe she's having a midlife crisis and thinks she's got herself a toy boy,' his mum had said. 'She'll be sick of him soon, wait and see.'

Before Tom was released from the nick, his nan had put her arms around Ellis and held him tight until he squirmed.

'I can't expect you to understand yet, but you'll see soon enough. Everyone will,' she'd whispered. 'I loved your dad more than anything in the world and that will never change. That's all you need to know for now.'

It was all a bit weird, and Ellis was glad to be at school, away from all the screwed-up adults.

Ellis wasn't one of the most popular boys in school. He didn't belong to the sporty set like Henry Farmer, who played rugby and lived in a massive house with an indoor swimming pool. But he was tall for his age and he handled himself well. He had a natural disrespect for the teachers – like his nan said Jesse used to – and backchatted them in class like the other kids wouldn't dare.

This gave him a certain status, and as a result he had collected a few hangers-on. A couple of them were proper psychos who'd been given several fixed-term exclusions for bad behaviour. They were the kind of kids most of his classmates steered clear of. But they came in useful now and again, and it was better than being a Nobby no-mates like the new kid. Ellis had seen his parents dropping him off yesterday morning. Seen him hug his dad and give him a high-five, something Ellis himself would never be able to do with his own dad.

He turned to Monty Ladrow, who was busy relieving a Year 4 kid of his lunch money. The word around here was that Monty's uncle ran a bit of an extortion racket on the local housing estates. If people paid him a monthly fee, their property miraculously remained safe. Due to missing so much school because of various exclusions over the last year, Monty had to have extra help in most subjects. He had no safety catch when it came to temper, and in Ellis's opinion, he was definitely someone it was best to have onside.

'See that new kid over there?' Ellis hissed in his ear. 'Thinks he's a proper tough nut, he does.'

Instantly interested, Monty released the whimpering Year 4 kid from a headlock. 'Yeah?'

Ellis nodded. 'I heard he's been bragging that his dad has done time in the nick, so he thinks he's rock hard himself. Reckons everyone here's scared to death of him.'

Monty frowned. 'You're joking? He's proper weedy.'

'Right. I told him, I said, you're not the only one whose dad has been sent down, Monty's dad has too, and you know what he said?'

Monty's face twisted and Ellis bit back a smirk. He was so easy to wind up. 'What? What did he say?'

'He said your dad was a pussy.'

'I'll kill *him* and then he'll not be saying anything,' Monty snarled.

'Well, I'd sort it out quick if I were you. People might get the wrong idea about your old man.' Seeing the dark expression that immediately fell over Monty's face, Ellis hastily added, 'I bet your dad would kill *his* dad if they had a fight.'

Ellis had never met Monty's dad, but he'd heard the other kids saying he was a nutter who'd been in and out of prison so many times Monty hardly knew him at all.

He watched as Monty stomped across the playground. He moved so fast, the new kid only spotted him when he was a few paces away. He dropped his foot down from the wall and stood very still.

Monty jutted his chin forward, then his arms shot out and he pushed hard. The younger boy lost his balance and stumbled. This immediately attracted the attention of other kids close by, and a small crowd swiftly gathered around them.

'Fight! Fight!' they began to chant in unison.

Monty easily wrestled the boy to the floor and managed to hit him in the face twice before a nearby teacher pulled them apart.

Ellis melted away into the shadows. His shoulders and neck felt more relaxed and his head wasn't banging any more. He felt better already.

31

Bridget

When I woke up, it took me a while to come around. I lay in bed longer than I should've done trying to drum up some energy and positive thoughts. An uneasy feeling radiated deep into my bones.

Tom had joined a swish new gym nearby. He was meeting one of his old boxing gym pals for a light brunch and then had booked his initial induction session with a personal trainer late morning. Before leaving the house, he'd dressed in the new Gymshark gear he'd ordered online. Slim-fit shorts and a sleeveless tee cut to show off his superb physique. His muscled calves looked like they'd been sculpted from steel, his shoulders wide and sturdy.

I felt uncomfortable about him getting back in touch with someone from his 'old life', as we'd started calling it. We were supposed to be making a fresh start together, the last thing he needed were hangers-on from the past dragging him down. But it was impossible to say something to him without sounding like Jill.

I'd felt my stomach catch as I watched him moving around the bedroom, humming to himself, packing his towel and water bottle into his gym bag. I wondered who else might be at the trendy gym. It was probably full of hot young women in their twenties and early thirties with firm, tanned bodies and glossy hair ...

'Can't wait for this.' He'd grinned, bending down and kissing my cheek before he left. 'There's a juice bar too, want me to bring you one back? The strawberry spirulina looks amazing on their website.'

'I'm good, thanks,' I said, forcing some brightness into my voice. 'Have fun.'

And then he was gone, taking his whirling youthful energy and sparkling enthusiasm with him. I felt tired and flat left lying there in our bedroom. I needed to redirect my thoughts.

I picked up my phone and opened Sunday's article in the *Daily Mail* again. I'd been really pleased with how the newspaper had portrayed us and they'd made a generous donation to Young Men Matter for the interview. We both looked great in the photograph, and I thought they'd written sensitively and intelligently about our relationship.

I scrolled down past the article and the sensationalist story adverts to the comments section.

Good luck to them both. They look good together.

They deserve happiness. Best of luck to them.

A warm glow started in my chest, allaying my silly fears and insecurities about Tom going to the gym. We *did* look good together and we were going to be very happy.

I scanned the next few comments and the glow quickly faded.

Sick. How can you love someone who killed your kid?

Man, she's old enough 2b his mother!

He's so hot ... why on earth is he with a wrinkly woman nearly twice his age??

People were so judgemental. They probably had such sad little lives they detested seeing others happy. There were plenty of folk out there like that, Jill Billinghurst being a prime example. In fact, I wouldn't be at all surprised if one or more of the anonymous derogatory comments was from her. Little did she know the stuff that was happening behind her own back. She'd soon have far more important problems to deal with than worrying about her precious son.

I reached for the make-up mirror on my bedside table and studied my face. Tom had thrown the curtains open when he got up, and the sun streamed in, cruelly highlighting all my faults and flaws. I turned my head this way and that. Sunlight aside, there was no doubt about it. The lines from my nose to my mouth were deepening despite the monthly anti-ageing facial I'd had religiously since I turned forty-five. I had no frown lines thanks to my three-month Botox appointments, and my cheeks had the perky plumpness of youth courtesy of facial filler, but … Maybe I was meant to see those horrible comments. Perhaps the cruel reactions had actually done me a favour and this was a sign it was time to take my anti-ageing measures that little bit further.

I closed the article and threw down my phone, pulling the covers up over my head and curling up on my side. Bile rose in my throat. Sometimes fighting off the signs of ageing felt like trying to hold back the tide. It didn't matter how vigilant you became; the lines, the wrinkles, the dryness, the loss of elasticity crept up on you like weeds in the garden. How must it feel to not bother? To be so happy in your own skin you accepted the way you looked?

I allowed myself five minutes of misery and then shook it off.

I texted Coral and asked her to call round at the house before she went to work. I hadn't spoken to her since the disastrous dinner party, but I got a reply back right away.

When's best to call?

Her obviously curt tone irked me, but I tapped out my reply.

This morning at 11.30?

See you then.

There were some uncomfortable things that needed saying. I felt like we'd reached a bit of a crossroads in our relationship. I didn't care if I never set eyes on Coral again, but I had Ellis to think of and I wouldn't compromise my contact with him for anything or anyone.

I ran a moisturising bubble bath and applied an expensive Clarins firming and nourishing face treatment and tried to forget about Tom ogling fit young women at the gym.

I opened the front door to Coral a couple of hours later. She wore baggy leggings and an old sweatshirt covered in paint stains. She had made zero effort to make herself look even half-decent. It spoke volumes about how little she'd come to respect me.

I made her a cold drink and she sat sipping it, scrolling through her phone, sniggering at various posts she came across.

'Coral, for God's sake put that away for a few minutes, will you?'

She looked at me and tutted with disapproval. 'Don't treat me like I'm at school and you're my teacher. It's really irritating.'

'I'll tell you what's irritating,' I said, instantly breaking my promise to myself not to get annoyed. '*Irritating* is you using your spare key to let yourself in here and dump Ellis any time it's convenient so you can go off and do your own thing. Like you did the other day.'

'Do my own thing?' Coral said, doing a good job of acting the offended innocent. 'You said to bring him over here for tea!'

I tried to keep a check on my temper, but it pushed to get out. 'What you do with your own life is your business, Coral, but I'm concerned Ellis is spending too much time on his own. The only interaction he gets seems to be through one of his devices.'

'You know, that would be hilarious if it wasn't so sad and upsetting.' Her eyes glinted peevishly. 'You seem to worry about everything but the thing that's actually affecting him and causing him harm.'

'What the hell are you talking about?'

'Do I have to spell it out? One minute Ellis is your whole life; the next, you've married the man who battered his dad to death. How do you think *that* might be affecting him?'

'It was one punch, hardly a vicious battering,' I retorted through clenched teeth. 'I've had long talks with Ellis about Tom and me getting married, as you know. I've told him he's free to ask me any questions or chat more as and when he feels the need.'

'You only told us a few days before Tom got out; there's been no time to get used to it. And there's the age thing, too. Tom could be your *son*, think about that. Think about how that cringey newspaper interview you've done might make Ellis feel ... his nanny and her toy boy! That's what the kids are spreading around his school, do you know that?'

I winced. It was a low blow. 'Tom is an adult and Ellis wouldn't even give our age gap a thought if—'

'Other people do, though! Are you so out of it you haven't thought about the gossiping that's happening around town? You must have seen it online, the sniping, the revulsion that you've married your son's killer. People are sickened. You're holed up in your nice house away from it all, but we have to live in the real world.'

I felt a flutter of nerves at what she was saying. I'd seen a few nasty comments but not full-blown gossip on social media. I'd been busy though. With Tom. Still, I wasn't about to let her see I had any concerns.

'Our marriage is nobody's business. Not yours, not the kids at school. Not bloody Facebook's. I'll speak to the head teacher if it's a problem for Ellis.'

'I've already spoken to her,' Coral said smugly. 'She rang to tell me that Ellis has been in trouble at school again.'

'What's happened?' My fingers fluttered to my throat. We'd had some behavioural problems with Ellis about a year ago. They'd had a 'father and son day' at school last autumn and he'd got quite down about the fact he'd never known his dad. He said some of the other boys made nasty comments and he'd reacted by bunking off lessons or asking to use the bathroom and then not returning to class. Mrs Cresswell, the head, was very understanding and got Ellis some help from the school counsellor. But it sounded like he'd started his old tricks again.

'Is someone bothering him?' I asked, feeling knotted up inside. I'd love to go down there and bang some heads together.

'Ellis has been picking on a new boy.'

'Bullying him, you mean?'

'Not directly, he got another boy to do it. Very nasty, actually, and it has to stop.' Coral looked resolved. 'You might as well know, I've spoken to both Mrs Cresswell and the school counsellor. They agree that for now, it might be best if I protect Ellis from your new relationship with Tom. It's too much for him to deal with, Bridget.'

'Oh really?' I felt heat rising inside me. Coral and the school talking about *my* business and how it might be affecting Ellis. 'Protect him how, exactly? We're married, and everybody has to deal with that, including Ellis.'

'I think you're rushing Ellis. It's too much, too soon, and it's started to affect him at school.'

'You don't know that! None of you do, it's guesswork.'

Coral hesitated. 'I don't want to fall out about this, Bridget, but I think it's best Ellis has a break from coming here. For a little while.'

'No way.' I slammed a hand down on the arm of the sofa. 'Ellis can handle it if only you'd stop treating him like a five-year-old. I'll have another chat with him; leave it with me.'

'That's the point, though, he *can't* handle it. His behaviour proves that. It's too much pressure for him. He acts tough, but he's just a kid.'

'In your opinion! I don't need to remind you that I can and will make your life difficult if I have to.'

Coral remained infuriatingly calm, which wasn't like her at all. One threat of removing the privileges I paid for and she was usually sucking up to me big-time. Not today.

'You marrying Tom has made everything so complicated. Why can't you admit that? Whether you like it or not, Ellis needs a little space.'

Everything I had been through, the effort it had taken to claw my way out of the black bog that had threatened to finish me when Jesse died ... there was no way I was going to let Coral McKinty dictate to me. She and Jesse had only been dating a year when he died, and as far as I knew, it hadn't been a serious relationship. If it hadn't been for the fact she was pregnant with Ellis, I'd happily never have seen her again.

'It's not at all complicated, Coral; it's actually very easy. Ellis is my grandson and there will never be a time when I tell him to stay away from his home.' I waved a hand around the room. 'That's what this place is. Ellis's home.'

'No, this is *your* home, Bridget. Yours and Tom's. Ellis's home is with me. *I'm* his mother, remember?'

'Do not continue with this, because if you do, you will lose. I guarantee you that.'

She was mocking in her response. 'Oh, let me guess. You're about to remind me how you pay my rent and allocate me an allowance each month.'

I burned with resentment at her bare-faced ingratitude. 'All of that is true.'

'Don't you think I know that?' she yelled. 'I think about it every day because *you* never let me forget it. But enough is enough. You think slipping me the odd few quid gives you the right to speak to me like dirt. Well, soon I'm not going to need your money.'

She sucked air in as if she'd let out something she shouldn't. The words hung in the air.

'And why's that then? Are you going to actually get yourself a full-time job like the rest of us instead of a few hours in that crappy restaurant?'

'That's a low blow!' she hissed. 'I'd lose my benefits if I did more hours.'

'Maybe. But there's no reason you can't work and support yourself. You're not ill and Ellis is fairly self-sufficient now.'

She hesitated. 'Yes, I'm getting a full-time job.' She was a terrible liar. Fidgeting, blinking too fast. All the signs were there. 'I want you to stop treating Ellis like he's your son, not mine.'

'He's one step away from it.' I took great pains to keep calm when it would have been easy to throw her out of the house. 'Ellis is all I have left of Jesse, and he isn't yours to take away.'

Coral's face lost its fury and her voice softened, almost to a plea. 'Look, I want to live my own life, Bridget. One where you're not looking over my shoulder, telling me how to raise my son. Dictating what I should do and how to do it when it comes to Ellis. You've put me off dating for years because you don't want another man around him, and then you bring Tom into his life. How hypocritical is that? I want a life!'

'Well, let me help you with that,' I snapped back. 'Have your life, and you can fund it yourself too.'

'Fine!' she said tartly. 'It's time I stood on my own two feet anyway. I'm sick to death of your charity.' She seemed to stand up straighter as she drew on some hidden reserve of confidence. 'Whether you like it or not, Ellis won't be coming around here for a while. He doesn't cope well with being in the same vicinity as Tom. He's told me about you sending Tom to school to walk home with him, and yet you know how bitter Ellis feels about him.'

'It's not your decision to make. Ellis is old enough to—'

'It *is* my decision, though. I'm his mother.'

'I'll take you to court. I'll get a court order stating I can see him, I'll—'

'Don't try to scare me with that empty threat, you have no legal right to see him, you know that. It's my decision and that's what's happening.' She turned and walked to the door, and I found myself wondering where all this new-found confidence had suddenly appeared from. 'I'm sorry, Bridget, but you decided to marry Tom without a thought for Ellis's feelings, and now you've forced me to protect him.'

Before I could respond, she'd left the house. The worst thing was, I knew she'd spoken the truth. As a grandparent, I had no real rights in the eyes of the law. As Ellis's mother, Coral was legally responsible for him.

I burned with fury. I should have let her slide after Jesse's death. When she was unable to cope, I could have applied for custody of Ellis. I'd made a terrible mistake in neglecting to safeguard my connection to my grandson.

Coral had the upper hand and she knew it. Unless I did something radical, I'd be left with the possibility of losing Ellis altogether.

I wouldn't let that happen. I'd do anything it took to ensure she didn't restrict me seeing him.

In the meantime, it was someone else's turn to suffer. I had a secret to reveal.

32

Jill

After seeing the photo shrine to Jesse in Bridget's house and now the publicity-grabbing interview in the newspaper, I found myself battling a growing sense of unease.

I knew I had to find something to distract me, to stop me going crazy.

Tom was a grown man, but he was naïve when it came to women, particularly someone as manipulative and determined as Bridget.

Nobody else seemed the least bit concerned about this, including Tom himself. I needed something solid to convince him Bridget wasn't genuine.

On Saturday afternoon, I'd made a couple of appointments in the interests of looking after myself again. I'd also arranged for the local handyman, Joel, who'd freshened up the hallway to come over and fit me some shelving. When he arrived on Monday morning, portly and jolly in his tan canvas dungarees and hobnail boots, I explained to Joel what I wanted and left him to it. He'd done work for us over the years and I trusted him implicitly.

'Lock up when you've finished and pop this back through the letterbox,' I told him, handing him a spare door key. Robert had student appointments all day until late so I knew Joel would be left to work undisturbed.

When I got out to the car, movement behind the trellis fence caught my eye. 'Hello, Jill, everything alright?' It was Nazreen. 'It's just ... we saw Tom in the paper.'

She raised her eyebrows and waited. If she was hoping I'd spill the beans on Tom and Bridget's relationship then she would be sorely disappointed.

'Yes. Hope you're OK, Naz. I'm so sorry but I have an appointment in town. Catch up soon!' As I reversed off the drive I caught the annoyance on her face. Since Tom's release, I'd noticed more neighbours than ever before walking slowly by our house and looking in, as though I might rush out and spill all the juicy gossip.

I visited a new hairdresser in the middle of town. Swanky and twice as expensive as Fiona, the mobile hairdresser who'd popped over to the house every few months to give me a cut and colour for the last ten years. I was lucky enough to get a cancellation. A slim young man with a ring in his bottom lip introduced himself as Andre and asked me what I'd like him to do.

'I haven't a clue,' I said. 'Surprise me.'

We had a 'consultation', which sounded fancy but was actually a quick chat. 'I would suggest a cropped bob with some discreet caramel highlights pulled through to soften the face,' Andre said, talking with his hands. 'How does that sound?'

'That sounds perfect,' I said, more confidently than I felt. 'Let's do it.'

I watched my transformation in the mirror, and at the end of it I was very, very happy. I not only looked pleasantly different but, I thought, younger and trendier. Next, I called into Boots and stopped by a few make-up counters. I emerged an hour later with a bag full of brand-new cosmetics that I'd been shown exactly how to use by the beauty counter staff.

As I came out of the shop, I bumped, quite literally, into Tom's old primary school teacher, Mavis Threadgold, and her little dog.

'I'm so sorry, dear,' she said, stepping back and pulling on the lead. 'I saw you in the hairdresser and walked back with Harry here to catch you when you left ... then you disappeared into the chemist.'

'Oh! Well, here I am,' I said. It seemed a little odd that she'd been skulking around, watching where I went. 'How are you?'

'I'm fine. I wondered if you had time for a quick chat.' She nodded over the road to a small, grassed area with a wooden bench.

She was obviously a bit lonely, and I was in no rush. It might actually be nice to reminisce about when Tom was younger.

'Very nice, by the way,' she said.

'Sorry?'

'Your hair. Very modern.'

'Oh yes, thanks. I wanted something neat and easy to maintain.' I patted my hair self-consciously, hoping I hadn't gone too far with the caramel highlights. It was quite dramatic compared to my usual flat brown. I felt nervous about what Robert might say, and then a twinge of annoyance at myself for feeling nervous. I'd done it for *me*, not for Robert.

We crossed the high street and headed for the bench, where Harry sniffed around our feet. The grass was well maintained, with a footpath meandering through it and small circular flower beds dotted here and there. It was surprising how peaceful it felt when the hustle and bustle of the town was so close. It was a dry, fine day but cold, as you might expect, in late October.

'When I saw you sitting there in the hairdresser's, I knew I had to speak to you,' Mavis said, owl-like behind her round metal-rimmed glasses. 'What a whirlwind this must have all been for you. Tom getting out of prison at last and then you finding out he'd married Jesse's mother.'

Her blunt manner would have probably annoyed me a few days ago, but now her candour was a relief from the sly looks and overly polite conversation I'd encountered from neighbours. As Tom's ex-teacher, Mavis was someone who'd warned that Tom should be vigilant about blindly following Jesse's often impulsive behaviour when they were younger. I still had doubts about an incident Tom took the rap for when they were fourteen. The idea that he'd forced Jesse to trespass in a local factory beggared belief. Somehow I'd managed to keep Robert from finding out about that.

I trusted her implicitly.

'I'm not going to deny it was a shock, Mavis. They'd embarked on some justice programme that brings victims and perpetrators together. From what I can gather, after growing closer over time, they got married in prison without telling anyone.'

'Shocking.' Mavis frowned. 'I take it Tom hasn't fully explained it all to you?'

'Sort of, but I'm not convinced. It doesn't make sense to me.' I sighed, not really knowing where to start. 'Robert doesn't want to talk about it. He doesn't care, if I'm honest.'

'I see,' she said. 'Well, I'm happy to listen.'

I shivered in the cool breeze and looked down at my feet as I considered this. Mavis certainly wasn't known to gossip, her closest confidant was her little dog. It would be such a relief to discuss it with someone else, and she had always seemed to want the best for Tom. I had Audrey to talk to, of course, but Audrey seemed distracted at the moment.

'This programme at the prison, it's called restorative justice and it's all about the victim's family working together with the criminal to finally begin the healing process,' I began.

Mavis said, 'I would imagine that's rather a tough process to go through for most people.'

'Quite. But Tom and Bridget have both said it was during this time they grew close and fell in love. It delves deep, I think. Gets them talking about and working through their feelings.'

'And who instigated this programme?'

'The prison staff asked him if he'd be interested and Tom said he was. It all grew from there.'

'Hmm,' Mavis pondered. 'May I ask what *your* thoughts are, Jill … about what happened that night in 2009?'

I paused a moment, surprised that she was referring back to the actual night of Jesse's death. It was a while since anybody had.

'Obviously I only know what Tom told me, and I believe that unreservedly,' I said. 'Jesse had been knocking back the drink and bad-mouthing the security team in Movers. Unsurprisingly, that got the boys thrown out of the club. Jesse was determined to try and get back inside and Tom tried to stop him. Jesse turned nasty and pulled a knife, so Tom did what anyone would do in that situation. He defended himself.'

'He punched Jesse very hard,' Mavis said carefully.

'Yes, but it was just the one punch. Jesse slipped and fell and the rest is history, as they say. Tom didn't know he would crack his head on the concrete.'

'I read that the judge was particularly harsh in his sentencing because Tom was a boxer,' Mavis remarked.

I nodded. 'They consider a boxer's hands to be lethal weapons, you see. Apparently, they always deliver a tough sentence.'

'Did you appeal against the judge's decision?'

'Yes, of course, but we lost. Instead, I focused on Tom's release, every hour of every day, and then he floors me with the news he's got married in prison to Bridget bloody Wilson.'

'Certainly, that must have been quite a blow,' Mavis said kindly.

I'd been hoping that chatting to Mavis would somehow help me feel a bit brighter about the situation, but I felt lower than ever. Harry pressed against my legs, his furry body warm and comforting.

'I don't know what to do,' I said. 'I can't really do anything at all, but I'm struggling to accept that. I keep thinking there must be something, because this whole thing seems so off.'

'I'm a big believer in listening to your gut, Jill. Sometimes, when your gut says stay out of something rather than get involved, it's not easy to do but it's the best thing all round.'

I nodded, but it was much easier to say this sort of thing than actually do it.

'My gut is doing the opposite,' I told her. 'It's screaming at me to *do* something. Anything. I want to get involved in my son's life while everyone else is telling me to back off.'

'As I recall, Jesse had a girlfriend,' Mavis said thoughtfully. 'She was pregnant when Jesse died.'

'That's right,' I said, surprised that she seemed to know so much. 'Her name is Coral.'

'And you've met her?'

'Oh yes, we knew her back then, too. She used to hang around with the boys when they were younger. I saw her again a few days ago, at Bridget's house. Understandably, she was a bit cautious, with me being Tom's mother, but she made it clear she disapproves of the marriage too.'

Mavis nodded. 'Would you like my advice?'

'Of course.' I reached down and scratched the back of Harry's long neck. 'You know I have a lot of respect for you, Mavis, and it helps to get the perspective of someone not directly involved.'

I expected her to tell me to get on with my life, to try to swallow my resentment and work at growing closer to Tom and Bridget. Instead, she said, 'Speak to Coral. That's my advice.'

I frowned. 'Why Coral?'

'Well, it seems to me that all the time Tom has been in prison, she's been the person closest to Bridget because of their shared care of her son. Get a bit friendlier with her. You never know what she might tell you about the situation.'

Coral had made a comment at the dinner party that perhaps I should be scared of Bridget. She'd tried to deny she meant anything by it but I got the uncomfortable feeling there were things that had happened or *were* happening that I was completely unaware of. Things Coral didn't want to talk to me about. She'd also made it clear she thought we'd never be friends because of me being Tom's mother. But there was a lot of tension between Coral and Bridget, so maybe Mavis had a point and I should try again.

'Thanks, Mavis,' I said, standing up from the bench. 'I appreciate the chat.'

'Any time, dear.' Mavis stayed seated, looking around her at the bodies rushing past, talking on phones, drinking coffee as they walked briskly by. 'People always seem too busy to pass the time of day any more, but us invisible oldies … well, we see a lot more than people give us credit for.'

33

I drove across town to the budget restaurant I knew Coral worked at part-time. There was still fifteen minutes before the end of her shift. I managed to park in a spot on the road where I had sight of the restaurant door and also the alleyway that ran down the side of it in case she exited out of the back.

I took out my Kindle and read the same page repeatedly. I couldn't focus on it for more than a few seconds. At last Coral sauntered out, absently scrolling through her phone as she walked. When she reached the corner, she stopped and leaned against the brick wall, then lit a cigarette and tapped at her phone.

I got out of the car and crossed the road, approaching her from the front so as not to creep her out by suddenly appearing from nowhere. Pungent spices filled the air as I got closer, and the noise of the traffic ebbed and flowed behind me. Coral wore the brown checked uniform of the restaurant chain, and had scraped her hair up into a bobble, revealing her natural dark roots against the harshness of the home-bleached blonde. With her face devoid of make-up, she looked pale and tired. When she looked up and saw me, her hand jerked in surprise and the long funnel of ash at the end of her cigarette fell to the floor, disintegrating on the pavement between us.

'Hi, Coral, sorry to startle you.' My friendly smile was not returned. 'I wondered if you had time for a quick chat?'

'What's all this about?' Nervously she looked up and down the street. 'Has Tom sent you … or Bridget?'

It was a strange thing to say.

'No, of course not,' I said and pointed to a small café across the street. 'Fancy a coffee? Gets us away from prying eyes out here.'

She took another drag of her cigarette and studied me carefully. I imagined the thoughts clicking methodically through her mind. Should she trust me? What exactly did I want to talk about?

'I haven't got long,' she said, stubbing out the cigarette on the wall and tossing it into a nearby bin. 'I have to go into school to see Ellis's class teacher at three thirty.'

'That's fine,' I said, relieved she hadn't told me to get lost.

The café was dim inside, with dark walls and orange globe lights that hung on long pendant chains over the tables. It was only about half full, so there were plenty of spare seats.

'A latte OK for you?'

She nodded, and I ordered at the counter, leaving Coral to grab us a table. She chose one well set back from the door, and sat staring at her phone.

I came back with the coffees and placed them on the table. She'd put her phone away, looking thoughtfully towards the window.

'It feels weird, sitting in here with you,' she said without looking at me. 'Really weird. It feels all wrong.'

I pressed my lips together. 'As Tom's mother, I do understand we're never going to be best friends, Coral. But I'd like to think we can be civil to each other now that Tom and Bridget are married. We can't fail to see more of each other, so we might as well try and get on.'

'Do you know?' she suddenly demanded, the little colour she had draining out of her cheeks. She looked as if she wanted to be sick but was forcing herself to be brave. 'Has Tom told you?'

I frowned. 'Told me what?'

She hesitated, seeming to backtrack. 'About why they got married. I mean, did he warn you?'

'No, he didn't. I'd have tried to stop it happening.' Her face softened slightly. I wanted to win her confidence, so it was important to show her some honesty. 'I was devastated, Coral. I still am. It's been a terrible shock.'

'That makes two of us. Ellis is really suffering.'

'It's natural he'll be upset.'

Using a long teaspoon, she scooped some foam from the top of her latte directly into her mouth. 'The head teacher rang me to talk about Ellis's behaviour at school. That's why I've got to go in.'

'I'm so sorry it's affecting him badly,' I said evenly. Jesse always used to be in some kind of trouble at school. Sometimes Tom was dragged into it by default simply by being present when Jesse decided he didn't like the look of someone's face or reacted to a teacher telling him to stop doing something. Mavis Threadgold had alerted me to what was happening early on. I'd spoken to Bridget about it, but of course it had fallen on deaf ears.

Coral put down her spoon and dabbed at her mouth with one of the tiny square paper napkins that came with our drinks. 'What was it you wanted to talk to me about, Jill?'

I was surprised at her forthright manner. Away from Bridget's domineering nature, she had a quiet confidence about her.

I tapped the side of my latte glass with a fingernail. Coral was no fool and I knew I had to tell her the truth about my feelings. 'I don't know if you're aware that Bridget and I used to be best friends. We raised our boys together, but after what happened and so many years passing, I feel like I don't know her any more.'

Coral made a conciliatory noise as though she knew how that felt. 'But what's that got to do with me?'

'Well, without putting too fine a point on it, you know her far better than I do now. Speaking to you as a mother, Coral, I'm asking you to put aside your feelings about the night Jesse died, for a few minutes.'

'If only it were that easy,' she muttered.

'It's a big ask, I know,' I said. 'I wanted to speak to you confidentially about Bridget.' For all I knew, she would leave here and go straight back to Bridget, tell her everything I'd said. But, as Mavis had suggested, I went with my gut feeling that any loyalty Coral had once possessed had dissolved when Bridget secretly married Tom. 'I wondered what your thoughts were on the two of them marrying. On whether Bridget is … serious, for want of a better word.'

'You're asking me if she's got a hidden agenda,' Coral stated simply.

I hesitated before replying. If it got back to Bridget that I'd been asking these kinds of questions about her, it might destroy any chance I had of staying close to Tom. Like it or not, I knew she had the greater influence on him at the moment. But if I wanted to get to the truth, there really was no sense in me holding back. 'Yes, that's what I want to know. I won't repeat anything you tell me and I hope you'll do the same. I'm asking for you to help me understand, I feel you're the only person who can.'

Coral cradled her cup in both hands and stared down into her drink. 'I'll be totally straight with you, Jill. Bridget has been really good to me. I know it's only because she wants Ellis in her life. Although I wouldn't give her the satisfaction of hearing me say this, she stopped me sliding too far down after Jesse's death. I often suspected he cheated on me, but his death hit me hard. I dread to think where I might have ended up without Bridget.'

'You must be very grateful for that,' I said. Despite her saying such positive things, I felt there might be a 'but' coming.

'But there's been a price to pay. Bridget never lets me forget it.' Coral bit her lip. 'There are things that have happened that you're not aware of. You seem like a nice person, and what Tom did that night is no reflection on you. Nothing that's happened is your fault, and I certainly don't blame you. It's never going to be possible for us to be friends, but as a mother, I want to say I do understand you're worried for your son. Whatever Ellis does, I'll always be there for him and hope to protect him.'

She drained her coffee and I felt desperate to keep her there.

'When you say there are things I'm unaware of, do you mean things Bridget has done?'

'Sorry, I can't talk about it, but you're better off not knowing.' She stood up. 'I don't know why Bridget married Tom. She didn't confide in me before doing so and it was as much of a shock to me as it was for you.' I felt my face fall and she hesitated. 'Maybe you're looking at the motives of the wrong person.'

I frowned. 'Who else is there but Bridget?'

'Tom has made his choices too, Jill,' she said gently. 'You shouldn't forget that.'

34

When Coral had left the café, I ordered another coffee and sat thinking for a while.

Everything in my life had changed. Robert's workload had increased so that he was regularly getting home too late for us to eat dinner together. He was avoiding any opportunity to talk about Tom and Bridget.

I'd informed the estate agent Tom was no longer interested in the flat, and I rejected the temporary job offer on his behalf.

I was so exhausted when I got into bed at night, I'd fall straight asleep even without reading a few pages of my book. But around 2 a.m., I'd spring awake and the relentless thinking would start. Old memories resurfacing.

When Tom was still a baby, we very nearly lost him. For the first three months of his life he was a healthy, bouncing child. He slept like a dream and had a happy, smiling countenance when he was awake. Everyone commented what a pleasant little soul he was and we loved to watch him playing boisterously with his toys. Then he started waking several times during the night and he'd be hard to wake up in the morning. He went off his food and lost some weight. He stopped playing with his toys.

The health visitor reassured me. 'Babies often go through these stages during their first year,' she said. 'Keep an eye on him over the next week or two, and if you still have concerns, pop him down to your GP. Just to be on the safe side.'

Tom's condition continued to deteriorate. He turned a strange colour, his rosy cheeks and creamy complexion disappeared overnight. He ate very little, slept lots during the day and became listless and quiet when he was awake.

We took him to the local surgery and the doctor told us exactly the same thing as the health visitor. It felt like a cop-out.

'I want him checked out,' I remember saying calmly but firmly. 'I'd like a second opinion.'

The GP was visibly annoyed and Robert squirmed, but I refused to budge. 'I'd never forgive myself if something happened to him. I want him thoroughly checked out. Something's not right. I feel it,' I said.

'You *feel* it?' the doctor repeated in a patronising tone, the corners of his mouth twitching.

'Yes,' I said. 'I feel it.'

And so it began. Days of travelling to and from the hospital. Each time, they'd tell us nothing was wrong, that Tom was 'one of those sickly children' but that he'd grow out of it.

'It's time to put a stop to this, Jill,' Robert said after the fourth day. He sat me down, looked at me like you might do to a kind aunt who you suspected was turning a bit batty. 'It's not fair of us to keep dragging Tom to hospital only for him to be poked and prodded and then discharged again. You've got to accept this is just the way he is. You heard what the doctor said.'

But when I looked into my baby's dull, pleading eyes, I knew. I just knew.

'I'll take him back on my own if you don't want to come,' I said. 'This time, I'm not leaving the hospital until they find out what's going on.'

To give Robert his due, he stuck with it, and the next day, after a terrifying dash to the hospital in the middle of the night, we finally got an answer that made sense.

Tom had a heart murmur that was getting rapidly worse. He needed an operation, and it was a bigger one than if they'd acted sooner. I wished I'd been more insistent earlier in the process. He recovered well, but the surgeon told us that, left untreated, the condition might easily have killed him. Like one of those healthy sixteen-year-old boys we've all read about who collapses out of the blue on the football pitch.

I'd known there was something wrong all along. When everyone had tried to shut me up, I knew it. Like Dad had once said, it was all about keeping tight control on what you cared about.

I'd internalised that rule. Lived by it. Now, I was beginning to realise how it had utterly exhausted me over the years.

I knew there were things happening around my son and I was determined to find out what. No matter how many times they all told me I was imagining it.

The café was only about a ten-minute walk from Second Chances, across the other side of town. It was a cold but dry afternoon, so when I'd finished my coffee, I decided to leave the car where it was and walk over there. I'd call in and surprise Audrey, find out what she thought about the cryptic things Coral had said.

It was actually a bit cooler than I'd thought, so I buttoned up my jacket and set off. The sky was grey and the breeze was persistent, but after a few minutes walking briskly, I warmed up a bit.

I took a short cut through the quieter side roads until I reached the bustle of the main shops again. I wondered how Tom would get on in his new job at Bridget's charity. It sounded so much fancier than the humble archiving clerk position I'd lined up for him. I wished I felt more pleased for him, but judging by the article Audrey had shown me, Bridget was making full use of Tom's link to Jesse's death to highlight the work of the charity. My son being pushed into the media spotlight for all the wrong reasons.

As I neared the shop, I felt a little nervous, hoping Audrey would be pleased to see me. All friendships had sticky patches. Maybe I'd been more absorbed in my own life than I'd realised. I thought she had things going on in her life she hadn't wanted to burden me with.

The shop looked empty from the street, but when I opened the door, prompting the old-fashioned bell to chime out, Audrey and the single customer who stood with her at the desk both turned round.

'Jill!' Audrey's eyes widened and she quickly stepped away from the other person. 'This is unexpected!'

She was babbling, but I was already too distracted to take any notice of her.

The customer stepped forward.

'Jill,' Bridget said. 'What a nice surprise. You look ... different. Your hair!'

To my knowledge, Bridget had never been in the shop before. I kept my voice level. 'Am I interrupting something important?'

'No! Of course not.' Audrey sprang into her smooth managerial patter. 'Bridget popped in to say hello and to—'

'I wanted a look around the shop,' Bridget added laconically. 'I've always wondered what it was like in here.'

'Really?' I took a few steps forward. 'Audrey, you were showing her, I presume?'

Audrey picked up some wire hangers and put them down again. She didn't know where to look or what to do with herself.

Bridget sighed. 'Look, to tell you the truth, I came in to ask Audrey if you were OK. Last week's dinner party wasn't the success I'd hoped it would be, and ... I thought Audrey might know how you were feeling.'

I folded my arms and stared at her. She must think I'd fallen off a Christmas tree.

'Why didn't you simply ask *me* how I was feeling, Bridget?' I turned my attention to Audrey. Her usually calm demeanour had vanished. Her face looked hot, her eyes darting around the shop as if she was searching for an escape route. 'I didn't know you were in touch with Bridget, Audrey.' My measured tone belied the relentless thumping on my chest wall. I was desperately trying to piece it all together, but I was drawing a complete blank.

'I should go,' Bridget said. 'Thanks for showing me around the shop, Audrey.'

'Hang on,' I called as she walked quickly to the door. Something was wrong with this picture. It wasn't only that my best friend was talking to my biggest enemy. There was something else more subtle out of place. I was the outsider. The one in the dark.

Another customer came in at that moment and Bridget took the opportunity to slip out.

With the new customer still browsing, I moved in on Audrey. 'Don't lie to me. I know something weird was happening there.' I made a real effort to dampen down the emotion, but it still slipped through, showing itself in my shaking voice. 'You're my oldest friend and I'm asking you to level with me. Did she send you round to the house yesterday to taunt me with that article?'

'Of course not!'

I wanted Audrey to tell me the truth, but I wanted that truth to be something innocent. Something that didn't threaten our friendship or complicate my life even further. The things I'd told her about Bridget, about my deepest feelings ... had she really been betraying me? Because that was what it looked like.

Audrey looked suddenly gaunt. 'Can you watch the shop for me while I make us a drink?'

'I don't want a drink. I want you to tell me why Bridget Wilson was here and what you were talking about.'

Audrey glanced anxiously at the customer browsing the scarf rack. 'When she's gone, I'll close up for half an hour and we'll talk. I promise. I'll make that drink. Your hair looks great, by the way. You look years younger.' She disappeared into the back of the shop. I heard crockery rattling in the kitchen and I willed the customer to leave quickly.

Bridget had said she was asking Audrey if I was OK, which was ridiculous. To my knowledge, Audrey hadn't spoken to Bridget since Tom went to prison. The two women knew each other, of course, and there had been family occasions where they'd met and exchanged pleasantries in the years before. But in the end, they had both been *my* friends, never friendly with each other. For years, all the meeting up and socialising Bridget and I did was based around the children, and Audrey didn't have kids.

'Hello?' the customer called out. 'I'd like the price of the long purple scarf, please.'

'Sorry, I was miles away.' I picked up the scarf and saw there was no little price sticker. The next one was the same. 'These must have been put out before they were priced up. One moment, I'll ask my manager.'

The customer nodded and moved on to the belts. I walked to the doorway that led through to the kitchen and back office.

'Audrey, can you come through to the shop for a moment?'

There was no answer. I heard the hot water urn spluttering and hissing.

'Audrey? A customer has a query about the scarves.'

Silence.

I glanced back into the shop. Our policy was to never leave it unattended when a customer was present. I walked down the short hallway, ensuring I still had sight of the woman. The kitchenette was empty. I pushed open the door to the office, expecting to see Audrey caught up on a phone call or looking at something on the computer, but that was empty too.

Which left only one place. The cloakroom.

'Audrey? You in there?' I rattled the handle, expecting it to be locked, but the door opened and Audrey wasn't in there.

I dashed into the office again with new eyes. Her handbag and coat were nowhere to be seen. The fire door leading to the back yard was closed, and I wondered if she'd popped out with a rubbish bag to the bins we shared with the neighbouring shops and inadvertently locked herself out.

I pushed down the emergency bar and the heavy, solid door swung open. A cat jumped out of an over-full bin and scurried out of sight, but other than that, the area was empty.

Audrey was nowhere to be seen. It seemed like she'd simply vanished into thin air.

I closed the fire door and rushed back into the shop, ready to explain to the customer that I had to close up, but she'd obviously got tired of waiting for me and had already left.

In the back, I searched through each room again and there, on the kitchenette worktop, was a note in Audrey's handwriting:

So sorry, Jill, feel unwell and had to leave. Will explain everything about Bridget very soon. Please close the shop for me. Will be in touch when I feel better.

What kind of explanation was that for doing a disappearing act without a word? It was outrageous – totally out of character for Audrey, who was a stickler for opening up and closing at the correct times.

I pulled my phone out of my bag and called her number. It was turned off and my call went straight to answerphone. I left a garbled message. 'Audrey? Where are you? Why did you take off like that? Call me when you get this message.'

I followed it up with a text as an insurance policy, so that she'd see at least one of my messages when she turned the phone on:

What happened? I'm worried about you! Contact me asap or I'm coming over.

At the counter, I scribbled a hasty note on a sheet of printer paper with black marker pen: *SORRY! SHOP TEMPORARILY CLOSED DUE TO UNFORESEEN CIRCUMSTANCES*. I stuck it to the glass with Sellotape – one of Audrey's pet hates – and then engaged the latch, bolted the door and pulled down the blinds.

I'd give her a couple of hours and then I'd go to the house. If she wasn't there, I'd wait. In the meantime, there was somebody else that owed me answers.

35

Bridget

When I got back home from the charity shop, Tom was watching football in the living room.

I'd driven around a bit after leaving the shop and I felt calmer now. I breezed in and kissed him on the cheek.

'Is it too early for a gin?' he called as I walked past. 'I've been dying to tell you all about the gym. Where have you been?'

'Here and there,' I said vaguely. 'I'll jump in the shower and then we can have a drink. Can't wait to hear all about it.'

Upstairs, as I soaped my skin and washed my hair, I tried to eradicate the altercation in the shop from my mind but it wasn't working. Audrey Denton's shocked expression was still in my head. I'd told her exactly what I'd seen, given her the date and time, and she was unable to deny it. She knew I was on to her now.

When Jill turned up at the shop like that it was my turn to be shocked. She'd had her hair styled and coloured and she was actually wearing make-up for once. It seemed to give her a new confidence. I'd beat a hasty retreat but now I'd have to think of how I was going to explain it all to Tom.

I stepped out of the shower, towel-dried my hair and wrapped a soft white bath sheet around me. Still damp, I padded through to the master bedroom, luxuriating in the soft cream carpet beneath my bare feet and the weak sunlight streaming in through the floor-to-ceiling window, drenching the room in a pale golden glow.

I gasped when I almost walked straight into Tom. He'd obviously crept up and waited for me. He looked like a cowboy, stripped to the waist. I spotted the small scar on his chest he'd told me was from a childhood op. Tousled hair, a five o'clock shadow and a slight smirk on his full lips. He looked ... *edible*, and within a second, my entire body ached for him.

'Hello. Is there something I can do for you?' I said saucily, letting the towel drop to the floor. He didn't say a word but pulled me towards him, his fingers tracing the back of my neck down to the damp, warm hollow at the bottom of my back. Everywhere they touched, they left a tingle of electricity. God, this man made me feel so *alive*.

Suddenly impatient to show him I was worth ten of those ditsy young women he'd no doubt seen at the gym today, I tugged at the waistband of his jeans and he took a few steps back as I shimmied forward. He lost his footing and stumbled backwards onto the bed, and we giggled as I launched myself on top of him, lost in the passion surging through me.

Then the doorbell rang. A long ring followed by a couple of staccato blasts.

Tom pulled his face back an inch, but I grabbed the back of his head.

'Ignore it,' I gasped, sealing my lips over his again. He smelled of nutmeg and soap.

He flipped me over so that he was on top, his muscular arms holding his weight off me, and I closed my eyes, feeling myself unwinding inside. A couple of seconds later, someone started to hammer on the front door.

'What the hell?' Tom froze above me.

A fist banging, then the doorbell, then the fist again ...

'Jeez!' He rolled off the bed and went to the window. He looked out, cursing in disbelief.

'What's wrong?' I sat up and reached for my damp towel from the floor. 'Who is it?'

His strong, tight body seemed to deflate in front of me. 'It's my mother.'

'Oh, perfect timing.' I groaned but my mouth went dry. I hadn't even mentioned my run-in with Jill to him yet.

'I'll have to go down,' he said, starting to dither around looking for his T-shirt. 'She'll see the cars and know we're in.'

'Tell her we're busy.' I gave him a little grin, tried to relax. 'Say she'll need to come back another time because you have some very pressing business to attend to.'

He didn't laugh. He made a sort of heavy puffing sound before muttering, 'I don't know about that. My mum can be very determined.'

'Yeah? Well so can I,' I was in no mood for Jill's power games right now. Her stalking into the shop like she had authority over who stepped through the door. I knew she'd hate to think I'd been speaking to Audrey, because Audrey was *her* friend and I was in the shop *she* worked at. Her urge to control everything and everyone around her was frightening.

Still, thanks to her impromptu visit, I had to think on my feet. I wasn't ready to tell Tom what I'd confronted Audrey with yet.

I slipped on some underwear and a loose white cotton shift dress and combed through my wet hair while Tom scuttled off to get the door. It infuriated me, the way he still jumped to attention when Jill clicked her fingers. No wonder she still thought she was in with a chance of telling him what to do with his life.

Tom might spend his life being nervous of her, but I'd be damned if I let Jill Billinghurst put *me* on the back foot. It was the perfect chance to put her in a bad light. What did Jill know about my chat with Audrey, really? Nothing! I would front this out, and hopefully, if I did a good enough job, Jill would come out of it looking much worse in Tom's eyes.

I walked across the expanse of biscuit-coloured carpet and descended the stairs, standing barefoot where I'd be able to listen to what was happening but I wouldn't be seen.

Tom had already opened the front door, and I heard a muted conversation taking place inside the hall. After a short time, their voices became louder, more heated.

'Something's going on with those two and I'm not leaving until I find out what it is,' I heard Jill hiss.

I took a step out into the open.

'Hello, Jill,' I said.

She glared at me and resumed her conversation with my husband without even acknowledging my greeting. 'Like I said, I just need to know if she's here, Tom.'

'I already told you, Mum,' Tom said firmly. 'She's not.'

'Who are we talking about?' I said innocently.

'Audrey.' Tom shrugged his shoulders, confusion furrowing his brow. 'She's gone missing from the shop, apparently. You didn't say you'd been there.'

'I called in when I was in town earlier. I didn't even realise it was the place you worked, Jill, until I saw Audrey behind the counter.'

'Rubbish! Why are you lying about it?' Jill's face burned crimson.

'Mum!' Tom's face clouded.

'Perhaps Bridget can help me out.' She looked at me expectantly. 'I wonder if you'd care to shed any light on why you and Audrey were huddled together, whispering in the shop?'

'I'd hardly call having a casual chat *huddled together*, Jill.' I adopted a puzzled expression. 'As I said, I didn't know it was your place of work until—'

'Oh please.' Jill threw back her head and laughed. 'Tom, even you must see she's lying through her—'

'I think you should leave, Mum,' Tom said curtly. 'Come back when you're feeling a bit calmer, yeah?'

Jill was unfazed.

'Let Bridget answer my question, please. What were you talking about with Audrey?'

I stared back at her and said nothing.

Jill addressed Tom. 'They were obviously both shocked to see me. Bridget ran out almost immediately and Audrey went to make a drink and did a disappearing act without saying a word to me.'

'Are you feeling OK, Jill?' I looked at her hot flushed face with concern. 'Audrey was fine when I left – and I certainly didn't run out. I saw you were agitated, so I thought it best to leave.'

'Don't you lie like this.' She spat out the words, stepping forward until she was almost toe to toe with me. 'You are a sly, underhanded—'

'Mum! Seriously, you need to leave.' Tom placed his hands on her shoulders and oriented her carefully but firmly towards the door.

She wailed and tried to resist his pushing, and I realised this was my chance.

'Wait, Tom!' I called out. 'Let me explain properly what happened.' They both turned to face me. I hesitated before continuing. 'Jill, I honestly didn't realise it was the charity shop you worked at. The trustees at work have been talking about the possibility of the charity opening our own shop to help raise funds locally, and the window display looked attractive. I just called in there on the off chance.'

'There you go, Mum,' Tom said, relieved. 'Perfectly reasonable.'

Jill's face darkened, but I continued before she interrupted. 'Audrey was in there and we got chatting. Nothing cloak-and-dagger; I'm afraid that's all in your head, Jill.' I forced my lips into a smile. 'While I was there, I took the opportunity of asking her if you were OK, because you'd been a bit prickly at the dinner party. That's all it was.'

'OK, Mum?' Tom let his hands fall away. 'Happy now?'

'No! I'm not happy at all. I don't believe a single word that comes out of her mouth. She—'

'I hadn't got around to telling you yet, Tom, because it didn't seem that important. I saw Audrey, said hello, asked about you, Jill, and that was it.'

Jill's face brightened as she sensed a loophole. 'So why did Audrey leave like that without saying a word? She even left a note asking me to lock up instead of facing me after you'd gone.'

'I think you'll have to ask Audrey that, Jill,' I said softly, touching the top of her arm as if I cared about her. 'I think she's been a bit worried about you, too.'

Jill turned then and opened the front door.

'You're a liar, Bridget Wilson, and you've got some kind of hidden agenda that nobody else can see.' She looked at an aghast Tom, then back at me. 'But I know you're up to something, and I *will* find out what it is.'

36

Tom

He'd watched as his mother huffed off back to her car. The new hairstyle suited her and he felt pleased she was looking after herself a bit more but she'd gone off on one for no reason. In a way she'd done him a favour turning up like that.

Fortunately for him, Bridget hadn't had the chance to ask any really awkward questions when Tom had said he'd forgotten his new Chilly's water bottle and needed to pop back to the gym to get it.

'The gym's a way off,' Bridget had remarked. 'Why don't you buy another one?'

'It was twenty quid!' Tom had exclaimed. 'I earned a tenner max in prison, and that was if I worked all week.' In HMP Nottingham, he'd worked as a cleaner for a while and then moved on to maintenance jobs. For a moment he was back there with the slamming of doors, the shouting all night and the awful bland food that tasted the same no matter which option you went for. 'I won't be long,' he'd said, bringing the conversation to an end.

He hadn't forgotten his water bottle at all, of course, but he'd needed an excuse that would buy him some time away from the house while he sorted out something very important.

Something that, thanks to his mother, had now gone horribly wrong.

37

Jill

2006

After his childhood operation, Tom grew into a stocky, strong child. I'd felt so relieved that his early heart condition had had no detrimental effect on him. He was a good boy, always willing to help and try his best for us.

Tom adored his father, always clamouring for Robert to include him in anything he was doing. Robert had had a fascination with clocks from his own childhood. He was skilled at repairing the old-fashioned mechanisms, though as time went on and digital clocks became more fashionable, his talent for repairs became a bit of a dying art. It was strictly a hobby – in those days, he was a trained architect and had a good job in a firm that he hoped to make partner in one day – but nevertheless the clock repair requests came in steadily and it was something he enjoyed, got lost in.

It was natural that Tom would take an interest, and when he was very young – six or seven – it was Robert's party piece to hand Tom a tiny screwdriver and get him to attach a cog or two whilst our friends sat around nursing glasses of wine and making appropriate impressed noises.

Tom was top of his class in woodwork lessons. He had an eye for meticulous detail that proved to be an essential requirement for the repair of Robert's clocks. Over time, I watched as Tom's rather cute capabilities at seven became an intense irritation to his father as he grew older. I tried hard, I really did, but the more I saw Robert's jealousy of his own son, the more I felt the keen sting of resentment towards him.

Robert had always liked getting his own way. That didn't mean to say I'd been a pushover in my marriage as my mother had been, but I picked my fights. I'd have a go back if it was about something that mattered greatly to me. I found that a good way of keeping anxiety at bay rather than fretting over every last thing in our relationship.

One event marked out the step change in Robert and Tom's relationship.

The grandfather clock came in three days before Christmas the year Tom turned fifteen. Always happy to assist his father, he'd helped carry it into the garage, which Robert had converted years before into a workshop. It stood in the corner and I remember being summoned, together with several of our neighbours, to witness its beauty.

Robert was in his element, preening like a peacock while we all oohed and aahed at the ornate mahogany piece.

'Made on the east coast of Scotland, circa 1780,' Robert announced grandly, pointing out various features. 'It has an eight-day movement, a twelve-inch dial and rococo spandrels.'

I remembered wishing he still looked at me like he looked at that clock. Like most of our friends' relationships, the rigours of marriage, work and running a house and family had robbed us of the romantic efforts evident in our early relationship.

'How much is it worth, Dad?' Tom had asked.

'Good question. Probably around eight thousand pounds.' There were gasps from his small audience, but Robert held up a finger. 'If it's in working order, I should say. The owner would be lucky to get a couple of grand for it in this state, but I shall work my magic and return it to its former glory.'

The clock had apparently been in the client's family for generations, and Robert had been the first person he'd trusted enough to repair it. He told everyone that particular detail, too.

Everything went downhill rather rapidly after that. Despite him spending most of the Christmas break in his workshop, the clock evaded all Robert's efforts to repair it. From what I remember – he went into great detail explaining it to me, most of which I admit went over my head – it was some sort of complication with the eight-day movement.

As he'd piqued the interest of the neighbours, several of them popped round to see the finished product and were told that Robert suspected a manufacturing fault was to blame for blighting the piece.

'I've repaired enough clocks in my time to know when there's a bigger problem,' he told them. 'I've tried everything in my considerable repair arsenal and I've finally got to admit I'm beaten.'

The day after Boxing Day, Robert's old school buddy turned up at 6 a.m. to pick him up for their annual overnight festive fishing trip. It sounded silly, but Robert looked weathered, physically beaten from his constant battles with the clock.

'I don't know how I'm going to tell the client,' he said morosely at the door as I kissed him goodbye. 'He had such faith in me to repair it ready for his wife's sixtieth birthday next month.'

'Put it out of your mind and enjoy your break,' I told him, handing over his sandwiches and flask. 'If it's beaten you then nobody else will be able to help him. That you can guarantee.'

Placated, he left, and I breathed a sigh of relief. I was looking forward to the house being a little calmer, with no more baffling talk of the mechanics of that ruddy clock.

Mid morning, Tom sauntered into the kitchen dressed in warm clothes.

'I'm going to tidy up the workshop as a surprise for Dad when he gets back,' he said. 'Shout me when lunch is ready, Mum.'

I gave it no more thought, but I remembered being touched that he wanted to do something to help his father. After lunch, he went out again and I had to call him in three times before he appeared for tea. His hands were covered in grease and he went directly over to the sink.

'Whatever have you been doing in there?' I whipped away the clean hand towel I'd just hung on the rail. 'Rubbing the floor with your bare hands?'

He turned to me and grinned. His face was flushed, his eyes bright and sparkling, and I got this feeling in the pit of my stomach. He looked exhilarated, but something told me it was for all the wrong reasons.

'You're not going to believe it,' he said, rubbing his hands so vigorously the soap foamed up between his fingers. 'Guess what I've done?'

And then I knew. I swallowed down the lump in my throat and said, 'Have you touched that clock?'

'I've done more than touch it, Mum, I've mended it. It's working! It's running perfectly, Dad's going to be amazed.'

But Robert was not amazed at all. When Tom led his father into the garage, Robert's face turned puce. 'Who the hell gave you the right to start meddling in here without my permission?'

He stormed over to the clock, and even through his fury, I saw the shock and amazement that Tom had managed to get it working.

'I thought I'd have a quick look at it, Dad. I know you've spent hours on it and I thought if I got it working, you'd be—'

'You had no right. No right!' Robert grabbed hold of him, but Tom, now nearly as tall as he was, managed to slip free before his father slapped him.

'Robert, please!' I pleaded. 'Calm down. This is a good thing, isn't it? Now your client won't be disappointed.'

He turned on me then. 'You! You've encouraged him to humiliate me like this. So you can tell everyone your precious son succeeded where I failed.' He looked at me with such revulsion, I shrank back outside.

I hovered around the closed workshop door listening to them screaming at each other.

'Why do you hate me?' I heard Tom scream. 'It's not my fault you're rubbish at mending clocks!'

It was the first time I'd heard him answer his father back, but Robert's misplaced anger had loosened something in him.

Voices were raised and Nazreen next door called over the fence to ask if everything was OK. I reached for the door handle, and then I heard it. A tremendous crash followed by a terrible banging.

The sound of a hammer cracking into the precious timepiece. Centuries-old craftsmanship and delicate glass pulverised in a moment of jealous madness.

Tom cried out and I burst into the workshop to see Robert sitting on the floor, crying, the hammer hanging loosely from his shaking hand.

Within a month, the company he'd worked at for twenty years had let him go. The official reason given was redundancy due to a restructure but seeing as the irate clock client had taken his business elsewhere and Robert's job was the only casualty, it didn't take much to read between the lines as to the real reason behind his dismissal.

It hit Robert badly. He suffered a period of anxiety and mild depression. Counselling helped with his recovery and inspired him to retrain in the profession himself.

But things were never the same again between the three of us after that.

38

Nottinghamshire Police

October 2019

DI Irma Barrington sighed and pushed away the pile of folders in front of her. She had two members of her team off on long-term sick and a temporary replacement in the DS position, a young woman from London called Tyra Barnes.

When her boss, DI Marcus Fernwood, had retired last year, Irma had been promoted to detective inspector at the age of thirty-eight. She missed Marcus, had learned a lot from him during her days as a DS. Now she was the senior detective in charge of a team.

Tyra sauntered over to her desk. As usual, she was dressed stylishly in a navy fitted trouser suit and a white T-shirt. She wore her hair in a full Afro, which she'd flattened on top with colourful hair slides.

She waved a piece of paper at Irma. 'New in. We got ourselves a dead body. A woman.'

'Pulled out of the river?' Irma said distractedly, leafing through the folders she'd sidelined. 'An overdose?'

'Nope.' Tyra leaned forward and placed the note squarely in front of her. 'The deceased is a twenty-eight-year-old local woman, single mother of a nine-year-old son. She was found with a fatal head injury. Uniform said it looks like a possible hit and run.'

Irma sighed. What a terrible end for this poor woman, and with a young son, too. Though people were always upset by the thought of a hit and run, they tended not to be as shocked as they were by a face-to-face assault or murder. Yet the cruelty of this particular crime always got to Irma.

Only two years ago, her own dad, an alcoholic, had stumbled in front of a bus and met his end. The bus driver had been inconsolable and completely blameless. But this … to plough into someone knowing at the very least that you were leaving a broken body, abandoning a person who was possibly in tremendous pain and trauma, took a special kind of wickedness in her opinion. Somewhere in the area, a young boy had lost his mother and he didn't even realise it yet.

Irma picked up the note with details of the identity of the woman. 'Coral McKinty,' she said to herself. Frowning, she rolled the name around on her tongue for a second time, a growing feeling of unease taking hold. 'Coral McKinty.' Why did it sound so familiar?

'The body was found in a ditch by a dog walker. It's the road that skirts the edge of Blidworth Woods. Her car was nearby. She might have been out walking, but officers at the scene said she hadn't got walking footwear or suitable clothing on.' Tyra hesitated. 'They're checking to see if she'd broken down and was going for help or to get a phone signal.'

'Go on,' Irma said, sensing Tyra was suppressing something interesting.

'Well, I took the liberty of looking up her details, and we've spoken to her before. To be precise, *you've* spoken to her before. Ten years ago, in connection with an assault and eventually manslaughter charge involving her then boyfriend, Jesse Wilson.'

'*That's* where I know her name from,' Irma cried, drawing glances from some of the team working close by. 'Tom Billinghurst, Jesse's best friend, threw a fatal punch outside Movers. They were both local boys.'

'Movers?' Tyra wrinkled her nose.

'Used to be a nightclub in the middle of town,' Irma said. 'I think it's a Sainsbury's Local now or something.'

She began tapping on her keyboard, faintly aware of Tyra saying something about the place being a bit of a backwater, and how she missed the clubs in London. Her voice sounded distant as Irma read and absorbed the words on the screen in front of her.

'Well I never.' She gave a low whistle. 'Coral McKinty turns up dead near a wood with a head injury, and guess who was released from prison less than a month ago?'

'Let me take a wild guess,' Tyra said. 'Tom Billinghurst?'

'The very same. I haven't a clue why Billinghurst would want to do her any harm and it might be a coincidence,' Irma said. She turned off the monitor and stood up. 'But something you should know about me, DS Barnes, is that I tend not to trust coincidences and so this sounds like a very good place to start.' Coral McKinty's son had already lost his father thanks to Tom Billinghurst's lethal punch all those years ago. The grim reality was that this lad was now an orphan. 'Grab your coat, we're going to the crime scene.'

'Cool,' Tyra said, and dashed over to her desk to collect her things, leaving Irma with a hollow sense of hopelessness.

They might be able to find out what had happened to Coral and even charge the perpetrator, but they'd never give her young son his family back.

Sometimes, life was so incredibly cruel.

39

Jill

October 2019

When I started to drive away from Tom and Bridget's house after confronting her about why she'd been with Audrey, I saw my son still hovering at the front door, the bright hallway light like a halo around his broad shoulders.

My heart ached but I didn't linger there, didn't wave. For the first time, I felt as angry with my son as I did with Bridget. Angry that he couldn't see what was so apparent to me, that Bridget was keeping secrets from him, playing some kind of game with both of us.

I drove away without looking back and headed across town to Audrey's house. It was a twenty-minute drive, and on the way I tried calling her again, with exactly the same result as before. Her phone was off, but this time it wouldn't even let me leave a message, presumably because her voicemail box was full of all my previous pleas for her to get in touch.

When I arrived at her modest two-bedroom semi in Mansfield Woodhouse, I sat in the car and took in the house. It was fairly obvious Audrey wasn't home, because her car wasn't parked out front.

The house was neat but very plain, nothing to make it stand out amongst the other similar plots on the quiet street. It reflected Audrey's personality. She didn't like to draw attention to herself. She operated in the background in all areas. At the shop, she liked to hang back and let people browse to their hearts' content. She wasn't the sort to jump on customers the second they walked through the door and start the hard sell.

A reliable, sensible person, she was always there when you needed her. The perfect friend, or at least that was how I'd thought of her up to a few hours ago. Worry nibbled at the edges of my annoyance. Where could she have got to?

I got out of the car and walked up the short path. I rang the bell and knocked on the front door, but I wasn't surprised when there was no answer. I walked around the side of the house and leaned over the small gate to access the security bolt I knew she'd had fitted about halfway down.

I'd been in the small, neat back garden in fine weather many times over the years. Audrey would make us a simple chicken or prawn salad – never barbecue food, she hated the mess – and we'd sit out at her little round wrought-iron table and eat, laugh and put the world to rights, sometimes for hours on end. My heart ached when I thought about how long it had been since those days, way before Tom went to prison.

It shocked me to realise the enormous slice of time that had passed in my life with nothing to fill it. Ten whole years of nothing but waiting and planning for a fantasy future, and for what? For Tom to marry Jesse's mother and ruin any chance he had of living a normal life. To pass up having children of his own, grandchildren I'd visualised so vividly I almost felt I already knew them.

I'd been wasting my own life trying to plan his.

I cupped my hands around my eyes and pressed my face close to the kitchen window. The blind was up and the kitchen was tidy. I saw that Audrey still had the photograph pinned up of the two of us eating fish and chips on Padstow harbour, summer 2009. I felt a pang of regret.

With my warm breath smearing the glass, I looked around the rest of the kitchen to see if anything had changed since I'd last been there, but all seemed to be exactly the same.

Then something caught my eye on the shortest bit of worktop, by the kitchen sink.

My heartbeat lurched up into my throat and I pressed my forehead hard to the window, trying to convince myself that I must have made a mistake. I hadn't. The blue and white striped scarf I was staring at was too distinctive to confuse with any other, and I realised in one breathless rush that ripped through my body that I had been an utter fool.

I had been blind and so stupid not to see how Audrey had been betraying me.

40

Ellis

Ellis was trying to concentrate on his game but stuff kept getting in the way.

His mum had been acting very strange. It might not seem that way to other people, but Ellis knew her. He knew how she usually behaved.

When she'd got back from her meeting at his school, her phone had rung, and she'd jumped up and taken the call in another room. Ellis was fairly sure she'd arranged to meet someone – possibly a man. He wasn't sure what made him think that, maybe it was her pink cheeks and bright eyes when she came back in the room.

It had happened a couple of times before, too. She'd get a phone call and go out of the room to take it. Then, a short time afterwards, she'd casually mention that she had to go out somewhere and did he fancy going to his nan's house for an hour or two?

Ellis loved being at his nan's house, much preferred it to being at home most of the time. But things were now very different because *the murderer* had moved in. That was what he called Tom in his head because that's exactly what he was.

The living room door opened and his mum came back in the room.

'Hey, Ellis, I've got to pop out to pick up some bits. Fancy going to your nan's for an hour or so?'

Ellis had taken out his earbuds and frowned. 'Will the murderer be there?'

'Maybe, but you can stay out of his way in your bedroom like you did last time, yeah?'

'I thought you said school had told you I had to stop going over to Nan's for a while,' Ellis had said moodily.

'We'll have to see how it goes. She really wants to see you, and ... well, it suits me for you to stay there sometimes.'

Ellis had narrowed his eyes. 'Where are you going? Who was that on the phone?'

His mum had smiled and ruffled his hair. 'So many questions! I'm popping out on an errand, that's all. I won't be long. Be a love and grab what you need. I'll text your nan now.'

Ellis had huffed and puffed but he'd unfurled his lanky frame from the sofa and headed for the door.

Now, here he was at his nan's house again, lying on the bed in his room. He got loads more time on his Nintendo than he was allowed at home.

But his mum's behaviour still niggled at him. It wasn't only the unusual phone calls that were strange. At home, the fridge freezer and cupboards were suddenly full of the kind of food they usually only had as treats – pizza, ice cream and chocolate, and Ellis's favourite snack: big bags of corn chips with tubs of salsa and sour cream.

She'd been to the hairdresser's instead of buying a box dye colour like usual, and she spent ages on the laptop. Although she didn't realise, yesterday, Ellis had taken a peek at her search history when she went upstairs for a shower, and she'd been looking at houses ... at the coast! If his nan knew she was planning on moving house and taking Ellis with her, she'd have a proper meltdown.

Ellis didn't want to move to the seaside. Not the sort of place that rained a lot and had boarded-up shops, anyhow. But he wouldn't say no to amusement arcades and skateboard parks. No one would know him there so he'd be able to act super cool, as if he was used to having loads of friends.

He liked the thought of being someone else.

41

Bridget

I put on my noise-cancelling headphones and lay on the sofa, trying to focus on my relaxation app, which was a guided walk by the river.

I visualised looking out over the rippling water the narrator described, watched a couple of swans glide by … It should have been a serene moment, but I made the mistake of opening one eye, and saw Ellis squaring up to Tom.

I whipped the headphones off. 'What the hell is the matter now?' I yelled, and the two of them looked at me in astonishment. As soon as Jill had left, Tom announced he had to go back to the gym to get the water cooler bottle he'd left there.

I didn't think anything of it at the time, but I now knew he'd lied to me.

When he'd left the house and Coral had dropped Ellis off, I decided to put a load of washing in. I'd run up two flights of stairs and emptied out the contents of the linen basket in the en suite. I spotted Tom's gym bag was at his side of the bed, so I went to get his gym towel to add to the laundry.

I'd pulled out the towel and froze, staring at the new water bottle he'd apparently gone back to collect from the gym.

Now, I felt hot and empty inside. I didn't want to ask him outright what he was up to and alert him to the fact that I knew he'd lied. I had to be cleverer than that. For now, I was staying quiet and watching.

'He's trying to tell me what to do again,' Ellis said sulkily, folding his arms. 'He's always trying to tell me what to do.'

'He was playing that game when I left for the gym and he's still playing it now.' Tom folded his arms too. 'It's not good for him, Brid, and besides, he needs to clear some of this mess up.'

I cast an eye at the classy new coffee table I'd bought from Dwell about a month ago. The lacquered white surface was littered with empty cans of pop, congealing slices of pizza and Dorito chips. It was true Ellis should know better, but he was still a kid. With Tom around too, also apparently unable to pick up after himself, it was starting to feel like I had two kids.

'You can't jump on him every time he puts a foot wrong, Tom,' I said.

I wasn't stupid. I knew how much Ellis resented Tom, but I also understood it. Tom had robbed him of his father and also, Ellis was bound to be a bit jealous. It had been me and him for so long when he came over, and now we never had any time together without Tom's presence.

I appreciated Tom's efforts to play a role in Ellis's life. He'd seemed so genuine on every level, but now I couldn't think about anything else but the reason he'd lied to me. Where had he gone, if not back to the gym?

I glanced at my watch. Coral had said she'd be gone an hour, so she should have picked Ellis up way before now. I'd called her, texted her, but there had been no reply yet. I'd planned a relaxing evening with Tom, a few drinks to loosen him up before I tried to find out the truth of where he'd been. Coral was really pushing my buttons. One minute telling me I was affecting Ellis's wellbeing and it was best if he stayed away from the house, the next, abandoning him here at short notice and with little explanation.

I decided I'd take Ellis home myself soon, and if she was out, I'd wait until she came home to confront her. It wasn't her right to limit me seeing my grandson at the same time as acting so unreliably herself.

Tom and Ellis had another swipe at each other and I stood up, the headphones still clinging on around my neck.

'I'm not listening to this any longer. I'm going into the bedroom to do my relaxation session, and I don't want to hear a peep out of either of—'

The doorbell rang.

'Are you expecting anyone?' Tom bit his lip, probably worrying it might be his mother again.

'No one I can think of.' I walked to the front door and looked through the peephole. Two official-looking women stood outside, one in her late twenties, one older, probably late thirties. I felt sick. What might this be about?

Behind me, Ellis ran over to the kitchen, where he had a good view of the front door when I opened it.

'We're here to speak to Bridget Wilson,' the older woman said briskly.

'I'm Bridget Wilson. What's this about?'

'Nottinghamshire Police. I'm Detective Inspector Irma Barrington.' She held up ID. 'This is my colleague, Detective Sergeant Tyra Barnes. We'll need to come inside, if that's OK.' She glanced at the house next door.

I stood aside. 'Come in.'

'What's this all about?' Tom appeared in the hallway, his face pale.

'It's not about the bullying, is it?' Ellis asked in a fearful voice. 'I didn't do that stuff they said at school, I—'

'I think we can be fairly certain it's not about bullying, Ellis,' Tom reassured him. Sometimes he responded in such a caring way in the face of Ellis's obvious resentment.

I led the officers into the living room. 'This is my husband, Tom,' I said. 'And my grandson, Ellis.'

DI Barrington cleared her throat. 'If it's OK, I think it might be better if we speak to you and your husband alone. It might be a good idea for Ellis to sit in another room while we talk.'

Could this be about school after all? Maybe Ellis had hurt another child and not told us. Coral would relish the chance to pile more blame on me.

'Can't I stay, Nan?' Ellis pleaded with me.

'Bedroom, please, Ellis,' Tom said firmly.

'Fine!' Ellis pushed by him, knocking his arm. 'Don't tell me what to do.'

The detectives glanced at each other as Ellis's bedroom door slammed shut so hard, it was a miracle the hinges stayed intact.

'Sorry,' I said. 'Kids, eh?'

They both sat down, refusing Tom's offer of a drink. 'Coral McKinty is your daughter-in-law, Ms Wilson, is that right?' Barrington said, folding her hands neatly in her lap.

I frowned and looked at Tom, but he stared silently at the officers. 'Sort of. My late son and Coral were never married, but we're close and she's Ellis's mother. What's happened?'

If Coral had made some kind of complaint about me, I swear I'd—

'I'm so sorry to tell you that Coral's body has been found on the outskirts of local woodland, in a ditch. She had a head injury, but at this point in time, I'm afraid we have no further information.'

'Her *body*?' I repeated faintly. 'You mean ...'

Barnes nodded. 'I'm very sorry, I'm afraid she's dead, Ms Wilson.'

Tom cursed and then cried out as he clenched the drink he held too hard and shards of glass fell to the floor. He rushed to the kitchen, clutching his bleeding hand.

I fell back against the seat cushion, my hand flat on my chest. I glanced at the door and dropped my voice, praying Ellis couldn't hear anything. 'How did it happen? I mean, has someone … Who did this?'

'That's what we're currently trying to ascertain. We haven't got the full picture yet, but we're treating the incident as a possible hit and run.'

Tom re-joined us, a clean cloth wrapped around his injured hand. Both detectives turned to face him. He clasped his hands together in front of him to stop them from shaking, but it didn't work.

He'd barely had anything to do with Coral. What on earth was he so afraid of?

'We'll need to ask you both some questions, if that's OK,' Barnes said, her eyes trained on Tom's trembling hands. 'Ms Wilson, when did you last see Coral?'

'She dropped Ellis off a couple of hours ago. Hang on.' I checked the call log on my phone. 'She rang me at 15.52 and dropped him off about fifteen minutes after that.'

Barnes checked her watch. 'And now it's six thirty, so he's been here a couple of hours, give or take.'

I nodded. 'She didn't say where she was going,' I volunteered. 'Just that she had a couple of things to do and she wouldn't be long. About an hour, she said.'

'I see. And what about you, Mr Billinghurst?' Barrington turned to Tom. 'When did you last see Coral?'

'I … I had to pop back to the gym so I was out when she dropped Ellis off earlier,' he said. 'Let me think.' The room fell silent. Then, 'Sorry, my mind's gone blank.'

'It must've been the dinner party on Friday,' I said, and he nodded, relieved.

'Yes, of course. I saw her Friday evening.'

Barnes checked her notebook. 'You were discharged from Nottingham prison nearly two weeks ago, Mr Billinghurst, is that right?'

'Yes.' Tom's voice sounded defensive. 'What's that got to do with anything?'

'Just confirming our details, sir. You don't mind answering our questions, I take it?'

'Actually, I feel a bit shaky,' Tom said. 'I think I still have some glass in this cut. Is there any way we can do this tomorrow?'

'Sure, no problem,' DI Barrington said easily, standing up. 'It would be great if you both came to the station. Shall we say tomorrow at ten?'

42

Ellis

'I'm really sorry about your mum, Ellis,' Tom said when the detectives had gone and his nan had told him the news that made him want to die himself.

'Leave me alone … I hate you!' Ellis cried. He picked up his nan's empty coffee cup and threw it. It smashed against the wall and shattered around Tom's feet.

'Ellis, don't!' His nan dashed over and threw her arms around him. 'I know it's unfair, I know it's a terrible, terrible thing that's happened, but it isn't Tom's fault, love.' She pressed him close to her and he began to sob uncontrollably.

Tom took a step towards them both, but Ellis felt her gently shake her head and he backed off.

Ellis tried to pull himself together. He was nine years old now, he had to man up, as he was always telling the younger kids at school when they couldn't take the name-calling. But this was his *mum* … his beautiful, kind mum. She was gone forever and the pain was everywhere inside him. He was full of it, and there was no escape. It was as if his blood had turned to burning oil, the hurt seeping into every millimetre of his body.

'I can't bear to see you both like this.' Tom threw his arms in the air and then clutched his head with both hands. 'I want to hold you, look after you.'

Ellis decided, if Tom came anywhere near him, he'd kick him in the nuts. Tom was good at pretending he cared, but underneath, he probably hated him. Ellis had heard the way he'd spoken to his mum that day, and he wouldn't forget it.

He pulled away from Bridget and headed for his room.

'Ellis?' she called after him.

'Leave me alone.' He stumbled through his bedroom door and slammed it behind him.

Tom was always there in the house and the creepiest thing was that he often watched Ellis slyly. It usually happened when Tom thought he was engrossed in his game. He'd stare at him and Ellis thought it might be because he reminded him of Jesse.

What if Tom was secretly thinking he'd like to kill *him* too? What if he crept into his bedroom when his nan was sleeping and slit his throat? Then he'd be dead like his mum and dad.

Ellis had heard people talk about feeling empty inside. Adults said it a lot, both in real life and on TV. He'd even heard his nan tell his mum a few years ago – when they thought he wasn't listening – that before he was born, she'd felt like she wanted to die because there was nothing left to live for. It had been after his dad had been murdered by Tom.

Now she was married to him. The man who had once made her want to die.

It seemed to Ellis that adults often felt a certain way one day and a completely different way the next. Kids felt the same every day. He did, anyway. His body felt sort of tight and sore, and if anyone spoke to him or looked at him the wrong way, his chest surged like it was on fire. He wished everyone would leave him alone to lose himself in his games. They were so straightforward. They were always the same, no matter what day it was.

After the police officers' visit, he understood what it *really* felt like to be empty inside. He curled up on his bed and wrapped his arms around his body. It felt like he was hovering on the ceiling and watching himself. He didn't cry or feel angry. He didn't want to talk to his nan … he simply felt nothing at all. It was if something had sucked out all his insides.

His dad had died even before he was born, and now his mum was gone too. And nobody would tell him anything about it. Nobody seemed to know what had happened.

The worst thing was, when his mum had said goodbye to him a few hours ago, he'd barely answered her. He'd just wanted to get in the house and start his game.

He twisted and turned on the bed. It felt like pieces of him were breaking off, shrivelling and turning to dust. As though soon there might be nothing left of him at all.

'It's not that I'm keeping anything from you,' his nan had said when the police officers left the house. She'd come into his bedroom and shut the door quietly behind her. 'We don't know anything yet, we don't know exactly what happened. It looks like your mum might have been walking on the road and got knocked over.'

'Has someone said they hit her? Were they looking at their phone?'

His nan gripped his hand and kissed it, but she didn't meet his eyes and that scared him. And then he'd realised the obvious.

'They think someone might've killed her and not stopped? A hit and run?'

'Ellis, they don't know that for sure yet.' Her voice had sounded different to usual, like she was trying really hard to make him think everything would be OK but underneath she was as scared as he was. That made everything worse, because if the adults around you were scared, what hope did a kid have?

Whatever had happened, Ellis's mum was dead now. She was never coming back. He wondered about the thing she'd made him swear not to tell anyone … did that matter any more? Or was it more important than ever that he kept quiet?

One morning, a few days after Tom had been discharged from prison, his mum had asked Ellis to go to the shop to get some milk and bacon. He'd grumbled, but when she'd said he could connect his Nintendo Switch to the TV for an hour when he got back, he'd decided it was probably worth the sacrifice.

His mum had seemed desperate for the items, even though they still had a bit of milk left and didn't need the bacon until lunchtime. She'd almost pushed him out of the house. The local Co-op was about a twenty-minute walk from home and much further than that if you took the long way round through the skate park where there were sometimes older kids doing really cool manoeuvres on the graffitied concrete slopes.

Ellis had reached the main road, about seven minutes from home, when he realised he hadn't picked up the tenner his mum had left for him on the kitchen worktop.

'Shit!' He'd kicked a brick wall and hurt his foot, sending his fury to a new level.

Over the road, a woman stood glaring at him while her dog sniffed around a lamp post. He'd felt so angry inside at her interest, he remembered wishing there was a pile of rocks nearby to lob at her. He knew at the time it didn't make sense, knew it was unfair of him, but he couldn't help it. That was how he felt most of the time these days, since he'd had to face Tom every time he went to his nan's house. Like he wanted to hurt someone.

He'd bitten down on his tongue until he tasted the metallic tang of blood, and the pain calmed him down a bit. Then he'd turned around and started walking back to the house to get the cash.

As he'd turned the corner at the end of their street, he'd spotted a tall figure in jeans and a hoodie stop outside their house. The man opened the small front gate and walked up the path. The house was in the middle of a long line of narrow townhouses. They used to live in a big old Victorian semi with damp walls and dodgy electrics, but his nan had helped them get a nicer place. His mum had a sign in the bottom corner of the front window saying *No Uninvited Callers*, but this guy had blatantly ignored that. Ellis broke into a run.

The door opened and he saw his mum step aside and let the man straight inside. They didn't talk or anything, and it looked like she'd been expecting him.

Ellis got a feeling like indigestion in his chest. He wondered if his mum had a secret boyfriend and didn't want him to know. Coral was twenty-eight and she was pretty and slim, and he saw blokes look at her in the street all the time. It was gross to think about your mum dating guys, but he knew she was attractive and his dad had been gone a long time now.

He had dawdled back to a slow walk. What should he do now? If he burst in there, they might be … doing anything, like the couple in that rude picture Monty had brought into school. It was sickening but true. But if he didn't pick up the cash and get the stuff from the shop, he wouldn't be allowed to play his game on the television.

It had occurred to him to shout to his mum from the door and then she wouldn't be surprised. But then she might introduce him to her new boyfriend and that would be the worst thing ever.

Then he remembered that the ten-pound note was actually on the end of the kitchen worktop, right by the back door. They never kept the back door locked during the day as his mum liked to stand outside in the garden regularly for a smoke. He'd sneak around the back, open the door and take the money and she'd be none the wiser. Then, on his way back from the shop, he'd take a detour through the skate park, and hopefully by the time he got back, the man would've gone.

He walked past the front gate and took a right turn down the alleyway that led behind the houses, giving access to the narrow gardens. He opened the squeaky back gate and snuck inside, praying they weren't snogging by the patio doors in the kitchen. He pushed down on the handle and levered the door gently open. Stepping inside, he reached for the cash, then froze as he heard raised voices coming from the living room.

'Coral, please. Just listen, I—' He instantly recognised Tom's voice. Were his mum and Tom having an affair? Behind his nan's back?

He'd gripped the worktop as Coral's shrill voice rang out next.

'No! You listen to me instead. Save your lies, because we both know what the big secret is. Jesse told you the night he died.'

'No!'

'You didn't like what you heard, so you killed him. Pretended it was an accident.'

'No! I—'

'But the court saw through you, thank God. So you can drop the nice guy act with me because I know the truth.'

Ellis had covered his mouth, certain he was going to be sick at any moment. He turned and ran out of the kitchen, but his foot caught on the step and he tripped, knocking over the small metal watering can his mum kept there for the house plants.

'Who's there?' he heard his mum shout. 'Ellis?'

He'd got to his feet but didn't have time to run before his mum and Tom appeared.

'He heard us,' Tom said, staring at him in a dark, dangerous manner.

'I didn't! I—'

His mum had turned to Tom. 'Go now. I'll speak to him.'

'Are you going to tell him—'

'Go,' Coral said. 'And don't come back here.'

Then his mum had sat him down, forced him to listen to her.

'I don't know what you heard or how it sounded, but it's not what you think, OK?' Ellis glared moodily at the wall. 'OK?'

'No, it's not OK! You said he killed my dad because he knew something.'

'That's not what I said, Ellis.'

'You did! I heard you!' He stood up, his whole body shaking, tears stinging his eyes. 'Nan would never have married him if she knew he meant to kill Dad on purpose. Tom convinced her it was an accident and said he was sorry, and Nan believed him.'

Coral had placed her hands on his shoulders and pressed him down into the seat again. 'Listen to me, love. It's very important you forget anything you heard today. Whatever you thought I meant, you need to put it out of your mind. Unless you want to get me into serious trouble, you don't breathe a word to your nan, you hear me?'

She'd looked so scared, so desperate, he'd quickly nodded. 'OK,' he'd said.

'Good lad. I love you.' She kissed the top of his head.

'I forgot the cash. I've got to go back to the shop.'

She'd laughed. 'Don't worry, we'll manage. Hook your game up to the TV and enjoy it.'

He'd realised then that she'd only sent him to the shop because she knew Tom was calling round. The question was, why had she been protecting him? What did Ellis's dad tell him before he died?

A wave of misery washed over him, like a terrible cramp that reached every inch of his flesh. None of it mattered any more. He didn't care why Tom had been in the house that day. He didn't care what his dad had told him that night.

His mum was gone now, and that meant Ellis was officially an orphan.

He wished with all his heart he'd die too.

43

Bridget

Tom and I sat quietly in shock. I heard Ellis sobbing upstairs in his bedroom. I'd tried my best to explain the terrible tragedy, to comfort him. Tom had tried too, but Ellis wanted nothing to do with either of us right now.

'I can't believe it,' Tom whispered. 'I can't believe Coral is dead.'

I looked at him. 'Did you get your water bottle?'

'What?'

'The water bottle you went back to the gym for. Did you find it?'

'Hardly seems important now,' he said, incredulous that I'd asked. 'Yeah, I got it, thanks.'

'You're a liar.' I stood up and glared down at him. 'I found your water bottle when I went in your gym bag to get your towel. So where did you go, and why lie about it?'

He pressed his cut hand and grimaced. 'Can we talk about this later?'

'No, we cannot! It's a small glass cut, for God's sake. How bad can it be?' I reached down and tugged at the cloth around his hand. He let out a yelp as it came off. The wound was quite nasty, but it had stopped bleeding and was already knitting neatly together. The surface was level and there was clearly no glass in it like he'd told the detectives. I walked to the kitchen cupboard and pulled out the first aid kit. 'Why lie about it being so bad you couldn't answer the detectives' questions?' I selected a large plaster and applied it to the cut before sitting back.

'I don't know.' He ran his good hand through his hair and sighed. 'It was a knee-jerk reaction. When they mentioned that I'd just been released, it made me jittery.'

'Fine. I can see how that might be the case. Next question – where did you go when you lied about the gym?'

There were a few moments of silence, and then he said, 'I'm sorry, Brid, I can't tell you.'

'What?' My mouth dropped open. 'You can tell me. You *will* tell me!'

'I can't. Please, you're going to have to trust me on this one.'

'Trust you? When you're admitting you've lied through your teeth to me?' My blood was on fire. 'I don't want a liar under this roof, so why don't you crawl back to your mother until you can man up and tell me the truth?'

'What I mean is, I *will* tell you, but it has to be the right time.'

My hot-blooded fury turned to ice-cold dread. He had someone else. He'd met some hot young woman at the gym and he didn't want to break my heart when Ellis was here and I'd had the terrible news about Coral.

Somehow I managed to speak without choking on the words.

'You don't get to choose the right time for you.'

'Brid.' He covered his face with his hands. 'You can't possibly understand.'

'If it's another woman, you can tell me,' I said wretchedly. 'In fact I want you to tell me, I'd rather know.'

'You are so far from the truth.' He grasped my hand. 'I love you, Bridget. There's nobody but you.'

He must have seen the relief on my face, because he seemed to collect himself and spoke with some authority.

'I will tell you everything, I promise. But not now. We need to get things sorted with Ellis first.'

'Sorted how?'

'Well, he needs some stuff from home, surely? You said you had a key to Coral's house.'

'Yes, but … shouldn't we ask the police if it's OK first?' I fretted. 'We don't want it to look like we're trying to cover something up.'

'That's a strange thing to say.' Tom frowned. 'What is there to cover up? It's only Ellis's belongings we're after. Her house isn't a crime scene.'

'I don't know, I'm saying how it might look to them.'

'If we ask their permission, they might well say no, and then we're stuck,' Tom reasoned. 'If they're annoyed about it, we can play dumb.'

'I can't leave Ellis here on his own, not after the news he's had. Can you stay with him?'

'He'll get hysterical if I go near him when he's in this state. I can go to Coral's if you tell me what he needs.'

'I don't really know. I need to see his stuff so I can decide what to bring back,' I said. He was right about Ellis kicking off if he came out of his bedroom and Tom was there.

'OK, well, I'll call my mum to come over here while we're out,' Tom said simply.

'Your mother? I don't think so!'

He picked up his phone and pressed a key. 'Brid, don't be petty. Not now.' He held the phone up to his ear. 'Mum? Can you come over, quick as you can? We've got an emergency situation here.'

He told her briefly what had happened, but his voice faded out as I thought about Coral. How she'd been here, alive and well, and now she was cold and dead. The feelings that stirred in my stomach reminded me so much of when Jesse had died.

'You're crying.' Tom touched my cheek when he'd ended the call. 'Mum's on her way over. She should be here in fifteen minutes.'

'I feel so bad now, getting annoyed with Coral. I'd never have been so mean to her if I'd known ...'

'You weren't mean to her, Brid. Not really,' Tom said softly. 'Coral could be difficult. She was becoming obnoxious about Ellis.'

I stood up. 'I'll get ready to go.'

Upstairs, I made sure everything personal was put away. Who knew what Jill might rifle though, given the chance? The knowledge Tom was keeping a secret from me drove me crazy. I could barely think of anything else, even though Coral had just died. I was the definition of a terrible person.

Fifteen minutes later, Jill arrived. I heard Tom explaining everything to her as I went back downstairs.

'Hello, Bridget,' she said. 'I'm so sorry about Coral. I know you two were close.'

'Thank you,' I said. 'Are you sure you don't mind being here? Ellis is upstairs in his bedroom, first door on the left. I'm sorry we've dragged you out, but—'

'I don't mind at all, of course I don't. I won't bother Ellis, I'll put the television on and sit down here. If he needs anything, there's an adult around. Far better than dragging him out with you.'

I was taken aback by her helpfulness. I might even prefer her being spiteful, because I knew how to handle that. 'Thanks,' I said. 'That's very kind of you, Jill.'

'It's no trouble.'

'Thanks, Mum,' Tom said, clearly relieved we weren't tearing each other's hair out for once.

Part of me still wondered about the wisdom of leaving Jill Billinghurst alone in my house, giving her the opportunity to snoop around, but Tom was right. We should get Ellis's stuff out of the house straight away in case the police decided to search the property or make it inaccessible for a while.

44

Jill

When Tom and Bridget had left to pick up Ellis's belongings from Coral's house, I poured a glass of milk and took a biscuit out of the cupboard.

I went upstairs and tapped on Ellis's bedroom door. There was no answer, so after knocking again, I stepped inside. The blinds were drawn, and the boy lay on the bed on his side, with his back to the door.

'I brought you milk and a biscuit, Ellis,' I said softly. 'Try and have a little sip and eat something.'

He shifted position slightly but didn't answer me. I placed the refreshments on his bedside table.

From the back, it was easy to imagine Tom at the same age. His hair was a similar shade, with a tuft on his crown that grew at an odd angle and stuck up, although Tom had been shorter and stockier.

Before I realised what I was doing, I laid my hand on Ellis's head. He was warm and still and I was surprised he didn't shrink away from my touch.

'I'm so sorry to hear about your mum, Ellis,' I whispered. 'I know you're so very, very sad, but let me know if you need anything at all. I'll be downstairs.'

'Can you stay?' His words were muffled by the pillow and I thought I'd misheard him.

'Sorry?'

He turned slightly but didn't look at me directly. 'I'd like you to stay for a bit. I don't … I don't want to be alone.' His voice sounded dry and scratchy.

'Of course. Do you want to talk about—'

'No,' he said. 'I'd like to be quiet, if that's OK.'

I patted his shoulder and sat in the white moulded plastic chair next to his bed. Everything matched in his bedroom. The walls were covered in Marvel and Nintendo posters, and there was an IKEA-style white built-in desk and shelving unit along one wall. Even the headboard and pendant shade were white, giving a neat, streamlined effect.

Tom's room hadn't been quite as smart as this, but he'd liked spending a lot of time on his own when he was Ellis's age. Sometimes Jesse being there drove him mad, because it was simply impossible for Jesse to sit quietly. As I recall, he had to be the centre of attention or he grew restless.

I closed my eyes and began to drift slightly. The television played out very faintly downstairs and I found the distant voices comforting. I kept reliving the moment I'd walked into the shop and seen Audrey and Bridget together. The way they were huddled spoke of a familiarity with each other. And then peering through Audrey's kitchen window and seeing that scarf. I still couldn't get my head around it. Couldn't face the obvious conclusion I'd come to.

My eyes snapped open when Ellis stirred and slowly rolled over so he was facing me. His eyes were red and swollen, his skin pale. We regarded each other.

'Are you OK, Ellis?' I asked him gently. 'I know you're full of pain, but you are getting through each minute and that's what matters. That's all you need to do.'

'My mum felt sorry for you,' he whispered. 'She said you weren't to blame for what happened.'

'Your mum was a nice lady,' I said gently. 'You shouldn't upset yourself thinking about your dad, love. Tom never meant for him to fall that night, you know. It was a horrible accident. A very sad accident.'

'I keep trying not to think about this because I don't know whether I'm still not supposed to say anything.' Ellis shook his head and closed his eyes. 'But I heard him. I heard what he said.'

'What who said?'

'Tom. When he came to our house.'

I could hear my pulse in my ears. 'Tom came to your house?'

Ellis pushed himself up on one elbow. 'He came over after he got out of prison, but Mum said I couldn't tell my nan or there'd be a lot of trouble.'

There was a tightness at the back of my throat. 'What happened exactly?' His eyes darted away and I realised I'd probably sounded a bit stern. 'Don't worry, you're not in trouble, Ellis,' I added hurriedly. 'I'm trying to understand what you mean.'

'Mum asked me to go to the shop, but I had to come back again because I'd forgotten the money. I saw Tom go into the house through the front door. I crept around to the back to sneak in, to snatch the money off the side, but then I heard them arguing.'

I kept my voice light and unconcerned. 'Can you remember what they were arguing about?'

Ellis squeezed his eyes closed. 'I heard Mum say that she knew Dad had told Tom a secret the night he died. And Tom didn't like what he heard so he hit Dad on purpose. He wanted to hurt him.'

I sat bolt upright. 'What did Jesse tell him?'

'I don't know, but Mum said she knew what the secret was.' Ellis looked at me, his eyes dark and haunted. 'And now she's dead, too.'

My insides had turned to liquid. It was all nonsense, it had to be! If the police heard about this, they might think Tom had a reason to hurt Coral. *To shut her up.*

'People say lots of things when they're angry,' I told him gently. 'Your dad's death was an accident. It wasn't because anyone had been lying or trying to keep secrets.'

Ellis whipped his head around. 'He died because Tom punched him and he fell. Why did Tom punch him? Because he didn't like what my dad told him!'

I pressed my lips together. It was not my job to talk to Ellis about his father pulling a knife on Tom. I didn't know whether Coral had told him about that detail, but he would certainly find out when he was older, and that would be time enough.

'If Tom and your mum were arguing in the house, it probably sounded worse than it was, love. You must have seen it in disagreements with your friends at school. People get angry and say stuff to hurt others, and then it blows over.'

'I haven't got any friends,' he said gloomily.

'Oh, I'm sure that's not true! Come on now, have a drink of milk and eat your biscuit.'

'I don't want a stupid biscuit.' His arm swept out and knocked the glass of milk to the floor. I gasped and swooped down to snatch it up as his voice rose to a wail. 'I want my mum and I want my dad. And now they're both dead!'

I sat on the bed and wrapped my arms around him. I fully expected him to push me away, but he let me hold him and sobbed a hot wetness into my shoulder.

I felt something swelling in my own chest, moving up into my throat. I opened my mouth and a sob escaped, and then I was crying too.

Ellis pulled away from me and turned his back again just as a shrill ping rang out from my phone downstairs on the hall table.

'I'd better check that,' I whispered. He didn't answer.

I padded out and closed the door softly behind me, dabbing my damp face with a tissue. Downstairs, I grabbed my phone. I was expecting a text from Tom saying they'd arrived at Coral's house, but it was a follower's notification. From Facebook.

I opened the notification and read Bridget's most recent public Facebook post.

Thanks to everyone for your condolences. I will pass your kind thoughts on to Coral's son and my grandson, Ellis. We don't know anything more yet, but rest assured if the police establish that Coral's life was indeed taken deliberately, I will not rest until someone pays for it.

My last interaction with Coral had been at the café earlier today. She had later been involved in an accident by Blidworth Woods. Tom had said the police weren't sure how she'd come to be out of her car and walking on the road, but they were treating her death as a possible hit and run until they'd established exactly what had happened. An investigation would mean that they'd want to speak to the people who'd seen Coral most recently, and that would include me.

I looked at Bridget's status again. She must have written and posted it after leaving the house to head over to Coral's. Surely she'd had too much on her mind to think about updating her social media at a time like this!

I ached to speak to Audrey, to get her opinion. She had such great insight into people. But it seemed Audrey had either disappeared off the face of the earth — which was unlikely — or was deliberately avoiding me, and when I thought about what I'd spotted on her kitchen worktop, I felt sick to my stomach about what she might confirm when I did speak to her.

Then something else occurred to me.

Was Bridget planning to frame Tom for Coral's death in some way? Was this how she'd planned on getting her revenge all along … to get Tom back behind bars, to have Ellis live with her permanently. It might sound dramatic to some but actually, the idea would be quite brilliant.

But that still left the police the question of who, exactly, had killed Coral?

45

Tom

2009

The friendship group Tom belonged to had unanimously agreed that the year after their GCSEs was the best time at school.

Tom and Jesse and quite a few of the gang had moved on to college together. Not because they were interested in studying, far from it. Tom's mum was chewing his ear off about what he wanted to do as a job. It didn't really matter if he'd said he was going to be a doctor or a lawyer; his dad would've found something to criticise.

Opting for A levels had got his parents off his back for two years, and that was good enough for Tom, because he hadn't really got a clue yet what he wanted to do, and neither had any of his mates.

There was a group of about five or six students who took to hanging around together in the sixth-form common room in free periods and at lunchtimes: Tom and Jesse, Coral, plus a few other kids who'd gravitated to joining them most days.

They'd all managed to get jobs in the evenings and weekends at various places to afford nights out. Although Tom's parents were probably the best off of all his friends' families, his mum thought spending money on drink was wasteful and his dad firmly believed he was old enough to earn his own money.

'Hard work never hurt anyone,' was his frequent refrain. Or another favourite, 'My parents never gave me a penny.'

His dad redeemed himself once Tom started going out regularly with his friendship group. He'd sometimes offer to pick them up in his new, spacious 4x4, saving them the cab fares home. Tom and Jesse lived close to each other, but Coral lived the other side of town and one or two of the others, even further. The result of this was that whenever Tom moaned about his dad, the others would jump to his defence, reminding him how much worse off they'd be without him.

Then Jesse and Coral became an item. Tom had noticed them getting closer. Jesse would often choose to sit with Coral in the pub rather than next to Tom, and he'd be 'busy' when Tom asked if he fancied going to the cinema or maybe the bowling alley like they used to do.

For a while, Tom hung around with the two of them. They didn't seem to mind and Coral was quite good company as it happened. Sometimes when Jesse had a late class, she and Tom would grab a coffee together in the common room or go to the library if they needed to catch up on coursework.

One midweek evening, Tom and Jesse had arranged to have a gaming session together. Tom called around to Jesse's house, but it was Bridget who answered the door.

'He's out with Coral. He must've forgotten,' she said, and then, when Tom's face fell, 'Stay anyway. I'm watching *Jaws* on DVD and I've made a big pot of chilli you can help me scoff. What do you say?'

They'd had a brilliant night. Bridget was such a cool mum, so chilled, and she liked the same things they all did. But to Tom she was also like real family. They'd spent so much time together as he was growing up, he knew her inside out and she him.

She told him about a couple of disastrous dates she'd had and how she was now a committed singleton.

'It might be a bit early for that decision, Brid,' he'd laughed. He'd taken to shortening her name like that and she said she liked it.

'Trouble is, men my own age seem to have so much less energy than I do. They start off fun and then want to stay in every night watching serious films instead of the funny ones we like.'

Tom had agreed it sounded like hell.

As Jesse got more involved with Coral, Tom found himself round at Bridget's house two or three times a week, keeping her company.

'It's not right,' Robert remarked when he asked Tom why the group never needed a lift home any longer. 'Holed up with a woman your mother's age nearly every night.'

He was exaggerating, because it wasn't every night at all. Tom liked spending time with Bridget. She was funny and kind and made him feel wanted.

Jesse had got into a couple of scuffles with boys at school who'd said disgusting things about what they'd like to do with Bridget, calling her a MILF and asking him for her number. Tom would never think of her in such disrespectful terms, but it was true she was so much more interesting than girls his own age. He had taken a couple of them out and they'd spent most of the night pouting into their phone cameras or texting their mates. He'd felt like he had nothing in common with them at all.

Then suddenly Jesse seemed to be around a lot more, and it was the three of them, Tom, Jesse and Bridget, watching movies at the house. Tom had asked about Coral.

'I'm still seeing her, we're still together. Just giving each other a bit of space,' Jesse had said offhandedly.

Bridget and Tom had exchanged glances, raised their eyebrows.

A few months later, Jesse announced that Coral was pregnant. Tom's mum would have had a meltdown, but as usual, Bridget took it in her stride.

'I'm happy for you both. I can't wait to see new little Jesse, although I'm not too fussed about being a grandma when I look so young,' she'd joked.

Tom had bumped into Coral at school. She was sour-faced, and when he asked if she fancied a coffee and a catch-up, she'd hurriedly made some inane excuse and scuttled off. Something wasn't right but nobody was saying what, though that suited Tom. He didn't want to get pulled into the politics of their relationship.

When Coral was six months pregnant, Jesse suggested that he and Tom have a night out together. 'We need a good session, like the old days,' he'd said. 'Time we had a proper chat, don't you think?'

Tom had agreed. A bit of banter sounded like a good enough idea.

They decided they'd go to the Mayflower bar for a drink before going on to Movers nightclub in town.

Although he was concerned about his training session the next day, Tom felt a catch-up with his best mate was long overdue.

After all, what harm would a few drinks do?

46

Bridget

October 2019

I had an awful sense that time was running out in some way, but I didn't know why. My neck and shoulders tightened as we travelled towards Coral's house.

We hadn't actually discussed what would happen with Ellis now that Coral was gone. There really was nothing *to* discuss. Ellis would come and live with us and that went without saying. I felt numb when I thought about Coral's death. The things we'd said to each other recently, the animosity. It all loomed large in my head. She had certainly made her disapproval of our marriage known whenever she had the opportunity, but still, I certainly didn't wish her dead. She had always been there, since Jesse's death, and I'd never really given much thought to my feelings for her. I felt surprised at the depth of the hollowness in my chest.

If I didn't admit that something good had come out of Coral's demise, I'd be lying to myself. Her threat of keeping Ellis away from me, the influence of those do-gooders at school who had been trying to convince her it was the right thing to do. All the worry of that had evaporated with her death. Still, it was an enormous price to pay and my heart cracked when I thought about how on earth Ellis was going to recover from this crushing double blow. His dad, and now his mum, gone forever.

Whoever was responsible for this had to pay.

When we first got into the car, Tom was quiet and distracted. I would make sure the three of us were happy as a new family. Once Tom had come clean about why he'd lied about going back to the gym.

I would talk to Ellis at a point in the future when things weren't quite as raw, persuade him to give Tom a chance. He'd have more counselling sessions and I'd definitely take him out of Mansfield Academy now I knew how unsupportive they'd been of my new situation. It would do him good to start afresh somewhere else.

I parked up outside Coral's small house and we walked around the back. I unlocked the kitchen door and we went inside. It was a small, tidy room with white units and a black and white ceramic-tiled floor.

'I'll start with Ellis's bedroom,' I said, heading for the stairs. 'I'll put his clothes on the bed and you can take them to the car.'

Tom followed me upstairs and together we emptied out Ellis's wardrobe. I piled his underwear, T-shirts and jumpers on the bed. Fortunately, Coral was a bit of a clean freak, always organising her drawers and cupboards.

'They keep shoes under the stairs,' I told Tom, standing up straight and wincing as I rubbed at the bottom of my back. 'I'll sort those out in a minute, but you can start taking all this out to the car.'

Tom scooped up a big armful of hangers, grimacing when he caught his sore hand, before dutifully taking them downstairs.

When he returned, he looked doubtfully at the large pile still left. 'Maybe we should have hired a small van,' he said. 'The back seat of the Merc is almost full.'

'I'm sure we'll manage.' I gathered up a heap of clothing and followed him down. 'We'll bundle them in.'

Tom deposited his pile into the car and went back into the house. A few minutes later, I followed him back upstairs and saw he was in Coral's bedroom.

'What are you doing in here?' I asked, a strange feeling coming over me as he visibly jumped.

'I'm checking to see if there's any stuff to go from this room,' he said easily.

I glanced down at the mess of paperwork in front of him on the floor.

'Did you do that?'

'No. It was like that already,' he said without looking at me.

I bent down and started to sort through it. It was only old bills, a tenancy agreement for the house, stuff like that, and I waved him away. 'It's fine. You carry on taking Ellis's stuff down to the car. I'll sort this out.'

I happened to look up as Tom's hand slid furtively into his pocket. 'What have you got there?'

'What?'

'Did you put something in your pocket?'

He looked at me as if he didn't know what I was talking about, but his face had turned pale, two little rosy spots blooming on his cheeks.

'Let me see.'

'See what? I'm not a bloody kid, Bridget, leave it out!'

'I saw you put your hand in your pocket, as if you'd taken something.' I had to know.

'Christ! Here, this is all I have. Is that OK?' He pulled out his phone and held it up. 'You're paranoid.'

'Sorry. I … I'm a bit nervy, that's all. Let's get out of here before the police call round.'

Fifteen minutes later, we were back in the car and on our way home. I had Ellis's clothes. It was done.

I looked over at Tom and reached for his hand. He didn't squeeze back, but stared straight ahead like his mind was elsewhere.

'Everything OK?' I wished I hadn't been quite so snappy with him now.

'Yeah, everything's fine,' he replied, but his expression said something different. I hadn't seen him like this before. It felt like he'd frozen me out.

47

Audrey

Audrey parked down the road and checked to see the coast was clear before getting out of the car. When she'd left the shop, she'd driven out of town and parked up by the water to think things through. After much deliberation, she'd made a call and then headed here.

Soon, she would have to explain to Jill everything that had happened. She hoped that their bond, although not as unbreakable as it used to be, would see them through, and that Jill would find it in her heart to forgive her.

She and Jill had been friends for so long, it was difficult to remember what life had been like before she knew her. Although they had always been there for each other, their relationship had changed over the years, as relationships often did. They had grown a little further apart, saw each other less outside work.

Ten years ago, when Tom first went to prison, Jill had suffered terribly. Being a naturally quite insular person, she had seemed to fade quickly until she was a mere shell of her former self. Audrey had done her best to offer support, had tried repeatedly to get Jill to take some interest in life again, but in the end, she'd had to give up because it was sapping her own energy.

She'd tried to make Jill see that even though Tom had been incarcerated for a lengthy sentence, it might have been so much worse.

'He wasn't the one who died,' she'd told her for months after his conviction. 'Tom is still here and one day he'll be a free man again. Don't give your life up, Jill, don't grieve like you've lost him for good because that's not the case.'

Jill had spent the last ten years in complete denial of what had really happened that night. In her opinion, her son had been completely innocent. It was simple. Jesse had pulled out a knife and Tom had defended himself.

In reality, it was never as clear-cut as that. There were no witnesses, but Tom and Jesse had been friends all their lives, and a lot of folk around here knew instinctively that there must have been other complications at play.

In the end, Audrey had taken some of her own advice and realised that she too was in a kind of denial. Although she'd never want to give up completely on Jill, she accepted nothing she could do would stop her friend grieving for a son who had not yet died. Nor would Jill admit that her life would be so much better without Robert eroding her confidence.

After a few years, Audrey had taken a step or two back and turned her attention to someone else instead. In short, she had got herself in a bit of a mess and she wasn't sure how to get out of it.

She rang the bell and watched through the coloured glass panels of the Billinghursts' front door as someone appeared in the hallway.

She took a breath and steeled herself as the door opened.

'Come in,' Robert said, the mere sound of his voice turning her knees to jelly. 'She'll be out for a while. We've got plenty of time.'

48

Jill

When Tom and Bridget returned from Coral's house, it was clear to me something had happened between them. Tom brought in a great armful of clothes, heading straight upstairs to offload them. I recognised the dark eyes, the beetled brows. Something was bothering him.

'Did you get everything you wanted?' I asked as he passed me.

He nodded, then stopped and looked at me over the tangle of fabrics. 'You can get off if you like now, Mum. Thanks for watching Ellis.'

I wanted to blurt out what Ellis had told me about his altercation with Coral, ask him what it meant. Had something gone on between Tom and Jesse on the night Jesse died that Tom had never told anyone? What would he say if the police asked about his relationship with Coral? Would he tell them about the argument Ellis had witnessed?

As he climbed the stairs, Bridget appeared in the hallway, a smaller clutch of garments in her arms.

'I can help you unload the car?' I offered.

'No, no. We'll do it, thanks,' she said dismissively. Then, 'Has Ellis been OK?'

'Fine. He asked me to sit with him a while.'

'He did?' She lowered her arms and looked at me. 'Did he …
say anything?'

'About what?'

She shrugged. 'He's not been very talkative with me, that's all.'

'He didn't say much,' I said. 'If you don't need any help, Tom
said I should get off.'

'Yes, thanks again for staying,' she said. An awkward silence
settled between us, then she said, 'The police want to speak to us
in the morning at ten.'

'They want to speak to Tom, too?'

Bridget looked at me steadily. 'Yes, Jill, they do. At the station.'
A whirl of emotions rose inside me, and I took a step back. 'Are
you all right? You've gone very pale. They said it's only routine,
they have some questions about Coral.' I pushed away the images
of the police taking Tom back to prison. 'I wondered if you'd mind
having Ellis again. We'll drop him off at your house on the way
to the police station if that's OK.'

'Course, that's fine,' I said quickly. 'He's a lovely boy.'

Bridget beamed. 'He's very special. Being a grandparent is the
best feeling in the world.'

She locked her eyes onto mine. Was that the faintest of smirks
forming on her lips? Or was I imagining it? A flutter started in
my chest.

Tom came back downstairs. He walked past Bridget and she
glanced at him, but he kept staring ahead. They'd definitely had
a falling-out and I wondered what it was about.

I said a hurried goodbye to Bridget and followed Tom out to
the car. I had to play this cool, otherwise he'd shut down.

'I'm off home,' I said lightly, standing by the car as he leaned
into the back seat and scooped out more clothing. 'Any time you
fancy a cuppa, pop in. We'd love to see you.' I thought about the
strained relations between Tom and his father. '*I'd* love to see you.
We could have a proper talk.'

I expected him to wave my offer away, but instead he turned and looked at me. His posture sagged, his forehead crinkled. He looked like he had the weight of the world on his shoulders. 'Thanks, Mum,' he said. 'I know you care and I'm sorry I've caused you so much heartache. I want you to know—'

'Tom?' Bridget called from the front door, hands on hips.

He gave me a peck on the cheek. 'See you, Mum, thanks again.'

'But what were you going to say? You want me to know what?'

'Nothing important,' he said, turning away. 'I'll come over soon and we'll talk. I promise.'

Back home, Robert seemed nervy, offering to make me a drink which was unusual. He kept gravitating to the window and craning his neck to see up and down the street.

'What are you looking for?' I said, wishing he'd settle down.

'Nothing, nothing. Just wondering what the weather's going to do. Any news?'

I shook my head. 'Bridget and Tom have to go to the police station in the morning to answer some questions.'

'A terrible business,' he said. 'Let's hope Tom being recently released doesn't put him under more suspicion.'

That was Robert all over. Saying the first thing that came into his head without a thought for how I'd worry endlessly over it.

'I don't want to discuss it,' I said shortly. 'I'm sure Tom will show he's completely innocent.'

Doubtfully, he twisted his mouth to one side but had the sense to stay quiet.

When he'd disappeared into his office, I went upstairs and walked to the end of the landing.

I stepped inside the room and closed the door behind me. The space was unrecognisable. All the football posters, the Star Wars memorabilia and boxing trophies were gone. Reclaiming the space as my own had felt profound. I'd packed Tom's things safely away in the attic. They were there if he wanted them, but I'd finally set them aside to make space for myself.

As per my instructions, Joel had dismantled the wardrobe and bed but left the desk and chair and the drawers. My comfy armchair that had been sitting in the other spare bedroom, under a pile of Robert's old suits, was in here, as was my mother's lamp. For me, the best thing of all was looking around the walls. Floor to ceiling shelves that provided a home to my books.

'Have you lost your mind?' Robert had raged when he saw Joel's handiwork. 'Money's tight and you've designed yourself an elaborate hideaway!'

'I'm finding a space for all my books as you suggested all those years ago when you evicted me from the office, Robert,' I said coolly. 'Somewhere you wouldn't trip over them was your brief, as I recall.'

'Yes, but I didn't mean for you to incur all this cost!' he blustered. 'God only knows what Joel will charge for a full day's work.'

'Well, this is just the start,' I said. 'I've spent precisely nothing on myself for the past ten years and I intend making up for that now. Which reminds me. Can you order me a bank card for our joint savings account?'

I smiled to myself when I thought about him stropping like a two-year-old, slamming the door on his way out. I'd had no interest in the household finances for a long time now and that had suited Robert. He'd always liked to control the purse strings.

On one of the shelves next to my desk sat Gran's Dickens collection. When Joel had finished the room, I'd ventured out to the garage and heaved the box onto the sack barrow. I'd hauled it into the house and unpacked it.

Several of the books were damp and the ones on the bottom were slightly warped, their spine hinges broken. My grandma had treasured the books and, although Mum hadn't displayed them, she'd kept them packed and protected.

Now, thanks to Robert's carelessness, they were in a worse state than ever. I walked over to the drawers, pausing to look over the view of the garden before opening a drawer and taking out the box containing my book repair tools. Then I selected *Oliver Twist* – my favourite volume as a child – and sat down at the desk.

I worked methodically and precisely, cutting out the old stitching and trimming the rough edges. Carefully, I removed the old glue with a sharp craft knife. The front hinge of the cover had become detached through age and wear and tear but that was to be expected with all the joy it had given. My favourite illustrations had been in this particular book and I smiled again as I recalled the hours of contentment spent in my gran's arms as we'd pored over detailed pictures of Bill Sikes, Oliver and the Artful Dodger. A warm glow filled me up inside, banishing the dark hollow that had been there for so long.

A sense of peace and calm enveloped me and for the next couple of hours, I had respite from my many worries.

Sadly, once I'd emerged from my reading room and returned downstairs, my head felt full of Ellis telling me about his mum and Tom arguing. What was it my son had been going to tell me before Bridget whistled him back in the house like a puppy?

If the police asked Tom about his relationship with Coral, he'd have to tell them about visiting her house that day. He'd have to tell them what they had been arguing about.

And if that happened, even I had to accept Tom's prospects did not look good.

49

The next morning, I stood at my bedroom window waiting for Tom and Bridget to drop Ellis off when movement across the road caught my eye. A figure dressed in dark clothing lurked at the back of the bus shelter. It was not unusual for people to stand in there, of course, but two buses had sailed past and this person didn't stop either of them. Unless it was my imagination, he or she also seemed to be staring over at the house.

I thought about fetching the binoculars when Tom's silver car pulled up. At that exact moment, the figure emerged from the bus shelter and started walking briskly away.

I went downstairs and waved to Tom from the front door. He waved back but didn't get out of the car. I was desperate to talk to him, but now wasn't the time.

'It's good of you to have Ellis again,' Bridget said when she brought the boy to the door. Her eyes looked dark and dull and she wore only mascara, leaving off the heavy liner. 'Hopefully we shouldn't be too long. It will be routine questions, I'm sure.'

I nodded, not wanting to show my concern.

Instead, I said, 'I hope you're bearing up, Bridget. You and Ellis.'

Ellis scowled. 'I could've stayed at home on my own.' The attitude was clearly a cover-up. His bloated face and red-raw eyes told another story.

'Well, I like your company even if you're not fussed about mine,' I told him, before looking back at Bridget. 'We'll be fine. I hope everything goes well at the station.'

Bridget got back in the car, and I waved in Tom's direction again before ushering Ellis inside and closing the front door.

'Go through to the living room, Ellis, it's the first room on the right,' I said. 'Are you hungry?'

'No,' he grunted, the vulnerable boy of yesterday nowhere to be seen.

His face looked drawn. Now when I looked at him, I didn't see Jesse's arrogance or surly expression. I saw a sad young boy and felt a swell of pity and fondness instead.

He looked around the room, his gaze lingering on the framed photographs, mostly of Tom, dotted about on tables, shelves and the wall. There was a group photo of Tom and his friends, including Jesse and Coral. Ellis stared at it.

I heard the office door open and Robert came out. Ellis sat down and took his Nintendo console out of his small rucksack.

'Hello again, Ellis.' I'd assumed Robert would be grumpy at finding the boy here. He didn't like his routine disrupted. But he sat down at the other end of the sofa. 'I'm so sorry to hear you lost your mum. I knew Coral back when she was still at school. Did she tell you that?'

Ellis shook his head.

'Well, I'm very sad indeed to hear what happened. How are you sleeping?'

'I'm not, much.' Ellis stared at his console but he didn't turn it on.

'That's understandable, but it will get better, you know. The secret is to keep yourself strong. Drink lots of water, eat plenty of fresh food and if you can do a bit of exercise, that's brilliant. It will all help you sleep a little better and you'll feel more able to cope. Do you promise you'll try?'

Ellis nodded. 'I will.'

It was astounding to witness Robert with his counsellor's hat on. I felt quite touched that he was taking the time to help Ellis. If only Tom was here to see it.

Robert handed Ellis a business card. 'If you want to talk at all or get anything off your chest you don't want to bother your nan with, give me a ring, OK? Anything we talk about is confidential.'

'OK,' Ellis agreed.

I opened my mouth to say that might not be appropriate, but then decided against it. I imagined Bridget's wrath if she discovered Ellis was confiding in Robert instead of her.

'Good man.' Robert looked at me. 'I'm popping into work to pick up some client files.'

For once, I didn't feel irritated with him. I'd seen with my own eyes why he was so much in demand from the students he worked with. When he was in counsellor mode, he lost the fuddy-duddy attitude and actually talked to young people on their level. Ellis had seemed to respond to him in a way he didn't with anyone else.

Why wasn't Robert like this with Tom when he was growing up? What was it, really, that he disliked about his own son? Tom was such a lovely boy growing up and I'd seen another side to Ellis the last couple of days. In fact, he reminded me at times of Tom. I looked across at Ellis, took in his thick hair, his nose in profile.

The mad flurry of thoughts that came so quickly made me dizzy.

One after the other and barely making any sense. Until they began to join up and then, the resulting possibility nearly knocked me off my feet.

50

Nottinghamshire Police

'Will you be interviewing both of us together?' Bridget Wilson's voice was tense. Hesitant.

'We'll need to speak to you separately,' Irma said briskly. 'Shouldn't take too long. Mr Billinghurst first, please.'

Tom and Bridget exchanged glances, then she took a seat in reception while he followed the detectives through to Interview Room 3, a slightly larger than usual space that the team jokingly called 'the parlour' on account of the softer chairs and the yucca plant in the corner that broke up the scuffed wall-to-wall magnolia paint.

Tyra ran through the necessaries. '... and we'll be both voice-recording and video-recording the interview. Do you understand?'

'Yes,' Tom said.

She pressed some buttons and then nodded to Irma that the set-up was ready.

'Mr Billinghurst, can you tell us your whereabouts yesterday afternoon?'

'I was at home. As you discovered when you visited the house.'

'Of course. But did you go out at all before we called to tell you about Miss McKinty's death?'

'I popped out briefly. I wasn't gone long,' he said, pulling at the neck of his polo shirt.

Irma nodded. 'So let's talk specifics. What time did you leave the house and where precisely did you go?'

He thought for a moment. 'Honestly, I didn't notice the time when I left. I'd say it would've been about four o'clock. I got back about an hour before you lot came to the door.'

Tyra picked up a pencil and twirled it between her fingers. 'And where exactly did you go, sir? From leaving the house?'

'I'd been to the gym late morning and I had to go back again to pick up something I'd left behind.'

'Which gym is that?'

'Bannatyne Health Club on Briar Lane.'

Tyra made a note. 'Where did you go when you left there?'

'Straight home. I took the long way back.'

'The long way meaning where, exactly?'

'Around the area.'

'To local woodland?'

'No ... just around! I don't know, Blidworth, the surrounding area. It was a pleasant day, too nice to be cooped up in the house. It's a long time since I've had the freedom to drive, and I'm getting my confidence back after being out of it so long. I didn't go far.'

'So you *were* near Blidworth Woods?'

Tom frowned. 'I suppose so – in the vicinity, anyway. Blidworth is very close to Ravenshead, don't forget.' He hesitated. 'I want to make it perfectly clear, I didn't see Coral McKinty. I didn't see anyone I knew.'

'I see,' Irma murmured. 'Did it not occur to you yesterday to mention the fact that you'd been "in the vicinity" of the very woods we found Coral's body?'

'No. I mean ... why would it? I didn't know exactly where Coral had been knocked over. The woods are vast.' Tom ran his hand through his hair as his eyes darted between the two detectives. 'You drive around here and you sort of pass through places.

Ravenshead, Blidworth, Rainworth. You don't necessarily register exactly where you are.'

'It's reasonable to assume that if you'd heard about someone you knew well having an accident there, you might have given it a thought,' Tyra remarked.

'Well, I didn't,' Tom said firmly. 'I've got a lot on my mind right now.'

'Such as?'

He glared at her. 'Such as personal stuff that's nothing to do with you and nothing at all to do with Coral McKinty's death.'

Irma picked up a piece of paper, her eyes skimming over it.

'You were released from prison very recently. I can imagine there's an awful lot to sort out, particularly as you got married when you were inside. All change.'

'Do I need a solicitor?' Tom narrowed his eyes. 'Because I'm not sure I like your tone.'

'This is an entirely voluntary interview, sir,' Tyra replied smoothly. 'You're free to leave at any point.'

'It would look bad if I did, though,' Tom said curtly. 'You lot need little excuse.'

Irma regarded him with interest. This was a very different person to the polite, concerned young man she'd interviewed with Marcus all those years ago. It was only to be expected, but his opinion of the police had clearly soured during his time in prison. She'd seen it many times before: a first offender landing a lengthy sentence and getting a good education from the seasoned lags inside. Sometimes they only picked up the attitude. Other times it was a more sinister set of skills on how to evade police detection.

'We understand Coral McKinty went to the same school as yourself and Jesse Wilson,' she stated. 'You must have known her well.'

'I wouldn't say that.' Tom shrugged. 'She was a mate, sure. There was a group of us that hung around regularly. She was much closer to Jesse than me, obviously.'

'I'd imagine you might have found Coral was a little unfriendly towards you when you got out of prison,' Tyra suggested. 'You moving in with her son's grandma, I mean. The fact that you were responsible for her partner's death and also the boy never knowing his father.'

'And I paid the price for that,' Tom retaliated, his cheeks reddening. 'Ten long years for a single punch to defend myself from a knife attack.'

'A penknife,' Tyra murmured under her breath, earning herself a piercing glare from Tom.

'I suppose Coral might not have looked at it like that.' Irma's pleasant smile didn't quite reach her eyes. 'From her point of view, she'd been left without the support of her partner and forced to bring up their child alone.'

'Don't you think I know that?' The muscle in Tom's jaw flexed as he tried to control his temper. 'What exactly are you trying to say? I didn't agree to come here for you to put me through a second trial.'

He was agitated and it hadn't taken long. Irma wanted to keep pushing.

'Course not, let's move on.' She glanced at the sheet in front of her. 'Tell us about Ellis.'

Tom sniffed. 'He's Jesse's son, but you already know that.'

'How did he react when you moved into the house with your new wife … his grandma?' Tyra asked bluntly.

'Like you'd expect any kid to react.' Tom shrugged. 'He wasn't impressed and I tried to break the ice, but then you can't get much out of them at that age. They're only interested in gaming and pizza.'

'Would you say there were heated exchanges?' Irma pursed her lips. 'Perhaps a few fireworks between the two of you?'

'Yes,' Tom said honestly. 'But like I'd already said to Brid … Bridget, we have to give it time. He'll come round eventually, though he's had a massive setback now and that's not going to help.'

'*Another* massive setback,' Irma remarked. 'Lost his father and now his mum.'

'Yes.'

'What did Coral think to you spending time with Ellis at the house?' Tyra asked, sitting back in her seat. 'Did she object?'

'Yes. I think she and Bridget had words about it.'

'What kind of words?' Tyra pushed.

'You know, Coral saying that she wouldn't let him come around any more and Bridget telling her that wasn't going to happen.'

'Bridget must have got quite annoyed about it,' Tyra suggested. 'Coral telling her what to do.'

'Course.' Tom nodded. 'Ellis is all Bridget has left of Jesse, so it's a natural reaction.'

'Perhaps you also felt angry with Coral,' Irma said. 'Her being awkward must've scuppered your romantic new start with Ellis's gran.'

Tom laughed bitterly. 'Maybe I did, but I didn't hurt Coral, if that's what you're getting at.'

'Nobody is suggesting that, Mr Billinghurst,' Irma said solemnly. 'We're trying to understand where the tensions lay in the family. You marrying your victim's mother, it's quite an unusual situation by anyone's standards, I'm sure you'd agree. Probably a shock for everyone, particularly with the recent press interest.'

'I suppose so,' Tom sighed. 'But it's nothing to do with anyone else. All that counts is that it's what me and Bridget want. We knew there would be family resistance to start with.'

'Coral, Ellis ... who else has taken it badly?' Tyra asked.

Tom blew out air. 'My mother, Jill. She's been worse than any of them.'

Irma sat forward, interested. 'In what way?'

'Oh, you know, generally kicking off. Making up silly stories in her head about what might go wrong.' He grinned. 'Being a mum.'

Irma did not return the grin. 'What's your mother's relationship with Bridget like?'

'They haven't got a relationship,' Tom replied curtly. 'They used to be best friends, but that ended when Jesse died.'

'Did you tell your parents you were getting married in prison?' Tyra asked suddenly.

He shifted in his seat, looked at his hands. 'No. We thought it would be best to just do it. I knew what Mum's reaction would be, and she'd have tried to stop it.'

'And your father?'

'He doesn't care. He's never been interested in my life.' Irma noted the unmistakable tang of bitterness that was laced through his words.

'Did your parents have much contact with Coral when you were in prison?' Tyra broke the brief silence.

Tom shook his head. 'None. They knew her from when we all used to hang around together. I'd sometimes have people round to the house and Coral was one of them. My dad would ferry us around if he was in the right mood, but that was it. They didn't really *know* her. Not like they knew Jesse.'

Irma cleared her throat. 'And the boy, Ellis? What will happen to him now his mother has died?'

'He'll live with us, of course,' Tom said. 'We're his family now and we'll do fine once we get all this out of the way.' He indicated the detectives, the room they were in. 'He's a good lad. Been through a lot.'

'Indeed,' Irma said slowly, noticing the unexpected pride in his face. Some men might resent the boy's presence, having to take him in at this crucial stage in a new relationship. But despite Ellis's anger towards him for what had happened to his father, it struck Irma that Tom looked as though he was looking forward to having him around.

Rather curious, really.

51

Tyra repeated the interview legalities, introducing herself and Irma again. 'We have some questions about your relationship with Coral and the family, if that's OK, Mrs Wil … Billinghurst,' she said, correcting herself at the last moment.

'Bridget is fine.'

'Thank you. We understand you and Coral were quite close, is that right?'

'Well, she was the mother of my grandson, so yes,' Bridget said, a little tightly. 'I'd like to think that if she were here now, she'd tell you I'd been a big support to her after Jesse's death.'

'You mean emotional support?' Irma said.

Bridget smiled. 'I mean emotional, financial, practical. She told me more than once that she didn't know what she'd have done without me.'

'I see,' Irma said. 'Would you say you've helped raise Ellis? Sort of taken Jesse's place as a parent figure, in a way?'

'Absolutely,' Bridget said without hesitation.

Irma got the distinct impression that Bridget Wilson – Billinghurst – was a determined, independent woman. She knew about her charity work, the way she'd fought for Jesse's image after his death. She admired her for that. And yet she sensed an edge of steel that she'd seen before in people who would do almost anything to get what they wanted. Sometimes not constraining themselves within legal boundaries.

'What was Tom's relationship with Coral?' Tyra asked.

Bridget frowned. 'Tom didn't have a relationship with Coral.'

'Maybe not after Jesse's death, but the two of them used to be in the same friendship circle, I understand?'

'That was years ago, when they were still kids.' Bridget sniffed.

'Perhaps he tried to get a little closer to her when he came out of prison?' Tyra suggested.

'Tom didn't like Coral, OK?' Bridget snapped, and then seemed to realise that what she'd said didn't sound good in light of what had happened. 'They didn't get on, for obvious reasons.'

'Mr Billinghurst told us he'd felt resentment from both Coral and Ellis,' Irma added. 'I suppose it might have made the atmosphere at home quite unpleasant.'

'We expected all that,' Bridget said in an off-hand manner. 'That's why we got married in prison, to force them all to deal with it.'

'Including Jill Billinghurst?' Tyra asked.

'Especially her.' Bridget wrinkled her nose. 'Interfering, bitter woman. It was my son who died, yet you'd think she was the one doing all the grieving.'

'Grieving the loss of her son for ten years in prison, I'd imagine,' Tyra said. 'It's a long sentence.'

'Yes, but now he's out. He gets a new life while Jesse is still six feet under in the cold earth. I'll never get *my* son back.' It was a startling moment, and silence cloaked the room before Bridget spoke again. 'That's what Jill needs to realise.'

'If you don't mind me saying so, you seem quite … bitter about Jill Billinghurst,' Tyra said softly.

'The woman annoys me, that's all. She's so controlling. Tom is nearly thirty years old and she still wants to call the shots in his life. She thinks I'm out to destroy him, use him for my own ends. You know, older woman, younger man kind of thing.'

'Mr Billinghurst told us he popped out on the afternoon Coral died,' Irma said. 'Can you tell us what time he left and where he said he'd been?'

There was a clear hesitation from Bridget. 'I can't really remember the timing of it; I was busy in the house and I'd been out and about myself.'

'He went back to the gym to pick up something he'd forgotten?' Tyra prompted.

'That's what he said, yes.'

'We've checked and the gym is about a ten-minute drive each way,' Tyra said. 'And yet Tom was out of the house quite a bit longer than that.'

'I didn't really give it much thought. As I said, I was busy.'

'After our visit, though, you must have talked about where he'd been?'

Bridget pulled a face. 'We were reeling from the news that Coral had died, and my priority was Ellis. Tom said he went to the gym and that was good enough for me.'

Irma sensed a reluctance on Bridget's part to talk about her husband's alibi. She said, 'Ellis and Tom's relationship. How would you describe it?'

Bridget rolled her eyes. 'Fraught, tense. Tom has tried to make inroads with Ellis, but he's been difficult. Like we expected.'

'Ellis will live with you and Tom now Coral has passed away?' Tyra asked.

Bridget nodded. 'Tom's been brilliant with him, never raised his voice or got annoyed. He seems to have a real affection for him.'

'That's unusual. I expect most men would find Ellis's anger towards them a little disconcerting.' Irma's interest was piqued again.

'Not Tom,' Bridget said, looking pleased with herself. 'He's all for us being a little family unit. He said it's what he's always dreamed of having.'

52

Tom

When they left the police station, Tom turned to Bridget.

'We'll pick Ellis up and then I'll drop you both off at home. I'm going back to see my mum.'

'What?' Bridget's eyes burned into his. 'Tom, this is no time to go running back to your mother's apron strings. We need to discuss everything the police asked us.'

His hands tightened on the steering wheel and he stared straight ahead without speaking. She was right, of course, in an ideal world he should be at home with his wife and with Ellis, who had lost his mum. But this was not an ideal world and he had to sort things out with his own mother. The truth he'd known he must one day tell her had been a glimmering light in the distance for years, but now it shone in his face like a powerful spotlight. It would not wait a day longer.

'The police think I'm good for Coral's death,' he murmured, his chest pounding.

'Did they say that?'

'Not in so many words, but I could tell. The way they spoke to me, looked at each other.'

'It's your trip to the "gym" that's screwed you.' Bridget hooked her fingers around the word. 'That's what happens when you lie.

And if you didn't go to the gym, where did you go? Are you ready to tell me the truth yet? Because I'm waiting and I'm fast losing patience.'

That word again. People all wanted the truth from him, but the irony was that once they had it, they wished they'd never got it.

This feeling – like his insides had liquidated, his brain unable to think straight – was pure panic. He felt incapable of facing the prospect of another ten years in prison. He'd rather die.

It was a real possibility. The police were sniffing around; they already suspected that Coral's death was not the simple accident it had first appeared to be. And Bridget was right about the trip to the gym. When the police checked – and he knew they would – they'd realise immediately that he'd been lying and would come and arrest him. The gym was kitted out with security cameras; it would be obvious he hadn't been there again in the afternoon.

He'd been somewhere else instead. He'd been to Coral's house.

If the police found out the truth, it would lead them straight to him as the main suspect in Coral's death, and that was why he had to speak to his mum right now.

He didn't know how much time he had before they came for him, but he suspected it wouldn't be long.

Jill's face floated into his head wearing that same expression he'd seen a thousand times before. It said, *Son, I want to believe you're telling the truth. I want to believe you are a good person.*

Except right now he felt like the worst person in the whole world, and soon everyone else was going to know it too.

53

Audrey

She watched Tom and Bridget pull up outside the house. Bridget went to the door and Ellis came out. Then they all drove away again. Tom didn't get out of the car at all.

Audrey waited five minutes, then knocked at the front door. Jill took a few minutes to answer. Her cheeks looked puffy and damp and she seemed out of sorts.

Jill's face hardened when she saw her.

'Hello, Jill,' Audrey said.

'Why did you disappear from the shop without saying a word?' she replied stiffly.

Audrey stood on the doorstep. 'I wasn't ready to tell you there and then. The shock of you walking in like that, seeing Bridget there … I panicked. It felt like fight or flight, and to my shame, I chose the latter. Sometimes you don't know what your reaction is going to be until you're under big pressure.'

'You might've said *something*. I was worried about what had happened to you as well as being put out, having to close the shop up.'

Audrey lowered her eyes. 'You were already so worried about Bridget ruining Tom, I honestly thought it would send you over the edge if I told you the truth. I drove out of town for a while at first, to get my head around things. Can I come in?'

Wordlessly, Jill stepped aside to allow Audrey to move inside. They went into the living room.

'I'm sorry, Jill. I didn't mean—'

'I'm not interested in empty apologies!' Jill's voice rose in alarm. 'Tell me about you and Bridget!'

Audrey took a deep breath. 'It's not what you think. We're not friends. She came to the shop because she thought I was having an affair with Robert.'

Jill watched her steadily. 'I came to your house looking for you and I saw his striped scarf on the side in the kitchen. *Are* you having an affair with Robert?'

'No! That would be laughable if things weren't so serious.' Audrey sighed and perched on the sofa. 'Look, I need to explain everything for it to make sense. From the beginning.'

'Do you know Coral is dead?'

'Yes. Look, Jill, I'm begging you, let me speak first.' Audrey patted the sofa cushion next to her. Jill sat down in the chair. 'I can see you're low, but there are some things I need to tell you. Things I should have told you years ago and I'm sorry now that I didn't. But I had my reasons.'

Jill looked at her but didn't respond. She seemed to be holding her breath and Audrey wondered if she was strong enough to do this, but it was too late to stop now. The truth had to come out.

'I don't know what happened to Coral. I don't know how she died. But I have something to tell you, and when I've finished, I'm going directly to the police to tell them too.'

Jill's eyes widened, but still she remained silent.

'These past few years, I've got to know Coral well. I didn't recognise her at first. We got talking in the shop and I treated her like another customer. But then of course, I quickly realised who she was and, over time, we forged a bit of a friendship, mainly me being a sounding board for her rather turbulent life. Anyway, once I did know, there never seemed to be a good time to tell you, because you were so tied up with Tom being in prison.'

'Don't tell me you think Tom had something to do with that girl's death, because I won't believe you.' Jill's voice rose in panic. 'And if you're in cahoots with Bridget Wilson too, then you should have the guts to tell me to my face.'

Audrey placed her hand on her friend's arm. 'Jill, come on now. I know you don't really think that of me. Please, let me finish. What I have to say is very important. About a year ago, Coral told me about someone who loomed large in her life. I was shocked, because all the time I'd known her, she'd never mentioned anyone … a man. I'd misunderstood, though. I'd assumed this man was a romantic attachment, but it was the opposite. She hated him.'

Jill frowned. 'So what was the problem?'

Audrey felt irritation swell in her chest. 'The problem was, the man she hated, who was such a presence in her life … he was Ellis's father.'

Jill's forehead wrinkled as she wrestled with this information that didn't match up to the facts she'd internalised. 'But *Jesse* was Ellis's father.'

Audrey reached for her hand, held it tight in her own. 'No, he wasn't.'

'I don't want to hear it.' Jill snatched her hand away and stood up, her face reddening. 'Please leave now, Audrey.'

'Jill, no! I haven't finished. I have to tell you—'

She covered her ears with her hands and raised her voice. 'I don't want to know. Do you hear me? Go! I want you to go.' She turned and ran out of the room.

Audrey called after her, but she already heard Jill's feet hammering on the stairs. Then the bathroom door slammed shut.

She took the sealed envelope with Jill's name on it from her handbag and propped it up on the mantelpiece. She prayed when her friend opened it and read the shattering contents, she would find it in her heart to forgive her for the terrible secret she'd kept from her.

54

Jill

The front door opened and slammed closed again. From the front bedroom window, I watched Audrey scuttle away from the house, her coat done up, head down.

My insides cramped. I'd thought I knew Audrey as well as I knew myself. I would have wagered this very house against the chance she'd ever betray me. Now I knew she'd been in league all this time not with Bridget, but with Coral.

I watched until she reached the bend in the road and disappeared from sight. I went back downstairs, poured a glass of water and took it through to the living room. The instant I stepped through the door, I saw it. A long white envelope with *JILL* written on it in thick black letters, large enough to read from across the room.

I put my glass down on the coffee table and picked up the envelope, turning it over in my hands. The flap was sealed and I felt a substantial fold of paper inside, more than one sheet.

I didn't want to hear what she had to tell me because I already knew. I knew what she was going to say about Ellis's father and the life-changing implications of that ... I couldn't bear it.

I jumped at a sudden noise in the hall – the front door opening. I rushed to the window and saw the silver car on the drive.

'Tom!'

He stood in the doorway and slid the door key into his pocket. 'I had to come back to speak to you, Mum. I can't go on like this, so many things not being said.' He glanced at the envelope in my hand. 'What's that?'

'Audrey was here. She left me this envelope. I ran upstairs because I didn't want to hear the rubbish she was spouting.' But I knew my words meant nothing. I felt the truth towering over us as each second passed.

Two red spots appeared on his cheeks. 'Rubbish about what?' he whispered.

I hesitated. Then, sick of all the pretence, I wailed, 'About who Ellis's father is! She was going to tell me something I don't want to hear it. Do you understand?' I looked at him meaningfully. 'I don't want to know, from you or her. I can't take it, I—'

'Oh, Mum.' He stepped forward and wrapped his arms around me. I sobbed into his warm chest, crushing the sealed envelope between us.

I'd waited so long to have my boy back again. My affectionate, loyal son. I didn't care about Audrey and her petty little secrets.

'Let's sit down, Mum. It's time for us to talk.'

I pulled away. 'No.'

'It's long overdue,' Tom said carefully. 'And there are things you should know. Things I should have told you way before now.' He sat down, but I stayed standing. 'Let me have the envelope, and then we'll talk.'

With shaking hands, I held it up. 'I know already, Tom. I know what I'm going to find when I open this.'

'Give that to me, Mum,' he said steadily, his eyes trained on the envelope that held the awful reality I had no choice now but to face. 'Don't open it.'

'Why? Because it's going to tell me *you're* Ellis's father, not Jesse?' I tore at the seal.

'Don't do this until we've talked about it,' Tom yelped, jumping up from his seat.

'What have you done?' I yelled as I backed away. 'Have you given away my grandson? Is it going to tell me that Ellis is *my* boy, not Bridget's? He heard you and Coral arguing about the secret Jesse told you that night.'

I gripped the back of a dining chair for support. For the first time in twenty-eight years, I saw what Robert had been telling me all this time. That Tom, my beloved son whom I'd defended, fought for and believed above everyone else, was actually a liar and a cheat and, to cover up his terrible deed, had deprived me of knowing my grandson for the first nine years of his life.

I gulped in air and broke into pieces from the inside out.

'Mum, please. Let me explain.' He walked towards me and I backed towards the door, still clutching the envelope. 'I'll tell you everything myself, from the beginning. You don't want to find out from a piece of paper.'

For a couple of seconds, I actually thought about it. I yearned to sit down with my son, the two of us, to talk honestly. It was all I'd wanted to do since his release from prison, but I'd been so naïve. He'd already been lying to me for years.

I bolted for the downstairs cloakroom. He moved fast behind me, gaining ground, and then there was a crack and he yelled out in pain. Maybe he'd collided with a chair or the table in his rush to get to me, but I didn't stop to see if he was OK like the old Jill would have done. I bashed the cloakroom door open and slammed it shut behind me, snapping on the light and locking the door. Moments later, he banged on the door like a madman.

'Mum, what the hell's got into you? Open this door.' His fist hammered so hard I feared the wood might splinter. 'Open it now!'

I hadn't got much time. With my heart banging too fast and too hard, I ripped open the envelope and pulled out the folded sheets within. The banging stopped.

'This is your last chance to save yourself the heartache, Mum. Your last chance to let me explain everything. We can sit down together, you and me … what do you say?'

'I've listened to your lies too long, Tom,' I cried out.

I felt sick and dizzy, but I unfolded the sheets.

I stared at the letter in front of me. It was from some sort of laboratory, addressed to Coral McKinty, and the words leapt off the page at me:

We have analysed the DNA samples you submitted and the results are a match. Please see below for further details of the …

Like a star popping out in the night sky, the shining truth I'd suspected and dreaded in equal measure was now facing me. It was the only thing amid all the lies, deceit and confusion that made absolute sense.

'Mum?' I heard Tom call hoarsely from the other side of the door. 'Are you OK?'

I blinked rapidly to clear my eyes of the tears welling there. Nine years. Nine long years I'd had a precious grandson and Bridget Wilson had filled my role. She'd loved and cared for Ellis, seen his first smile, watched him crawl and walk and run. These were *my* gifts that were now lost forever.

'Mum! Open the door.'

I gathered myself and refocused on the letter.

Please see below for further details of likely DNA relationship between the two samples: Tom Billinghurst and Ellis McKinty.

Close family members, possibly siblings.

I frowned. *Close family members, possibly siblings*? I was expecting to see 'father and son'. I tried to make sense of the wording.

'Mum?' All the urgency and anger had gone from Tom's voice. 'Open the door. Please.'

I read the results again, mouthing the words silently.

… likely DNA relationship between the two samples:
Close family members, possibly siblings.

I slumped like a lead weight, sinking down into the floor. I twisted around and unlocked the door. A moment later, Tom stood in front of me, his face wretched and sagging.

'Ellis is my half-brother, Mum. That's what I've tried to protect you from all these years.'

I looked up. The shape of my son was blurred and vague. I blinked and tears rolled down my cheeks, clearing my vision.

Tom crouched down in front of me and took my hands. His fingers were warm and reassuring as he squeezed them gently.

'It was Dad who betrayed you,' he said. 'It's Dad who's been lying through his teeth all this time. Not me. Dad is Ellis's father.'

55

Tom

'Remember all those times Dad offered to pick us up late from our nights out? We couldn't quite believe he was being so helpful?' Jill stayed tight-lipped and silent. 'Coral told me she had sex with him twice.'

A small sound of disbelief escaped Jill's lips. He had no choice but to carry on now, he had to say the terrible things.

'She was drunk both times. He didn't force her; she was a willing partner. To her it was something that happened a couple of times at the end of the night and she knew Dad really well because ...'

'Go on,' Jill whispered.

'She'd been going to him for counselling sessions. Through college. She said that Dad was really kind to her and that they'd chat on the way home. She said he made her feel safe, ironically.' Tom hesitated. 'It's hard to explain but all my mates really liked Dad. He was ... so different with them than he was with me. I used to wonder what was so wrong with me that he wasn't like that at home. I know you probably can't imagine it, Mum, but he was.'

'I've seen it with my own eyes,' Jill said softly. 'He's like that with Ellis, too.'

Tom felt a surge of inadequacy, but he battled it back. He had to get this all out. It might be his only chance if the police came for him.

'Anyway, she forgot to take her pill she said and fell pregnant. She was pretty certain the baby was Dad's because she and Jesse had been going through a rocky patch for a while and they hadn't slept together.' He paused for a moment before continuing. It was beyond weird to be discussing all this with her. 'She said she felt like Jesse didn't care about her any more, and there had even been rumours he'd been seeing other girls. When she found out she was pregnant, she seriously considered not going through with it.'

'Did she tell Robert?'

'Yes. And he told her to get rid of the baby. Coral said it was like he'd flipped a switch and all the compassion and kindness disappeared in an instant.'

They looked at each other. They both knew only too well that this side of Robert existed even though he didn't show it to the world.

'Dad told her he wouldn't see her for counselling and the lifts home were done. He completely cut her off. Then Jesse died and Bridget immediately became territorial about the baby, promised Coral she'd look after both her and the baby. So Coral said nothing to me or to Bridget and decided instead to pass the baby off as Jesse's.'

Jill frowned, the cogs turning in her head as she struggled to process the awful facts. 'So, Jesse never knew about Robert?'

'That's the thing. On the morning of the day Jesse died, Coral found texts on Jesse's phone. He'd been secretly seeing another girl. They had a terrible argument and Coral lost her temper, threw the truth of what she'd done with Dad at him to hurt him. That's why Jesse wanted us to go out that night. To tell me about Dad and Coral.'

Jill shook her head, unable to comprehend it. 'She actually told Jesse that Robert was the baby's father?'

'Yep. Even though she wasn't a hundred per cent sure, she said it in the heat of the argument. Jesse was excited about the baby and she wanted to really hurt him after finding out he'd been unfaithful.'

'She didn't have DNA proof back then?'

Tom shook his head. 'That didn't happen until years later. When Jesse died she was terrified of the truth coming out and Bridget disowning her and the baby. But needing to know the truth tortured her and when Ellis was five, she had his DNA analysed. The result in itself didn't mean anything, but she kept it for a reason.'

Jill frowned. 'She was waiting until you got out of prison.'

Tom nodded. 'She never saw Dad again and she didn't want anything to do with him, either. She had Bridget to help her financially. But as Ellis got older, Bridget became more and more controlling, and Coral got to the stage where she wanted out.'

'Bridget truly believed Ellis was Jesse's son and she was his blood grandparent,' Jill whispered, and Tom saw the realisation dawning on her face that she wasn't the only person who'd been terribly betrayed. 'And why wouldn't she?'

'Jesse told Coral that day he was going to tell me what Dad had done and he was going to punish Robert, ruin him. Coral never got a chance to speak to me before I was arrested for Jesse's manslaughter. But when Ellis was five, she wrote to me in prison and said that if I had a DNA test done too when I got out of prison, it would prove we had the same father and I was Ellis's half-brother. It would be her passport to getting rid of Bridget. But there was another consideration. She didn't want to let her nice life go, the life Bridget supported. So, together with Audrey, who she'd befriended at the shop, she came up with a plan. She realised that once she had the DNA evidence that Ellis was Robert's son, she had the ability to make Dad pay – literally.'

His mother frowned. 'Pay maintenance for Ellis, you mean?'

Tom laughed sadly. 'Oh, she wanted a lot more than that. Between them, she and Audrey cooked up a plan to blackmail Dad. Maintenance payments would be peanuts, but if Dad was faced with losing his marriage, his job, his standing in the local community, he might be persuaded to sell the house and pay her a good lump sum for her silence.'

Jill's mouth fell open. 'He asked me to sign something … I didn't read it. Something to do with the mortgage.'

Tom shook his head. 'Don't worry about that now, Mum. We'll have to sort everything out. The first thing is to get the truth out there.'

'Audrey knew, you knew,' Jill said in a small voice. 'The people I loved the most.'

'I had to make a decision in prison. If I'd told you on one of your visits it would have nearly killed you, sitting there in that awful visitors' hall. You were so low, so desperate for us to be a family again. You, me and Dad. It was an easy decision for me, it had to wait until I was released.'

'And Bridget?'

'I'm going to speak to Bridget when I leave here,' he said with a weary sigh.

'Hang on a minute.' Jill raised a finger as a thought occurred to her. 'You married Bridget knowing that Ellis was probably your half-brother.'

'Yes,' Tom said quietly.

'Did you marry her so you'd be close to him?'

He felt sad to see the hope in his mother's eyes. Hope that he'd reveal he didn't have feelings for Bridget after all.

'No, Mum. I married Brid because I love her. But I'd been desperate to keep on good terms with her because of Ellis. I wrote so many letters during that first year. In one of them, at my lowest point, I told her the truth about Dad being Ellis's father. But she destroyed that letter and all the others without reading them. So the truth never came to light. Then when we did the restorative justice programme together, we got closer and I fell in love with her. I married her for the right reasons.'

'I see,' Jill said softly. Then, 'I'm glad about that. I'd hate to think you'd been so cold and calculating. That's not the way I raised you.'

Tom nodded. 'Apart from that one letter, Coral never made contact with me again in prison and I had to put up with that. It got easier as time went on to push the truth about Ellis to the back of my mind, but then when my release date got closer, it loomed large again.'

'And once you did get out?'

'I spoke to Coral straight away. I'd had a DNA test done in prison as part of the restorative justice programme. They fund certain procedures if they think it will help an inmate's mental health and privately, I'd told the programme's counsellor I had doubts about my own father. I didn't know Coral was involved with Audrey and that she'd come up with a scam to get money out of Dad. When I saw she'd given you a sealed letter today, I knew it would be the truth about the DNA match showing that me and Ellis shared the same father. I never wanted you to find out that way.'

'But still, you've never said a word until now. Until Coral was dead.'

'It killed me to see you hating Bridget so much when you were living with the enemy under this roof all that time. But I struggled exactly how to do it. I knew so many people would be shattered by the truth: you, Bridget, Ellis … the list goes on.'

'And Coral?' Jill said carefully. 'Do you know exactly what happened to her?'

He looked her in the eyes. 'No. I don't know what happened, Mum, but once I've spoken to Bridget, I have to tell the police the truth about Dad.'

56

Bridget

'There's something I have to tell you. Something I should have told you a long time ago,' Tom said.

'You're scaring me now.' I swallowed, my wet fingers fluttering to my throat. 'What is it?'

My shoulders and neck had been tight and painful when Tom had dropped Ellis and I back at the house after visiting the police station. Ellis had gone to his room to catch up on sleep and Tom had insisted on going back to see his mother alone. I'd got in the hot tub to ease the tension and dissipate the fury I felt towards Tom for lying to me about the gym and then sloping off to see Jill when we badly needed his support here.

He had returned from his mother's house looking like a beaten man, and when I refused to go back inside the house and talk to him, he'd got in the tub with me.

'We should have had this conversation before now but I didn't know how, Brid.'

He touched my arm. His eyes looked haunted in the soft light reflecting off the water. The smell of chlorine seemed overpowering all of a sudden and I struggled to breathe. On some level I felt – I *knew* – he was going to tell me something profound.

I almost told him to stop, to say nothing, but I didn't speak or move. I sat there, the sound of the water rushing in my ears, and stared at him. Silently pleading with him not to end my world.

'I love you Bridget,' he said sadly. 'I've loved you for a long time and it's because of that – and everything that's happened – that I have to tell you the truth about the night Jesse died. I can't keep quiet about it any longer, because it's the gateway to the truth about everything else.'

Everything else?

'Oh no, no …' I whimpered, covering my face with my hands.

My entire body ached. Was my worst fear about to be realised? What if I loved a man who had killed Jesse on purpose? Who had intended knocking him unconscious with that punch, fully aware it might finish him?

He pulled gently at my hands, forcing me to look at him.

The water frothed and bubbled all around us, the firm underwater jets shooting into the bottom of my back. What usually felt relaxing pained me now, my entire body feeling raw. Exposed.

The lights set around the edge of the tub danced innocuously through their repeating spectrum under the dark sky. The colours merged into one swirling mess in front of my swimming eyes.

Tom's face looked pale and damp as he began. 'As you know, that night we had a drink in the Mayflower bar first. We were chatting normally about sport, gaming, all the usual stuff, but I could tell there was something bothering Jesse. It's hard to explain, he wasn't his usual self. Then later, he was drinking more than usual, shots with his pints, but there was something else, too.' He pressed his lips together and frowned, reaching for the words that would better articulate what he meant. 'He was naturally a chatty guy, but when we got to the club, he hardly drew breath. He sounded almost … I don't know, *manic*, somehow. Like he was regurgitating all the words he knew so there was no space to think at all.'

He'd told me this before but my muscles felt tight as a drum, braced for the shock that might be coming.

'It was quiet in Movers, so we didn't have to queue. When we got in, we landed a booth, which was unusual.' Tom seemed to slip into a world of his own momentarily, staring out over the garden as he remembered the details of that terrible night. 'That's when Jesse started drinking in earnest. He ditched the pints and switched to vodka plus the shots, which were all on two-for-one as it was midweek. I told him to slow down, reminded him I had a training session the next morning, and he called me a wuss. But I kept trying to pull him back because I saw whatever was up with him, the drink was making it worse.'

I opened my mouth and a strange noise came out, halfway between a cry and a wail.

Tom looked at me. 'I know this must be really painful for you, Brid, but you have to know.'

I focused on keeping my face from crumpling. I imagined the two of them sitting together in the nightclub, the music almost too loud to speak, so loud, you felt the bass beat reverberating off your face, your body. I'd been in Movers twice in my twenties with some of the other office cleaners when someone had a birthday, so I visualised the interior as it was back then.

I couldn't help wondering why Tom hadn't told me all this in the two years I'd been visiting him. We'd covered the night Jesse died in the restorative justice programme. He was supposed to recall everything, and yet he'd said nothing resembling this detail. He'd seemed so transparent, like a puppy dog, too innocent to lie to me. As an experienced older woman, I'd always thought I'd see through any deception, any lies.

He began speaking again. 'After about half an hour of what felt like Jesse drinking himself into oblivion, I shouted over the music for something to say, "How're things between you and Coral?" He screamed back, "Hey, thanks for asking, mate! Nice to know how much you care," and then, for want of a better word, he went ape – out of nowhere. It's the only way I can describe his bizarre behaviour.'

'What made it so bizarre?' Jesse had a crazy side, both Tom and I knew that, and I'd always loved him for it. It made him different. Quirky.

'He sprang up off his seat, ran to the dance floor and threw a few wild moves before coming back and draining his glass. He did that several times. I mean, I kind of realised that me mentioning Coral had flipped a switch somewhere in his head. I thought that was what must have been wrong with him all night, that maybe they'd had an argument and were splitting up or something.'

'But you said in court he got you thrown out of the club. So did he get worse?'

Tom nodded. 'He got himself another round of vodka and shots. He didn't even sit down; he brought them back to the booth and drank them all standing up. Then he stood there looking down at me, this expression of pure fury on his face. I said, "Chill out, will you, mate, what's up with you tonight?" And he started doing stupid kung fu moves, punching and kicking and getting pretty close to my face. I thought ignoring him was the best policy, and I made my mind up to leave after I'd finished my pint, but then the security guy came over. He told Jesse to sit down, and Jesse retaliated, calling him some pretty nasty names. The next thing I knew, this guy had hold of Jesse by the scruff of his jumper and had dragged him across the dance floor. I followed, trying to reason with him, but then another doorman grabbed me, the emergency exit doors flew open and we were both pushed out onto the street.'

I reached over and turned off the water jets. The garden around us fell deathly quiet, I hadn't realised how noisy the tub had been. I felt so hot now, like I was overheating. I wanted to climb out but I couldn't break Tom's flow. I had to hear this.

'Jesse was straight up on his feet, spoiling for a fight. Threatening what he'd do to the security staff when he got hold of them. He wanted to go back to the entrance and try to get admitted to the club again.'

'But you stopped him.'

'I tried, but he was like a man possessed. Then suddenly, he seemed to forget about it and turned his attention to me instead. He said, "You might as well know, me and Coral are splitting up." I said I was sorry, but part of me wasn't surprised. Even though Coral was pregnant, he'd messed her about a bit. He was always chatting up other women when we were out on our own.'

I shifted in the water. It was still uncomfortable for me to accept that Jesse had had that side to him. I didn't like being reminded of it. 'Then what happened?' I pressed, hoping Tom would move on.

'Well, he stared at me for a few moments and then he said, "You know she's pregnant, right?" I laughed and said, "Course I do!" I mean, she only had a few months to go; it was fairly obvious to anyone with eyesight.'

'And then?'

'Then he went ice cold on me. Within a couple of seconds he seemed sober as a judge, looking me straight in the eye. And then he said, "Funny, is it? You knowing all this time the baby isn't mine?"'

'What?' I whispered, feeling choked. 'Whose baby did he think it was?'

Tom held up a hand to signal for me to let him finish, but my head swirled dangerously. I felt sick to my stomach.

'That was my reaction, too. I said, "What? Don't be stupid, man. Course the baby's yours, Coral thinks the world of you!" I mean, he'd been so excited about being a dad, you know that yourself, Brid.'

'Tell me what he said next,' I muttered between clenched teeth. Underneath the water, my fingernails dug into my thighs. If I didn't get out of here soon, I was going to faint.

'Jesse started crying. He said, "She told me herself this morning. The baby isn't mine." So I said, "OK, so whose is it then?" trying to reason with him, 'cos he was clearly plastered, and that was when he said ...'

Tom pulled back a sob and I realised that all the time he'd been talking, in a tone that would suit a discussion about the weather, he'd been holding the emotion tightly in. Tears streamed down his face and a terrible feeling started in my guts. It gathered speed so quickly that within seconds it was inside my head.

Fear. Fear of what he was about to say. Was it ... was he about to tell me he was Ellis's father? I started to get out of the tub. I didn't want to hear it.

'Brid, please.' Tom grasped my arm.

'Let go of me!' I shook him off and stood up, and then he opened his mouth and the words coiled out of him like a slippery eel.

'Coral told Jesse that Robert was the baby's father. My dad is Ellis's dad, too. When he'd been giving her a lift home, they ... they'd had sex twice, in Dad's car and ... Ellis is my half-brother, Brid.'

The strength drained from my legs in an instant and I went down. I slipped under the water, gulping in mouthfuls of chlorine and chemicals, gasping and choking as I tried to drag in air.

I felt Tom's strong arms plunge down and grasp me under my arms, and after that, there was nothing. A deep, dark nothingness.

57

When I woke up, I was back inside the house, wrapped in a big soft towel and lying on the sofa in the kitchen. Tom crouched down, staring at me.

I sat up. I shivered. Then I remembered Ellis was upstairs. 'We can't talk about this now, not with Ellis here and—'

'It's OK. I've been up to check, and he's fast asleep,' Tom said. 'That lie you told me about going back to the gym … what was all that about?'

'I went to Coral's house to get the letter I knew she had that proved my sibling DNA link to Ellis. But Coral wasn't in.'

'Were you looking for it in Coral's bedroom when we picked up Ellis's things?' I'd been so certain he'd put something in his pocket despite his assurances that wasn't the case.

Tom nodded. 'In the paperwork, I found one of Dad's counselling appointment cards Coral had obviously saved. I slipped it in my pocket.'

I stared at him. He'd lied so convincingly, seemed affronted I'd accused him of such a thing.

'I needed the DNA letter to explain everything to you and my mum. To prove it. I didn't know at the time, but Audrey had a copy – Coral had given it to her to help her get money out of Dad. Audrey gave it to Mum today, although she hadn't opened it when I went round. She'd asked Audrey to leave because she thought it was going to confirm I was Ellis's father and she felt she couldn't handle it.'

'I thought that's what you were going to tell me, too,' I croaked, my throat burning from swallowing chlorinated water. I glanced nervously at the door to check Ellis wasn't there. 'In the end, though, the result is the same. Ellis isn't Jesse's son. He isn't my grandson.'

Where there had been warmth inside, there was nothing. I felt completely empty.

'I'm so sorry, Brid. I'm so sorry I didn't tell you before now, but I couldn't do it to you or Mum. It had to wait until I was a free man again and able to explain and face everyone's heartbreak. I did actually put it in a letter to you once when I was in the first year of my sentence. I was at a real low point and I convinced myself you should know. When you told me you'd shredded the letters, I was so relieved. Then years later, we fell in love and—'

'Is your love real, Tom?'

'What?'

'Is your love for me real or did you want to be close to your brother?'

'My love is as real as it comes.' He perched on the edge of the sofa and grasped my hands. 'I love you with all my heart, Brid. Please believe that. Can you forgive me for keeping the truth from you?'

It wasn't Tom's fault that Coral had slept with Robert. It wasn't his fault that Jesse wasn't Ellis's father. And it wasn't Ellis's fault that I wasn't his blood grandparent.

'I wish you'd told me before now but I can imagine how difficult that was. You were in a no-win situation, I get that.'

'And Ellis? How do you feel about him?'

I didn't have to think about my answer. 'You don't need a blood connection to love someone with all your heart. Ellis is my grandson and I'm his nan and nobody can take that away from us.'

'Can we do it, do you think, Brid?' Tom said softly, a tear trickling down his cheek. 'Can we make a little family, the three of us?'

I touched his face. 'We can try,' I whispered.

58

Nottinghamshire Police

After Tom Billinghurst's call, it didn't take Irma's team long to locate his father, Robert.

'He's at home,' an officer told her. She called Tyra over and five minutes later, they were leaving the station.

When they arrived, Jill Billinghurst stood at the front of the house, the door wide open.

'He's in the office. He only got back about half an hour ago, I've been holding in everything I want to say to him because I didn't want him to realise you were coming,' she said. 'I'll get him for you now.'

The officers waited outside. The usual signs of neighbourly interest started around them. An upstairs curtain twitching next door, someone suddenly deciding to sweep the path over the road.

'Robert?' Jill called out in the hallway. 'Some people here to see you.'

Irma and Tyra stood right by the open door. Close enough to hear Robert Billinghurst's annoyed response to his wife. 'I told you I'm busy. What is it?'

Jill turned and walked towards them. Irma stepped inside.

'Mr Billinghurst, I'm Detective Inspector Irma Barrington …' He babbled over her, but Irma raised her voice. 'And this is Detective Sergeant Tyra Barnes.'

'Jill, what the hell is this? What's going on?'

'You're Ellis McKinty's father, Robert,' Jill said smoothly. 'That's what's going on.'

'Now hang on a minute. That's not true, I—'

'Save your breath and tell the detectives at the station.' Jill turned her back on him. 'I'll pack up your things while you're gone. You won't be coming back here.'

'Jill! What's got into you?'

'We need you to get into the police car now, please, sir,' a young officer said from behind the detectives.

'Jill! I can explain everything. Just give me a chance, I'll—'

'Bye, Robert,' she said. 'Don't come back here. Ever.'

Irma looked at Tyra and raised an admiring eyebrow.

In a couple of hours' time, Robert Billinghurst sat opposite Irma and Tyra in an interview room.

'Tom killed her,' he said soon after Tyra had started the video recording. 'I didn't want to say in front of his mother but he mowed Coral down and then begged me to take the rap for it.'

Irma regarded him coolly. 'And what reason would your son have for killing Coral McKinty in cold blood like that, Mr Billinghurst?'

'He … he … I don't know! But he's been trouble all his life and I wouldn't be at all surprised if he hadn't got something to do with it. You've seen the kind of man he's turned into, killing his best friend and then marrying Jesse's mother, who's not far off twice his age. It's appalling.'

Irma ignored his comments and relayed to him the evidence they had so far. The DNA proof that Robert was Ellis's father, Tom's testimony that Coral had told him about the lifts home Robert provided but also that the sex had been consensual. 'And on top of all that, we expect to have your car in the pound for forensic examination before the day is out,' Irma added. 'What evidence will we find on that, I wonder?' It was clear Billinghurst was responsible for Coral's death but Irma had yet to find a solid motive.

Billinghurst's face crumpled. 'I swear, it was a complete accident,' he whispered. 'I never meant to hurt her. I wouldn't do that, not purposely.'

'Did it not occur to you to telephone for the police and an ambulance, Mr Billinghurst?' Tyra asked coldly. 'Did it not occur to you to stay with the victim, to offer some comfort to an obviously dying young woman?'

'The road, it was so quiet … there was no one around at all.' Robert covered his face with his hands for a moment. Then, 'I panicked. I had to get away. It was such a strong compulsion, there was no fighting it.'

The two detectives said nothing for a few seconds. The horror of Billinghurst intentionally leaving Coral McKinty dying in the road hung like a toxic fug in the air. Irma considered him carefully. The epitome of a decent, responsible citizen to look at, and yet underneath the facade he was a cruel, callous individual who had even tried to pin the blame for a young woman's death on his own son.

'Let's go back a few years,' Irma said. 'How many times did you have sex with Coral when you offered her a lift home?'

She saw him bridle slightly at her blunt question.

'Twice,' he said quietly. 'That was all it was, a quick fumble each time. We'd park up on a dirt track I knew near her home. I had a nice big car then, plenty of room if you see what I mean.'

Irma battled to keep her nose from wrinkling with distaste.

'She was eighteen years old and you were …' Tyra checked her notes, 'forty-two. Is that right?'

Billinghurst sniffed. 'Yes.'

Irma enunciated her words carefully. 'Twenty. Four. Years. That's one hell of an age gap from an eighteen-year-old girl's point of view, Mr Billinghurst. In fact, if Coral had been just three years younger, we'd be charging you with rape of a minor.'

'That's ridiculous,' Billinghurst snorted. 'That little slapper knew exactly what she was doing.'

'That's a very interesting response from a man who currently works with female students of a similar age to Coral McKinty back then.'

And also an interesting response from a man who found his son's new wife's age so distasteful, Irma thought privately.

'Now look here. This is all getting out of hand.' Billinghurst affected a *let's not overreact* tone. 'Coral McKinty was of a legal age to have sex, so please don't try pinning exaggerated charges to me.'

'But Coral was also one of your clients, wasn't she?' Tyra remarked. 'As her counsellor I think you'd agree that's totally unethical.'

Billinghurst's face turned puce and he clamped his mouth shut.

'Did you know Ellis McKinty was your son?' Irma changed tack.

'Yes, of course I did. She … Coral, told me when she found out. But she was sleeping with her boyfriend too, although she swore the baby was mine. I told her to get rid, that I wanted nothing to do with her or the brat and I thought that was the last of it. Then she began to blackmail me, to extort money.'

Irma glanced at Tyra. 'I'm sorry, who blackmailed you?'

'Coral McKinty! She approached me anonymously years ago, threatening to tell my wife and expose the lies to my employer.'

'And you paid her?'

'Of course I paid her! She only asked for two hundred pounds a month. Nothing really, so I played along. I let her think I didn't know it was her who was benefitting from the money. It was a cheap solution to keep her off my back.'

'How long did you pay her this money for?' Tyra asked.

'Five years. That's all she asked for. Never could quite work that one out.' Billinghurst's brow furrowed. 'Anyway, after five years I stopped the payments and I never heard another thing … until she came back for more a few months ago.'

'Coral got in contact with you for more money?' Irma clarified.

'Yes … well, actually, she got Audrey Denton to do her dirty work. That hag has never liked me, she's been waiting to take a chunk out of me since I married her best friend.'

'What happened between you and Audrey?' Irma said, steering him back on track.

'She contacted me at college a couple of months ago, said Coral had told her I was the father of the boy and that they had proof of that even without me agreeing to a DNA test.'

'Because your son and Ellis are brothers,' Irma clarified.

'Yes, that's right.' Billinghurst dropped his head briefly. 'I agreed for Audrey to come to the house to talk about it. I was hoping to appeal to her better side, to tell her it would destroy Jill if this were all to get out and that she should remember it was also Jill's money that she was demanding.'

'Your money was in a joint account?' Tyra asked.

'Most of it. Always good to have a little salted by your wife doesn't know about though, eh?' It occurred to Irma that the ghastly grin on Billinghurst's face seemed so disrespectful in the context of Coral's recent death. 'Go on,' she said, her voice steely.

'Jill was out for the afternoon and it would have been easy to say Audrey had called to see her if she'd returned early. The first thing she did was to deny that Coral had blackmailed me for five years. She said she'd have known about it, that Coral would have told her. I knew she was lying through her teeth, of course. Audrey told me that unless I wanted Coral revealing all to my family and to the college, which would mean losing my job, I had to double the monthly payments. I tried to get out of it but Audrey's savvy.'

'Tried to get out of it, how?' Tyra pushed him.

'Well, I'd paid a few months at the lower amount and it had nearly ruined us. I earn nothing like what I used to and Jill had noticed money was scarce. I told Audrey that if she continued to fleece me like this I'd have to speak to my wife about selling the house, which would destroy Jill. Do you know what she said?'

Tyra and Irma waited without commenting.

'She said it would be the best thing in the world for Jill. That hopefully she'd make a fresh start without me!' His face darkened. 'That girl didn't have to keep the child. She was the one who chose to have him so why should I be made to suffer?'

'Her name was Coral,' Tyra snapped. Her fingers were laced so tightly together, the knuckles looked fit to burst through her skin. Irma caught her eye and signalled for her to relax and breathe.

'And so did you agree to pay up?' Irma pressed him.

'I said I needed some time to think about it but I knew then that they'd never stop. Whatever I did, whatever I agreed to, they were going to ruin me. I knew that's what Audrey wanted.'

'Why did Audrey dislike you so much, do you think?' Irma had to stop herself adding, *apart from the fact you're a misogynistic, entitled pig, that is?*

Briefly, the arrogance disappeared from his face and he actually looked a little rueful. But it didn't last long.

'I don't know,' he said, offhand. 'Probably some innocent comment I made that she took the hump over. She's very over-sensitive, like most wom …'

His voice trailed off as he caught Tyra's murderous expression. Even Irma had a brief twinge of fear that her colleague might decide to lunge across the desk and throttle him.

'What comment?' Irma said.

'I don't know, probably some comment I made a few years ago when Tom was about halfway through his sentence. A little joke that she took the wrong way.' Irma raised her eyebrows in anticipation and he fidgeted in his chair. 'I'd said something about my wife being out of action and might Audrey be up to fulfilling some of her ... marital obligations.'

'By "out of action" I assume you mean her GP had diagnosed your wife with anxiety and depression and so you weren't having sex?' Tyra said bluntly.

'Heavens!' He grinned and looked at Irma. 'They don't train them in subtlety these days, do they?'

Finally, Audrey's duplicity was making sense. As Jill's lifelong friend, Irma had been trying to work out why Audrey had embarked on a persecution of Robert that also seemed to betray her friend. Now the pieces were slotting into place.

'Did you think about telling the police you were being black-mailed? Or at the very least, did you consider speaking to your wife?' Tyra said.

'That would've meant massive implications for me.' Billinghurst folded his arms and scowled. 'I was in a straitjacket. I had so much to lose whatever option I came up with.'

'Except one, it seems,' Irma remarked. 'If you got rid of Coral, then maybe Audrey would be warned off and the problem would go away.'

'I told you, I didn't mean to kill her. I was angry with her but even so, I tried to resolve things amicably. I went round to Audrey's house first, tried once more to reason with her that the additional payments would ruin us but she seemed completely resolved and wouldn't be persuaded. I left her house – inadvertently leaving my scarf behind – and contacted Coral directly, asked to meet her and I told her not to mention it to Audrey or the deal was off. Coral was the one who suggested we met in a lay-by near the wood. We sat in my car talking, but she quickly got hysterical when I told her I wouldn't be selling the house to pay her. She started threatening me with all sorts of despicable things, said she'd tell Jill, tell my employer. Then she got out of the car and ran off. I waited a few moments to see if she reappeared, but she didn't. So I drove away, and that's when she dashed out into the road in front of my car. I'd glanced down, just for a second at my phone, and the next thing, there was an almighty thud and I'd hit her. My first thought was to call the police and then all the implications hit me and … I realised this insurmountable problem I had would die with her.'

There were a few moments of terrible silence as Irma thought about the horror of Coral left behind at the scene.

'But Coral wasn't the only person who knew all this about you. Audrey did too,' she pointed out.

'Crucially, Audrey also had a lot to lose. She'd lose her job at the charity shop if I revealed her part in the blackmail and that's basically all she has in her sad little life. Jill would obviously never speak to her again either.' He sighed. 'I didn't mean to kill Coral, but when I left the scene and thought it through, I realised it could work. It just might solve all my problems.'

'Except it hasn't done that at all, has it, Mr Billinghurst?' Irma remarked coldly. 'You have so many problems, and the day has finally arrived when you must face them all.'

59

Jill

One month later

When I closed the door behind Robert and the police that day, I'd sunk back against the wall. My breathing was erratic, my heart pounding and I felt like crying – tears of freedom, of relief.

At last he was gone and my life was my own. The house was up for sale and Robert was in custody awaiting trial, charged with the manslaughter of Coral McKinty.

Mid-afternoon, I sat in the kitchen with a gin and tonic talking to Bridget.

'You've heard that saying, *you don't know what you've got until it's gone*?' I said, and Bridget nodded. 'Well, I didn't know how much I needed to get rid of him until he walked out that door.'

Bridget nodded. 'Some things you have to find out for yourself.'

'I've certainly done that,' I agreed. 'What about you? What have you found out for yourself?'

Bridget thought for a moment. 'I think I've found out that no matter what I do, I can't keep Jesse alive. I started visiting Tom because he had so many memories of him, like me. I kept Coral around because I wanted Ellis, believed he was the part of Jesse that was still here. Though of course that wasn't the case at all.'

'I admire you so much for what you're doing. Making a new family with Ellis and Tom.'

'If I'm honest with you, Jill, I have my worries about whether it can work, the three of us together, but we're determined to give it a go. Ellis still isn't close to Tom, but he's getting better, and one day he'll find out the truth that Tom is his half-brother. But he's had so much trauma to deal with, we have to take it slowly. We start our family counselling next week. We'll tell Ellis the truth at some point, in the safety of that environment. I do feel like I have a lot more living to do yet.'

Nobody could accuse Bridget of trying to hide her lust for life. She wasn't your typical middle-aged woman.

'I love Tom and I'd never want any harm to come to him. I've forgiven him for his part in Jesse's death; the restorative justice programme helped us both with that. What about you, Jill? How do you feel now about me and Tom?'

'It's a relief for me to let Tom live his life and not keep tabs on his every move. We both know that life can deal some very tough blows, but things don't turn out as badly as you might think – in my case, anyway. I've spent what feels like my whole life expecting the worst at every turn, and sometimes the worst doesn't happen.'

Bridget nodded. 'It must be an exhausting way to live.'

'So exhausting. And trying to control every last detail doesn't work anyway, because stuff still happens. The feeling that you're controlling life is an illusion. Nobody can do that. Not even me. But for what it's worth, I think what you've done – accepting Ellis as your grandson and forgiving Tom for not telling you about Robert being his father – is very noble. It can't have been easy.'

'The way I look at it, Ellis *is* my grandson. I love him with all my heart. And Tom didn't tell me for all the right reasons. The same reasons he didn't tell you. He didn't want to hurt us. When I first found out about Ellis, I wondered if Tom had married me to get close to his brother, but he pointed out that if that was all he'd wanted, he would have made a play for Coral. We always had a connection, you know, even when the boys were growing up. Obviously completely innocent and platonic back then, but we were close, we've always cared about each other.'

'I know that,' I agreed. 'I loved Jesse too. I admit I used to feel jealous sometimes. Tom would come home and say what a great time he'd had at your house and that you were such a great mum.'

'That's understandable,' Bridget said. 'I can see now that I was too lax with Jesse. Teenagers are bound to think that's cool and push the boundaries.' She hesitated a moment. 'Have you heard from Audrey?'

I nodded and said simply, 'We've spoken.' Audrey had called at the house and begged for me to listen to her side of the story. She told me about the pass Robert had made at her which I'd been totally unaware of and how, when she realised she would never get through to me about the kind of man he was, that she'd rather help someone who did listen.

I'd also confided in Audrey that I had a policy maturing when I was fifty, a nice lump sum that as yet, Robert was unaware of. 'I knew then you'd be OK for money if Robert paid Coral,' she'd said. 'And she really needed the money to stop Bridget controlling her.'

'I don't know if I can trust her again, Bridget. I've had enough people lying to me to last a lifetime. She wanted to help me, save me from Robert and she wanted to help Coral, too. Audrey is stuck in a different hell, involving herself in other people's lives and how she thinks they should live them.'

'I suppose while she's sorting out everyone else's problems, she doesn't have to dwell on her own lonely life,' Bridget murmured.

I thought she had a point. 'For as long as I've known her, Audrey has always fought for the underdog, seen it as her life's mission to help others out, find solutions. At college she'd fight the popular causes and rush to someone's defence if she felt they'd been slighted. I asked her once why she did that stuff but she shrugged and said she was just that kind of person who hated any kind of injustice. Now I realise any David and Goliath situation, where one side is more powerful, well, that really pushes Audrey's buttons. When she met Coral, she admitted she felt sorry for her and then probably saw a way to get back at Robert, who'd never liked her and now we know why. But I think she really did care about Coral in the end and wanted to make him pay.'

'I saw Audrey and Robert at the door of your house when I was driving past on the way to town. I went into the shop to let her know, to have the satisfaction of doing it. I'd heard she'd been bad-mouthing me around town. I did really think she was having an affair with Robert.'

'Me too,' I said. 'When I looked through her kitchen window and saw his scarf, it all seemed to fit. There's still one little mystery I'd like to unravel.'

'What's that?' Bridget said, taking a sip of her gin.

'Well, money has been tight for a while now, and after they took Robert into custody, it came to light he'd been paying a thousand pounds to Coral for a few months. I searched his office, found all his bank statements going back years. Turns out this payment business isn't new. He'd been paying out two hundred pounds every month for the first five years of Tom's sentence then inexplicably, it suddenly stopped.'

'What was he paying for?'

'Well, that's the mystery. He'd been drawing out cash on the last day of each month from the savings account. It wasn't for day-to-day expenses because he was also drawing cash from the current account. The regularity of it, the same amount, on the same day each month for exactly five years shows it was for something specific. Something I was completely unaware of. Twelve thousand pounds of our savings that I had no clue about.'

'Is it possible Robert siphoned money away from your joint accounts for his own use?'

I shook my head. 'DI Barrington asked him about it and he told her he'd been "anonymously" blackmailed about being Ellis's father for five years but that he knew it was Coral all along. That was why, when Coral made her new demands via Audrey, he assumed she'd got greedy and wanted to reinstate the agreement. That made him doubly angry and he demanded they meet to discuss it.'

'But you're saying, in fact, the five years previously wasn't anything to do with Coral?'

I shook my head. 'Audrey categorically denies it. She claimed Coral wouldn't have had the confidence or the knowledge to set that up on her own. It's one reason I still can't trust her, if I'm honest. I'd have thought more of her if she'd admitted it. Anyway, it's all water under the bridge now. I've had to draw a line with lots of things, and that's one of them. I'm moving on in every way. I want to get this place sold now and buy somewhere smaller.'

'Exciting times for you.' Bridget bit her lip before continuing, her voice softer. 'Jill, where do we go from here? I'd like us to be good friends again, to meet for a coffee and chat about old times and, if it's not too much to ask, to build some fresh memories.'

'We can set a time to meet up for a coffee,' I said. 'But I start back at the library next week so I'll have less time on my hands soon.'

'Wow! That's great.' Bridget looked genuinely pleased. 'Is it full-time?'

I shook my head. 'It's part-time for three months, and then there'll probably be a full-time position coming up if I'm interested.' I smiled, unable to keep the excitement from my face. 'Part of my duties will be book repair.'

We both glanced at the set of shining red and gold books that took pride of place on the shelf where Robert's community award used to live.

'They look amazing,' Bridget said admiringly. 'They must have taken so much work.'

I nodded. 'They really did but in a way they helped to set my mind straight, too. Something about clearing my head and immersing myself in the here and now … it made me realise how I'd been so stuck in the past and what had been, you know?'

Bridget nodded and said simply, 'I know how that feels. I've pared back the photographs and tributes to Jesse in the house. I don't need that stuff to remind me of my son and I know now he'd want me to live for the future, not what might have been.'

'For most of my marriage, I've thought I'd be nothing without my husband. After Tom went to prison, I became so insular. I honestly believed I needed Robert to survive.'

'And in reality you don't need him at all,' Bridget added.

I held up my drink. 'Cheers to that!' I said, and we clinked glasses.

60

The guest

Two months later

It was a small gathering in the garden of Jill Billinghurst's house, so it was so lovely to get an invitation, a totally unexpected treat.

The bride looked radiant and the groom so dashing. Jill had told her they had dressed in similar wedding outfits to their special day in the prison when nobody could celebrate with them. Jill looked the happiest I'd seen her in years and we got to chat a little bit.

'I feel like I've had a new lease of life,' she told me, 'now that I've got rid of that pain-in-the-backside husband of mine.' Oh, that made me chuckle!

There were lovely nibbles and proper champagne, and I confess I thoroughly enjoyed indulging in a glass or two. It was so heart-warming to see all these nice, genuine people having a merry time on the other side of such trauma.

There were so many good things about the party, but for me, the big bonus was being able to chat to Ellis. Such a handsome boy, and although Jill had confided he spent too much time playing computer games, like so many youngsters these days, once I got him talking, I discovered his love of drawing and writing his own stories.

'I really miss my mum, but one thing she always wanted was for me to play less on my screen, and so I'm trying to do more drawing and writing at my new school,' he said, touching my heart with his openness. Such a commendable young man after everything he'd been through!

I turned around when I heard my name.

'Oh, it's you, Tom!' I beamed as he walked over, tall and suave in his well-cut navy suit.

'Now this is a very special lady, Ellis,' he told the boy. 'Miss Threadgold used to teach both me and your dad. She was very strict but fair, and you'd do well to listen to any advice she gives you.'

'Oh nonsense, Tom. I'm sure you and Bridget do a wonderful job guiding Ellis. I hear he's a talented artist, and I wondered if perhaps one day I might pop over to the house to do some art together.'

'That's a wonderful idea, thank you.' Tom beamed. 'What do you reckon, Ellis?'

'Cool,' Ellis agreed.

'I'll speak to Bridget and we'll be in touch then,' Tom said brightly. 'Take care, Miss Threadgold, lovely to see you again.' And he was off, to circulate around his other guests.

Back home later that day, I looked around my little house and thought how lucky I was. I'd come a long way myself in recent years.

Seeing everyone today had brought back that fateful night when I'd heard Jesse telling Tom that Robert Billinghurst had fathered Coral's child. I'd been shocked and appalled, but the worst was to come.

Year after year, I watched Robert Billinghurst getting away with everything he'd done. Held up as a pillar of the community, quoted in the local newspaper as the voice of authority on the mental wellbeing of young people. And, earlier in the year, even some kind of accolade for work in the county presented by the town's mayor. I was finding it harder to manage without my salary,

and to see him, footloose and fancy-free after his wicked deeds …
well, it didn't seem fair.

Then I ran into an ex-student of mine, now a senior bank official
and working abroad. He relayed some entertaining anecdotes of
some things people got up to in order to shield their income from
tax. One of those things was to acquire an untraceable, numbered
bank account. It didn't take me long to set up something fairly
private for myself, although perfectly legal, I hasten to add. I
opened a completely separate bank account from my usual one
and also a PO Box address to enable cash to be sent.

Robert Billinghurst duly received an anonymous message
telling him that I was someone who knew all about Coral and the
baby and if he didn't want that shared with his employers and his
wife, then he'd have to buy his way out to save his squeaky-clean
image. With hardly any bother at all, he paid me a considerable
monthly sum for the five years I'd had to extend my mortgage by
and then, true to my word, I released him from his commitment.

I'd now paid my mortgage, thanks to my enterprising idea, and
I'd even salted some money away so that young Ellis would receive
a little nest egg of his own when he turned eighteen.

And now, after our lovely afternoon, Tom and his adorable
little family would take me into their hearts and home soon to
help young Ellis with his studies.

Like I'd prayed would happen all those years ago, everything
had turned out rather splendidly in the end.

A LETTER FROM
K.L. SLATER

Thank you so much for reading *The Marriage* and I really hope you enjoyed the book. If you did and would like to keep up to date with all my latest releases, just sign up at the following link. Your email address will never be shared and you can unsubscribe at any time.

www.bookouture.com/kl-slater

The idea for *The Marriage* began with my husband spotting a local newspaper story about a man who killed a stranger on a night out with a single punch. With the help of a restorative justice programme, he became good friends with his victim's mother.

The story ignited my interest, and when I get 'that feeling', I always invest some time to think around the idea. I started to play around with the facts. I thought, what if the man killed his best friend rather than a stranger, and what if he wasn't just friends with his victim's mother, but ended up marrying her! That became the real seed of the idea, and it grew rapidly in my head, which I think is always a good sign for a writer.

I always outline a new story to get things straight in my head and to let my editor see what I have in mind. But there is no real detail in the outline and it's only when I start to write that the characters come to life and things get interesting. As I developed the character of Tom, it became apparent that he'd had a problematic relationship with his father from childhood. I enjoyed exploring this angle of his character and seeing how seemingly disconnected events from someone's childhood can have implications in adult life. The Billinghurst family unit is complicated further when Tom's mother, Jill, takes it upon herself to try and keep the peace between family members. An exhausting and thankless task that perhaps many of us recognise!

This book is set in Nottinghamshire, the place I was born and have lived all my life. Local readers should be aware that I sometimes take the liberty of changing street names or geographical details to suit the story.

I do hope you enjoyed reading *The Marriage* and getting to know the characters. If so, I would be very grateful if you could take a few minutes to write a review. I'd love to hear what you think, and it makes such a difference helping new readers to discover one of my books for the first time.

I love hearing from my readers – you can get in touch on my Facebook page, through Twitter, Goodreads or my website.

Thank you to all my wonderful readers ... until next time,
Kim x

 KimLSlaterAuthor

@KimLSlater

KLSlaterAuthor

www.KLSlaterAuthor.com

ACKNOWLEDGEMENTS

Every day I sit at my desk and write stories, but I'm lucky enough to be surrounded by a whole team of talented and supportive people.

Huge thanks to my editor at Bookouture, Lydia Vassar-Smith, for her wonderful insight and editorial support. We start the process of a new story together, pooling ideas and thrashing out plots, and it's one of my favourite stages in the process!

Thanks to ALL the Bookouture team for everything they do, which is so much more than I can document here. But special thanks to editorial manager Alexandra Holmes and to Kim Nash, Sarah Hardy and Noelle Holten, who are all a pleasure to work with.

Thanks as always to my wonderful literary agent, Camilla Bolton, who is always there with expert advice and unwavering support at the end of a text, an email or a phone call. Thanks also to Camilla's assistant, Jade Kavanagh, for all her work on my behalf. And thank you to the rest of the hard-working team at Darley Anderson Literary, TV and Film Agency, especially Mary Darby, Kristina Egan, Georgia Fuller and Rosanna Bellingham.

Big thanks to the copy editor, Jane Selley, and proofreader, Becca Allen, for their eagle eyes and focused attention to help to polish up the book.

Thanks as always to my writing buddy, Angela Marsons, who has been a brilliant support and inspiration to me for many years now. Our careers have grown and flourished together from the early days when we'd keep each other's spirits up on the long road to becoming published authors, both of us dealing with disappointments and rejections along the way.

Massive thanks as always go to my husband, Mac, for his love, support and patience. For understanding when I'm at the mercy of deadlines, for not complaining if our plans have to suddenly change to accommodate my schedule. To my family, especially my wonderful daughter, Francesca, and Mama, who are always there to support and encourage me in my writing and have believed in me from the very beginning of my writing journey.

Special thanks to Henry Steadman, who has worked so hard to pull another amazing cover out of the bag.

Thank you to the bloggers and reviewers who do so much to support authors, and to everyone who has taken the time to post a positive review online or has taken part in my blog tour. It is always noticed and much appreciated.

Last but not least, thank you SO much to my wonderful readers. I love receiving all your wonderful comments and messages and I am truly grateful for the support of each and every one of you.